EIGHT SUPERB STORIES . . .

. . . to delight the heart of the avid SF fan and newcomer alike, edited and introduced by the acknowledged grand master of the genre, Isaac Asimov. These stories won highest honours in the 1972 competition run annually by the Science Fiction Writers of America – here is top SF chosen by top writers. So you can be sure they're good. *Very* good.

D1388644

Also in this series in Panther Science Fiction

Edited by
Isaac Asimov

Nebula Award Stories 8

Panther

Granada Publishing Limited
Published in 1975 by Panther Books Ltd
Frogmore, St Albans, Herts AL2 2NF

First published in Great Britain by
Victor Gollancz Ltd 1973
Copyright © Science Fiction Writers of America 1973
Made and printed in Great Britain by
Richard Clay (The Chaucer Press) Ltd
Bungay, Suffolk
Set in Linotype Plantin

CONTENTS

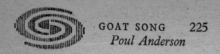

INTRODUCTION

SO WHY AREN'T WE RICH?

Isaac Asimov

On Saturday, February 17, 1973, I was at the Commodore Hotel in New York City, where I gave a speech to an international convention of *Star Trek* enthusiasts. The convention was the second of its kind.

At the first such *Star Trek* convention, a year earlier, 250 attendees were expected and 2,500 came. Learning by experience, the organizers planned for 4,000 attendees at the second convention – and 7,000 came.

And all this for a programme that has been off the air for some years and is only seen now, occasionally, as re-runs. Indeed, when I gave my talk (to an audience of at least 2,000) I asked for a show of hands of those who had never seen the programme when it was on the air in its original state, but had seen *only* re-runs. A sizeable forest of arms stretched towards the ceiling.

To the outside world this seems an amusing and inexplicable phenomenon. Why this manic devotion to a programme that no longer exists and that was not terribly successful in the ratings-fight when it did exist? After all, are there any conventions, any cults, any screaming excitements over other dead programmes such as *The Life of Reilly*, or *My Mother, the Car*?

Or, if you think that I'm loading the dice by picking two notoriously un-great programmes (though they probably did as well in the ratings in their day as did *Star Trek*) then let me ask where are the conventions attended by the fans of *I Love Lucy* which has been on the TV air, original and re-run, for twenty-two years non-stop? Or for *The Beverly Hillbillies*? Do you expect that even *All in the Family* will develop a cult that will survive its death? You know it won't.

It's *Star Trek* only, but why?

I was asked this question on that Saturday. There were television interviewers present all set to be amused at childish antics – except that a surprising percentage of those attending were quite adult, and there were no childish antics. You never saw 7,000 better behaved people, young and old, in your life.

They interviewed me and asked me how I explained this curious phenomenon and were, I think, more than a little disappointed when I told them it was no mystery at all, but was exactly what was to be expected. Facing the cameras coolly, I said, 'It is simply part of the science-fiction phenomenon and you are surprised by it only because you know nothing about science fiction.'

As most science fiction devotees know, there have been science fiction clubs ever since the mid-1930s, and they still exist in countless numbers. There were regular meetings of these clubs, that grew larger and more elaborate with time, and culminated in the First World Science Fiction Convention, held in New York in 1939. (In 1973, the 32nd World Science Fiction Convention is held in Toronto. There has been one every year – except for three years during World War II – and every year in a different city.)

These World Science Fiction Conventions, unpromoted outside the field, unsupported except by registration fees, unglamorized, unhokumed by any press agentry, collect over 2,000 attendees, some of whom come from distances of thousands of miles.

The fidelity, the fanaticism if you will, of the science-fiction fan (and 'fan' is short for 'fanatic' – look it up in the dictionary) is unparalleled of its kind.

Is it any surprise, then, that the enthusiasm of science-fiction fandom should carry over to *Star Trek*? The surprise, in fact, is not that so many people should flock to a convention honouring a dead science-fiction show, but that so few should.

After all, the World Science Fiction Conventions draw their attendees chiefly from those who read the science-fiction magazines and paperback books. The most successful science-fiction magazine has a circulation of roughly 100,000, and a science-fiction paperback is quite satisfactorily successful if it sells 200,000 copies. It is from this public that the 2,000 individuals at a World Science Fiction Convention are gathered.

Star Trek, however, was viewed by at least 20,000,000 people at one time or another; a hundred times as many as might read a particular paperback book; two hundred times as many as might read a particular magazine; yet the *Star Trek* convention attracts only four times as many people.

So you see, when I say that the enthusiasm of a *Star Trek* convention is part of the science-fiction phenomenon, I can go further and add that, proportionately, it is not even a particularly successful part.

Well, then, we ought to ask a different question, broadening our view. What is the explanation of the science-fiction phenomenon? Why does it create so fanatical a public?

The reason I would like to offer for this is that science fiction is relevant; it is important; it has something to do with the world; it gives meaning to life; and it enlightens the readers. And it has all these characteristics as no other form of literature has!

When I say this in public, and I frequently do, I am almost always greeted by some with an attitude, explicitly stated or implicitly implied, which can be put into words like this: 'Oh, come now, Dr. Asimov. You mean all that stuff about monsters and ray-guns?'

Of course, they're judging from the comic strips, and from the motion pictures and television programmes put out by twelve-year-olds writing and producing for twelve-year-olds. (Stupid twelve-year-olds in both cases, of course.)

The true science-fiction enthusiasts are more discriminating than that. It isn't *Lost in Space* or *Land of the Giants* or any of the other illiteracies that evoke fan-enthusiasm, regardless of TV ratings, but only *Star Trek* because that strove for intelligence and frequently attained it.

When *we* talk about science fiction, we talk about *good* science fiction, and it is *good* science fiction that is relevant, important, and so on. Those outsiders who disagree ought to read some – and if they then still disagree, let them consider matters carefully. The fault may be in themselves.

The fact of the matter is that the history of mankind is one of gradually accelerating social change. The rate of social change took a sudden jump when the Scientific Revolution of 1600 was followed by the Industrial Revolution of 1800. Science and technology formed the base for a vastly increased rate of social change, a rate that is *still* increasing today.

The rate has become so great that the world I live in today is enormously different socially and technologically from the world I was brought up in. The world in which the young people of today will find themselves middle-aged and elderly will be even more drastically changed.

It is part of the peculiar difficulty of our times that the racing tide of change must buck the fact that the average man cannot make himself believe that change is inevitable in the first place, and then, when the change comes, resents it bitterly. To the average man of my age, life as it was in his formative years is what it *should* be, so that the Archie Bunkers of the world have a horror of the young and feel a disgust for the world of the young.

This conflict between the generations is not new. Socrates is often quoted as having deplored the degeneration of manners among the young twenty-five hundred years ago. However, as the gap in social custom increases for a difference of thirty years, the hostility between the generations becomes ever more acute and dangerous.

That I escape some of the misery of finding myself living in a world I never made I attribute very largely to my own generation-long immersion in science fiction.

Of all forms of literature, science fiction is the only one that deals primarily and basically with change. It is the only one that routinely tells its story against the background of a different society – a colony on the Moon, a mythical world inhabited by monsters, an Earth after a holocaust. There are endless possibilities but all have this in common: they are nothing like the here and now.

The different society that forms the background of a particular science-fiction story may never come to pass; the author may not expect it to come to pass; that doesn't matter. It is enough that it is different. In the 1940s and 1950s, it was fashionable in science fiction to concentrate on engineering advances with a high probability of becoming fact, so that many of the notions of those days (nuclear bombs, computers, Moon-flights, etc.) have 'come true', but that is a detail. It is not the function of science fiction to predict the actual future, but rather to present alternate futures of any degree of probability from one hundred to zero, and to do so as intricately as possible.

Do you see the difference this makes? Young people may be excited by the action in detective stories, western stories, sport stories, war stories, love stories or any of the large variety of fiction that deals essentially with the world of today or yesterday. When all is done, it is only the action that counts and that, after all, is trivial.

But because science fiction deals with other societies and encourages a view of possible futures and a contemplation of possible change, it is bound to leave behind a wonder and a thoughtful contemplation of what Earth and man and the reader himself is coming to.

And because science fiction stimulates this kind of thought, it is relevant to the present as nothing else is and performs a service for mankind nothing else can.

If science fiction is increasingly relevant as time goes on and the rate of social change continues to speed up, does it not follow that ordinary fiction is becoming increasingly *ir*relevant?

It certainly does and the proof of that is plain to see. In the last quarter-century, we have seen the market for fiction, other than science fiction, steadily decline. The pulp-magazines have disappeared and the general interest slick-magazines are disappearing. And if this is blamed on economic factors that have nothing to do with fiction, then why is it that those magazines that survive print hardly any fiction and that publishers are increasingly reluctant to publish fiction which lacks the kind of sensationalism that will allow it to be foisted on the public for reasons other than that it is fiction?

But science fiction continues to flourish. There are changes within the field as paperback books increase at the expense of the magazines, but the thing itself remains.

This has resulted in an enrichment of the field since many young people, eager to write fiction, turn to science fiction as the one healthy outlet. Many of them would not have done so a generation ago, I suspect, for there would have then been other outlets they might have felt better suited to their talents. Now, however, their talents are at our disposal.

In general, the new writers are not as science-oriented as the writers of a generation ago. (In those days, one almost had to be science-oriented to want to write for so specialized a field.) The new writers have a stronger literary background and are more interested in stylistic experimentation and in the new freedoms with which sex and inner consciousness may be explored than the older writers were.

So the field is broader and more diverse (as this series of Nebula Award Stories anthologies demonstrates), and therefore better.

And yet the science-fiction field cannot be viewed entirely as something that is marching on from triumph to triumph. There are factors that sharply limit the extent of its victories.

Most forms of literature have as their climax an *act* – the gun, the fist, the baseball bat, the kiss. An exception is the classic mystery, in which the great detective has a *thought*. In the good science-fiction story there may be much action and violence but the crucial factor is the *idea*.

Science fiction, as a literature of ideas, appeals particularly to those who value ideas and find pleasure in considering them. It is not surprising, then, that even the most cursory consideration of science-fiction readers leads to the inevitable conclusion that their average intelligence is considerably higher than the average intelligence of the general population.

Because the science-fiction readers are more intelligent, thoughtful, and articulate, on the average, than the general population is, a surprisingly large percentage among them have the drive and ability to organize clubs, edit amateur publications, set up conventions, hand out awards, and turn to professional writing. The science-fiction reader makes noise, generates enthusiasm, and organizes drives far out of proportion to his numbers – as the television people found out to their amazement and discomfort when they tried to take *Star Trek* off the air after its first year.

On the other hand, the very factors that make the quality of the science-fiction reader so excellent, make his actual numbers low. Since they are drawn from among the more intelligent of the population, they are and will always remain a minority. Whatever forms of success depend on quantity of readers, rather than on quality, remain unattainable in the field.

In particular, when science fiction is considered as a source of income, we must ask how many science-fiction readers there are, and not how intelligent they are or how enthusiastic. And because there are not many, science-fiction writers, as a class, don't get rich.

Even if the monetary rewards were greater than they are, I doubt very much that science fiction would ever be a popular field of literary endeavour for those writers who are looking for something *easy*.

As it happens, science fiction is a particularly difficult form of writing; perhaps the most difficult there is.

To see why that is so, consider that every piece of fiction has both its foreground and its background. In the fore-ground are the characters, who are thinking their thoughts and doing their deeds. In the background is the society or sub-society in which the characters live and against which their thoughts and actions have meaning.

In every case, in a good work of fiction, the characters must not obscure the background, and the background must not drown the actors. Both must have their fair share of weight.

The writer of most kinds of fiction is ordinarily greatly

helped by the fact that the reader knows the background. The writer can depend on this knowledge and let it carry its full weight. No writer has to describe an automobile or an aeroplane or go into great detail about city streets, hotels, mountains, or cows. Even when a specialized bit of society is involved, a coal-mining society, a sixteenth-century English society, even a fantasy society, the writer can count on a substratum of basic knowledge.

Not so in science fiction. There, the background, by the very nature of the field, is *unfamiliar* to the reader. It must be explained to the reader almost from scratch and without interfering with the action. Conversation must be natural and yet somehow illuminate the background for which the speakers themselves require no illumination. References outside conversation must be complete and yet not intrusive.

If this can be done, the reward for the reader is great, for the unfamiliar background may be as essentially interesting as the characters and events in the foreground. The interaction of the two may allow a probing of mind and soul that would be impossible in the here-and-now.

But the *task* of doing so is inordinately difficult to do it really well requires either a specialized genius or a long and hard apprenticeship.

What is worse yet is that one science-fiction story does not necessarily help another. In other forms of fiction, a writer may establish his background; a particular police-station, the Mississippi backwoods, the Chicago of the 1930s; and use that same background in a hundred stories.

This can be done to an extent in science fiction as well, but the readers quickly tire of such a thing – and rightly. They are paying for novelty in background as well as in plot. We find, therefore, that science-fiction writers are compelled to invent different societies and backgrounds in almost every story.

The result is this –

A good science-fiction writer can, very probably, write anything else he wishes (and for more money), if he decides to take the trouble to do so. Many science-fiction writers have done so and a few have been lost to the field as a result.

On the other hand, a good writer who has never tried science fiction, but has learned his trade outside that field, will very probably find it impossible to write good science fiction, no matter how he tries.

It is uphill to science fiction; downhill to everything else.

Am I talking through my hat? Am I just boosting my own field?

No! In this one case I am the world authority.

I began by writing science fiction, yes, and for over thirty years, I've been considered a leading writer in the field. Nor have I lost my touch with age. This very year my novel *The Gods Themselves*, won the Nebula in the novel category.

But, in line with what I have said, I found that my training in science fiction made it possible for me to write anything. I have written mysteries, both novels and short stories, for instance. I have also written non-fiction books on every branch of science, both popularizations for the general public, and textbooks at both the graduate level and the grade-school level. I have written history books, discussions of the Bible, Shakespeare, Byron, and Milton. I have written satires and jokebooks. I have written about 150 books as of now and I tell you that of all the different things I write, science fiction is by far the hardest thing to do.

So when people urge me (as they frequently do) to write less of everything else and more science fiction, I wish they would consider this and have a little pity.

But then, if science fiction is so hard to do and pays so little – why do it?

Haven't you been listening? *Because* it's important, and *because* the difficulty of the challenge makes it fun.

Most of all, though, because there is no audience in the world more appreciative, more enthusiastic, more intelligent, and, all in all, more satisfying to reach than the science-fiction reader. And when we *do* reach them, then, money or not, we are *rich*.

A MEETING WITH MEDUSA

The science-fiction story which has, as its chief centre of interest, the development of science and technology and in which the characters are of interest primarily as wielders and victims of these developments, is now referred to as 'hard science fiction'.

There are many who look at hard science fiction as the 'real thing', the kind of story in which science fiction truly fulfils itself, since it is all science fiction and nothing else. There are others who feel that hard science fiction is passé; that it had its hey-day in the 1940s and 1950s, and that mankind has now passed beyond the simplistic enthusiasms of science.

Emotionally, I am on the side of the former and write hard science fiction myself. Nevertheless, in the science-fiction house there are many mansions and what makes a story good is not its type or category but its quality.

Among the writers of hard science fiction, Arthur Clarke is outstanding and has been for thirty years. It helps for a writer of hard science fiction to have a thorough knowledge and understanding of science, and in this respect Clarke qualifies as well as or better than anyone else in the field. As is well known, he combined science and imagination to describe the communications satellite back in 1948 and lived to see the space scientists accept his ideas exactly.

Can you find a better guide, then, on a trip to Jupiter?

A MEETING WITH MEDUSA

Arthur C. Clarke

1. A DAY TO REMEMBER

The *Queen Elizabeth* was over three miles above the Grand Canyon, dawdling along at a comfortable hundred and eighty, when Howard Falcon spotted the camera platform closing in from the right. He had been expecting it – nothing else was cleared to fly at this altitude – but he was not too happy to have company. Although he welcomed any signs of public interest, he also wanted as much empty sky as he could get. After all, he was the first man in history to navigate a ship three-tenths of a mile long. . . .

So far, this first test flight had gone perfectly; ironically enough, the only problem had been the century-old aircraft carrier *Chairman Mao*, borrowed from the San Diego Naval Museum for support operations. Only one of *Mao*'s four nuclear reactors was still operating, and the old battle-wagon's top speed was barely thirty knots. Luckily, wind speed at sea level had been less than half this, so it had not been too difficult to maintain still air on the flight deck. Though there had been a few anxious moments during gusts, when the mooring lines had been a few anxious moments during gusts, when the mooring lines had been dropped, the great dirigible had risen smoothly, straight up into the sky, as if on an invisible elevator. If all went well, *Queen Elizabeth IV* would not meet *Chairman Mao* again for another week.

Everything was under control; all test instruments gave normal readings. Commander Falcon decided to go upstairs and watch the rendezvous. He handed over to his second officer,

 Nebula Award, Best Novella 1972

and walked out into the transparent tubeway that led through the heart of the ship. There, as always, he was overwhelmed by the spectacle of the largest single space ever enclosed by man.

The ten spherical gas cells, each more than a hundred feet across, were ranged one behind the other like a line of gigantic soap bubbles. The touch plastic was so clear that he could see throu h the whole length of the array, and make out details of the elevator mechanism, more than a third of a mile from his vantage point. All around him, like a three-dimensional maze, was the structural framework of the ship – the great longitudinal girders running from nose to tail, the fifteen hoops that were the circular ribs of this sky-borne colossus, and whose varying sizes defined its graceful, streamlined profile.

At this low speed, there was little sound – merely the soft rush of wind over the envelope and an occasional creak of metal as the pattern of stresses changed. The shadowless light from the rows of lamps far overhead gave the whole scene a curiously submarine quality, and to Falcon this was enhanced by the spectacle of the translucent gasbags. He had once encountered a squadron of large but harmless jellyfish, pulsing their mindless way above a shallow tropical reef, and the plastic bubbles that gave *Queen Elizabeth* her lift often reminded him of these – especially when changing pressures made them crinkle and scatter new patterns of reflected light.

He walked down the axis of the ship until he came to the forward elevator, between gas cells one and two. Riding up to the Observation Deck, he noticed that it was uncomfortably hot, and dictated a brief memo to himself on his pocket recorder. The *Queen* obtained almost a quarter of her buoyancy from the unlimited amounts of waste heat produced by her fusion power plant. On this lightly loaded flight, indeed, only six of the ten gas cells contained helium; the remaining four were full of air. Yet she still carried two hundred tons of water as ballast. However, running the cells at high temperatures did produce problems in refrigerating the access ways; it was obvious that a little more work would have to be done there.

A refreshing blast of cooler air hit him in the face when he stepped out on to the Observation Deck and into the dazzling sunlight streaming through the plexiglass roof. Half a dozen workmen, with an equal number of superchimp assistants, were busily laying the partly completed dance floor, while others were installing electric wiring and fixing furniture. It was a scene of controlled chaos, and Falcon found it hard to believe that everything would be ready for the maiden voyage, only four weeks ahead. Well, that was not *his* problem, thank goodness. He was merely the Captain, not the Cruise Director.

The human workers waved to him, and the 'simps' flashed toothy smiles, as he walked through the confusion, into the already completed Skylounge. This was his favourite place in the whole ship, and he knew that once she was operating he would never again have it all to himself. He would allow himself just five minutes of private enjoyment.

He called the bridge, checked that everything was still in order, and relaxed into one of the comfortable swivel chairs. Below, in a curve that delighted the eye, was the unbroken silver sweep of the ship's envelope. He was perched at the highest point, surveying the whole immensity of the largest vehicle ever built. And when he had tired of that – all the way out to the horizon was the fantastic wilderness carved by the Colorado River in half a billion years of time.

Apart from the camera platform (it had now fallen back and was filming from amidships), he had the sky to himself. It was blue and empty, clear down to the horizon. In his grandfather's day, Falcon knew, it would have been streaked with vapour trails and stained with smoke. Both had gone: the aerial garbage had vanished with the primitive technologies that spawned it, and the long-distance transportation of this age arced too far beyond the stratosphere for any sight or sound of it to reach Earth. Once again, the lower atmosphere belonged to the birds and the clouds – and now to *Queen Elizabeth IV*.

It was true, as the old pioneers had said at the beginning of the twentieth century: this was the only way to travel – in silence and luxury, breathing the air around you and not cut off from it, near enough to the surface to watch the ever-changing beauty of land and sea. The subsonic jets of the 1980s, packed with hundreds of passengers seated ten abreast, could not even begin to match such comfort and spaciousness.

Of course, the *Queen* would never be an economic proposition, and even if her projected sister ships were built, only a few of the world's quarter of a billion inhabitants would ever enjoy this silent gliding through the sky. But a secure and prosperous global society could afford such follies and indeed needed them for their novelty and entertainment. There were at least a million men on Earth whose discretionary income exceeded a thousand new dollars a year, so the *Queen* would not lack for passengers.

Falcon's pocket communicator beeped. The co-pilot was calling from the bridge.

'O.K. for rendezvous, Captain? We've got all the data we need from the run, and the TV people are getting impatient.'

Falcon glanced at the camera platform, now matching his speed a tenth of a mile away.

'O.K.,' he replied. 'Proceed as arranged. I'll watch from here.'

He walked back through the busy chaos of the Observation Deck so that he could have a better view amidships. As he did so, he could feel the change of vibration underfoot; by the time he had reached the rear of the lounge, the ship had come to rest. Using his master key, he let himself out on to the small external platform flaring from the end of the deck; half a dozen people could stand here, with only low guardrails separating them from the vast sweep of the envelope – and from the ground, thousands of feet below. It was an exciting place to be, and perfectly safe even when the ship was travelling at speed, for it was in the dead air behind the huge dorsal blister of the Observation Deck. Nevertheless, it was not intended that the passengers would have access to it; the view was a little too vertiginous.

The covers of the forward cargo hatch had already opened like giant trap doors, and the camera platform was hovering above them, preparing to descend. Along this route, in the years to come, would travel thousands of passengers and tons of supplies. Only on rare occasions would the *Queen* drop down to sea level and dock with her floating base.

A sudden gust of cross wind slapped Falcon's cheek, and he tightened his grip on the guardrail. The Grand Canyon was a bad place for turbulence, though he did not expect much at this altitude. Without any real anxiety, he focused his attention on the descending platform, now about a hundred and fifty feet above the ship. He knew that the highly skilled operator who was flying the remotely controlled vehicle had performed this simple manoeuvre a dozen times already; it was inconceivable that he would have any difficulties.

Yet he seemed to be reacting rather sluggishly. That last gust had drifted the platform almost to the edge of the open hatchway. Surely the pilot could have corrected before this. . . . Did he have a control problem? It was very unlikely; these remotes had multiple-redundancy, fail-safe takeovers, and any number of backup systems. Accidents were almost unheard of.

But there he went again, off to the left. Could the pilot be *drunk*? Improbable though that seemed, Falcon considered it seriously for a moment. Then he reached for his microphone switch.

Once again, without warning, he was slapped violently in the face. He hardly felt it, for he was staring in horror at the camera platform. The distant operator was fighting for control, trying to balance the craft on its jets – but he was only making matters worse. The oscillations increased – twenty degrees, forty, sixty, ninety. . . .

'Switch to automatic, you fool!' Falcon shouted uselessly into his microphone. 'Your manual control's not working!'

The platform flipped over on its back. The jets no longer supported it, but drove it swiftly downward. They had suddenly become allies of the gravity they had fought until this moment.

Falcon never heard the crash, though he felt it; he was already inside the Observation Deck, racing for the elevator that would take him down to the bridge. Workmen shouted at him anxiously, asking what had happened. It would be many months before he knew the answer to that question.

Just as he was stepping into the elevator cage, he changed his mind, even if it took longer and time was the essence. He began to run down the spiral stairway enclosing the shaft.

Halfway down he paused for a second to inspect the damage. That damned platform had gone clear through the ship, rupturing two of the gas cells as it did so. They were still collapsing slowly, in great falling veils of plastic. He was not worried about the loss of lift – the ballast could easily take care of that, as long as eight cells remained intact. Far more serious was the possibility of structural damage. Already he could hear the great latticework around him groaning and protesting under its abnormal loads. It was not enough to have sufficient lift; unless it was properly distributed, the ship would break her back.

He was just resuming his descent when a superchimp, shrieking with fright, came racing down the elevator shaft, moving with incredible speed, hand over hand, along the *outside* of the latticework. In its terror, the poor beast had torn off its company uniform, perhaps in an unconscious attempt to regain the freedom of its ancestors.

Falcon, still descending as swiftly as he could, watched its approach with some alarm. A distraught simp was a powerful and potentially dangerous animal, especially if fear overcame its conditioning. As it overtook him, it started to call out a string of words, but they were all jumbled together, and the only one he could recognize was a plaintive, frequently repeated 'boss'. Even now, Falcon realized, it looked towards humans for guidance. He felt sorry for the creature, involved in a man-made disaster beyond its comprehension, and for which it bore no responsibility.

It stopped opposite him, on the other side of the lattice; there was nothing to prevent it from coming through the open framework if it wished. Now its face was only inches from his, and he was looking straight into the terrified eyes. Never before had he been so close to a simp, and able to study its features in such detail. He felt that strange mingling of kinship and discomfort that all men experience when they gaze thus into the mirror of time.

His presence seemed to have calmed the creature. Falcon pointed up the shaft, back towards the Observation Deck, and said very clearly and precisely: 'Boss – boss – *go*.' To his relief, the simp understood; it gave him a grimace that might have been a smile, and at once started to race back the way it had come. Falcon had given it the best advice he could. If any safety remained aboard the *Queen*, it was in that direction. But his duty lay in the other.

He had almost completed his descent when, with a sound of rending metal, the vessel pitched nose down, and the lights went out. But he could still see quite well, for a shaft of sunlight streamed through the open hatch and the huge tear in the envelope. Many years ago he had stood in a great cathedral nave watching the light pouring through the stained-glass windows and forming pools of multicoloured radiance on the ancient flagstones. The dazzling shaft of sunlight through the ruined fabric high above reminded him of that moment. He was in a cathedral of metal, falling down the sky.

When he reached the bridge, and was able for the first time to look outside, he was horrified to see how close the ship was to the ground. Only three thousand feet below were the beautiful and deadly pinnacles of rock and the red rivers of mud that were still carving their way down into the past. There was no level area anywhere in sight where a ship as large as the *Queen* could come to rest on an even keel.

A glance at the display board told him that all the ballast had gone. However, rate of descent had been reduced to a few yards a second; they still had a fighting chance.

Without a word, Falcon eased himself into the pilot's seat and took over such control as still remained. The instrument board showed him everything he wished to know; speech was superfluous. In the background, he could hear the Communications Officer giving a running report over the radio. By this time, all the news channels of Earth would have been pre-empted, and he could imagine the utter frustration of the programme controllers. One of the most spectacular wrecks in history was occurring – without a single camera to record it. The last moments of the *Queen* would never fill millions with awe and terror, as had those of the *Hindenburg*, a century and a half before.

Now the ground was only about seventeen hundred feet away, still coming up slowly. Though he had full thrust, he had not dared to use it, lest the weakened structure collapse; but now he realized that he had no choice. The wind was taking them towards a fork in the canyon, where the river was split by a wedge of rock like the prow of some gigantic, fossilized ship of stone. If she continued on her present course, the *Queen* would straddle that triangular plateau and come to rest with at least a third of her length jutting out over nothingness; she would snap like a rotten stick.

Far away, above the sound of straining metal and escaping gas, came the familiar whistle of the jets as Falcon opened up the lateral thrusters. The ship staggered, and began to slew to port. The shriek of tearing metal was now almost continuous – and the rate of descent had started to increase ominously. A glance at the damage-control board showed that cell number five had just gone.

The ground was only yards away. Even now, he could not tell whether his manoeuvre would succeed or fail. He switched the thrust vectors over to vertical, giving maximum lift to reduce the force of impact.

The crash seemed to last for ever. It was not violent – merely prolonged, and irresistible. It seemed that the whole universe was falling about them.

The sound of crunching metal came nearer, as if some great beast were eating its way through the dying ship.

Then floor and ceiling closed upon him like a vice.

2. 'BECAUSE IT'S THERE'

'Why do you want to go to Jupiter?'

'As Springer said when he lifted for Pluto – "because it's there".'

'Thanks. Now we've got *that* out of the way – the real reason.'

Howard Falcon smiled, though only those who knew him well could have interpreted the slight, leathery grimace. Webster was one of them; for more than twenty years they had been involved in each other's projects. They had shared triumphs and disasters – including the greatest disaster of all.

'Well, Springer's cliché is still valid. We've landed on all the terrestrial planets, but none of the gas giants. They are the only real challenge left in the solar system.'

'An expensive one. Have you worked out the cost?'

'As well as I can; here are the estimates. Remember, though – this isn't a one-shot mission, but a transportation system. Once it's proved out, it can be used over and over again. And it will open up not merely Jupiter, but *all* the giants.'

Wester looked at the figures, and whistled.

'Why not start with an easier planet – Uranus, for example? Half the gravity, and less than half the escape velocity. Quieter weather, too – if that's the right word for it.'

Webster had certainly done his homework. But that, of course, was why he was head of Long-Range Planning.

'There's very little saving – when you allow for the extra distance and the logistics problems. For Jupiter, we can use the facilities of Ganymede. Beyond Saturn, we'd have to establish a new supply base.'

Logical, thought Webster; but he was sure that it was not the important reason. Jupiter was lord of the solar system; Falcon would be interested in no lesser challenge.

'Besides,' Falcon continued, 'Jupiter is a major scientific scandal. It's more than a hundred years since its radio storms were discovered, but we still don't know what causes them – and the Great Red Spot is as big a mystery as ever. That's why I can get matching funds from the Bureau of Astronautics. Do you know how many probes they have dropped into that atmosphere?'

'A couple of hundred, I believe.'

'*Three* hundred and twenty-six, over the last fifty years – about a quarter of them total failures. Of course, they've learned a hell of a lot, but they've barely scratched the planet. Do you realize how *big* it is?'

'More than ten times the size of Earth.'

'Yes, yes – but do you know what that really means?'

Falcon pointed to the large globe in the corner of Webster's office.

'Look at India – how small it seems. Well, if you skinned Earth and spread it out on the surface of Jupiter, it would look about as big as India does here.'

There was a long silence while Webster contemplated the equation: Jupiter is to Earth as Earth is to India. Falcon had – deliberately, of course – chosen the best possible example. . . .

Was it already ten years ago? Yes, it must have been. The crash lay seven years in the past (*that* date was engraved on his heart), and those initial tests had taken place three years before the first and last flight of the *Queen Elizabeth*.

Ten years ago, then, Commander (no, Lieutenant) Falcon had invited him to a preview – a three-day drift across the northern plains of India, within sight of the Himalayas. 'Perfectly safe,' he had promised. 'It will get you away from the office – and will teach you what this whole thing is about.'

Webster had not been disappointed. Next to his first journey to the Moon, it had been the most memorable experience of his life. And yet, as Falcon had assured him, it had been perfectly safe, and quite uneventful.

They had taken off from Srinagar just before dawn, with the huge silver bubble of the balloon already catching the first light of the Sun. The ascent had been made in total silence; there were none of the roaring propane burners that had lifted the hot-air balloons of an earlier age. All the heat they needed came from the little pulsed-fusion reactor, weighing only about two hundred and twenty pounds, hanging in the open mouth of the envelope. While they were climbing, its laser was zapping ten times a second, igniting the merest whiff of deuterium fuel. Once they had reached altitude, it would fire only a few times a minute, making up for the heat lost through the great gasbag overhead.

And so, even while they were almost a mile above the ground, they could hear dogs barking, people shouting, bells ringing. Slowly the vast, Sun-smitten landscape expanded around them. Two hours later, they had levelled out at three miles and were taking frequent draughts of oxygen. They could relax and admire the scenery; the on-board instrumentation was doing all the work – gathering the information that would be required by the designers of the still-unnamed liner of the skies.

It was a perfect day. The southwest monsoon would not break for another month, and there was hardly a cloud in the sky. Time seemed to have come to a stop; they resented the hourly radio reports which interrupted their reverie. And all around, to the horizon and far beyond, was that infinite, ancient landscape, drenched with history – a patchwork of villages, fields, temples, lakes, irrigation canals. . . .

With a real effort, Webster broke the hypnotic spell of that ten-year-old memory. It had converted him to lighter-than-air flight – and it had made him realize the enormous size of India, even in a world that could be circled within ninety minutes. And yet, he repeated to himself, Jupiter is to Earth as Earth is to India. . . .

'Granted your argument,' he said, 'and supposing the funds are available, there's another question you have to answer. Why should you do better than the – what is it – three hundred and twenty-six robot probes that have already made the trip?'

'I am better qualified than they were – as an observer, and as a pilot. *Especially* as a pilot. Don't forget – I've more experience of lighter-than-air flight than anyone in the world.'

'You could still serve as controller, and sit safely on Ganymede.'

'*But that's just the point!* They've already done that. Don't you remember what killed the *Queen*?'

Webster knew perfectly well; but he merely answered: 'Go on.'

'*Time lag – time lag!* That idiot of a platform controller thought he was using a local radio circuit. But he'd been accidentally switched through a satellite – oh, maybe it wasn't his fault, but he should have noticed. That's a half-second time lag for the round trip. Even then it wouldn't have mattered flying in calm air. It was the turbulence over the Grand Canyon that did it. When the platform tipped, and he corrected for that – it had already tipped the other way. Ever tried to drive a car over a bumpy road with a half-second delay in the steering?'

'No, and I don't intend to try. But I can imagine it.'

'Well, Ganymede is a million kilometres from Jupiter. That means a round-trip delay of six seconds. No, you need a controller on the spot – to handle emergencies in real time. Let me show you something. Mind if I use this?'

'Go ahead.'

Falcon picked up a postcard that was lying on Webster's desk; they were almost obsolete on Earth, but this one showed a 3-D view of a Martian landscape, and was decorated with exotic and expensive stamps. He held it so that it dangled vertically.

'This is an old trick, but helps to make my point. Place your thumb and finger on either side, not quite touching. That's right.'

Webster put out his hand, almost but not quite gripping the card.

'Now catch it.'

Falcon waited for a few seconds; then, without warning, he let go of the card. Webster's thumb and finger closed on empty air.

'I'll do it again, just to show there's no deception. You see?'

Once again, the falling card had slipped through Webster's fingers.

'Now you try it on me.'

This time, Webster grasped the card and dropped it without warning. It had scarcely moved before Falcon had caught it. Webster almost imagined he could hear a click, so swift was the other's reaction.

'When they put me together again,' Falcon remarked in an expressionless voice, 'the surgeons made some improvements. This is one of them – and there are others. I want to make the most of them. Jupiter is the place where I can do it.'

Webster stared for long seconds at the fallen card, absorbing the improbable colours of the Trivium Charontis Escarpment. Then he said quietly: 'I understand. How long do you think it will take?'

'With your help, plus the Bureau, plus all the science foundations we can drag in – oh, three years. Then a year for trials – we'll have to send in at least two test models. So, with luck – five years.'

'That's about what I thought. I hope you get your luck; you've earned it. But there's one thing I won't do.'

'What's that?'

'Next time you go ballooning, don't expect *me* as passenger.'

3. THE WORLD OF THE GODS

The fall from Jupiter V to Jupiter itself takes only three and a half hours. Few men could have slept on so awesome a journey. Sleep was a weakness that Howard Falcon hated, and the little he still required brought dreams that time had not yet been able to exorcise. But he could expect no rest in the three days that lay ahead, and must seize what he could during the long fall down into that ocean of clouds, some sixty thousand miles below.

As soon as *Kon-Tiki* had entered her transfer orbit and all the computer checks were satisfactory, he prepared for the last sleep he might ever know. It seemed appropriate that at almost the same moment Jupiter eclipsed the bright and tiny Sun as he swept into the monstrous shadow of the planet. For a few minutes a strange golden twilight enveloped the ship; then a quarter of the sky became an utterly black hole in space, while the rest was a blaze of stars. No matter how far one travelled across the solar system, *they* never changed; these same constellations now shone on Earth, millions of miles away. The only novelties here were the small, pale crescents of Callisto and Ganymede; doubtless there were a dozen other moons up there in the sky, but they were all much too tiny, and too distant, for the unaided eye to pick them out.

'Closing down for two hours,' he reported to the mother ship, hanging almost a thousand miles above the desolate rocks of Jupiter V, in the radiation shadow of the tiny satellite. If it never served any other useful purpose, Jupiter V was a cosmic bulldozer perpetually sweeping up the charged particles that made it unhealthy to linger close to Jupiter. Its wake was almost free of radiation, and there a ship could park in perfect safety, while death sleeted invisibly all around.

Falcon switched on the sleep inducer, and consciousness faded swiftly out as the electric pulses surged gently through his brain. While *Kon-Tiki* fell towards Jupiter, gaining speed second by second in that enormous gravitational field, he slept without dreams. They always came when he awoke; and he had brought his nightmares with him from Earth.

Yet he never dreamed of the crash itself, though he often found himself again face to face with that terrified superchimp, as he descended the spiral stairway between the collapsing gasbags. None of the simps had survived; those that were not killed outright were so badly injured that they had been painlessly 'euthed'. He sometimes wondered why he dreamed only of this doomed creature – which he had never met before the last minutes of its life – and not of the friends and colleagues he had lost aboard the dying *Queen*.

The dreams he feared most always began with his first return to consciousness. There had been little physical pain; in fact, there had been no sensation of any kind. He was in darkness and silence, and did not even seem to be breathing. And – strangest of all – he could not locate his limbs. He could move neither his hands nor his feet, because he did not know where they were.

The silence had been the first to yield. After hours, or days, he had become aware of a faint throbbing, and eventually, after long thought, he deduced that this was the beating of his own heart. That was the first of his many mistakes.

Then there had been faint pinpricks, sparkles of light, ghosts of pressures upon still-unresponsive limbs. One by one his senses had returned, and pain had come with them. He had had to learn everything anew, recapitulating infancy and babyhood. Though his memory was unaffected, and he could understand words that were spoken to him, it was months before he was able to answer except by the flicker of an eyelid. He could remember the moments of triumph when he had spoken the first word, turned the page of a book – and, finally, learned to move under his own power. *That* was a victory indeed, and it had taken him almost two years to prepare for it. A hundred times he had envied that dead superchimp, but *he* had been given no choice. The doctors had made their decision – and now, twelve years later, he was where no human being had ever travelled before, and moving faster than any man in history.

Kon-Tiki was just emerging from shadow, and the Jovian dawn bridged the sky ahead in a titanic bow of light, when the persistent buzz of the alarm dragged Falcon up from sleep. The inevitable nightmares (he had been trying to summon a nurse, but did not even have the strength to push the button) swiftly faded from consciousness. The greatest – and perhaps last – adventure of his life was before him.

He called Mission Control, now almost sixty thousand miles away and falling swiftly below the curve of Jupiter, to report that everything was in order. His velocity had just passed thirty-one miles a second (*that* was one for the books) and in half an hour *Kon-Tiki* would hit the outer fringes of the atmosphere, as he started on the most difficult re-entry in the entire solar system. Although scores of probes had survived this flaming ordeal, they had been tough, solidly packed masses of instrumentation, able to withstand several hundred gravities of drag. *Kon-Tiki* would hit peaks of thirty g's, and would average more than ten, before she came to rest in the upper reaches of the Jovian atmosphere. Very carefully and thoroughly, Falcon began to attach the elaborate system of restraints that would anchor him to the walls of the cabin. When he had finished, he was virtually a part of the ship's structure.

The clock was counting backward; one hundred seconds to re-entry. For better or worse, he was committed. In a minute and a half, he would graze the Jovian atmosphere, and would be caught irrevocably in the grip of the giant.

The countdown was three seconds late – not at all bad, considering the unknowns involved. From beyond the walls of the capsule came a ghostly sighing, which rose steadily to a high-pitched, screaming roar. The noise was quite different from that of a re-entry on Earth or Mars; in this atmosphere of hydrogen and helium, all sounds were transformed a couple of octaves upwards. On Jupiter, even thunder would have falsetto overtones.

With the rising scream came mounting weight; within seconds, he was completely immobilized. His field of vision contracted until it embraced only the clock and the accelerometer; fifteen g, and four hundred and eighty seconds to go. . . .

He never lost consciousness, but then, he had not expected to. *Kon-Tiki*'s trail through the Jovian atmosphere must be really spectacular – by this time, thousands of miles long. Five hundred seconds after entry, the drag began to taper off: ten g, five g, two. . . . Then weight vanished almost completely. He was falling free, all his enormous orbital velocity destroyed.

There was a sudden jolt as the incandescent remnants of the heat shield were jettisoned. It had done its work and would not be needed again; Jupiter could have it now. He released all but two of the restraining buckles, and waited for the automatic sequencer to start the next, and most critical, series of events.

He did not see the first drogue parachute pop out, but he could feel the slight jerk, and the rate of fall diminished immediately. *Kon-Tiki* had lost all her horizontal speed and was going straight down at almost a thousand miles an hour. Everything depended on what happened in the next sixty seconds.

There went the second drogue. He looked up through the overhead window and saw, to his immense relief, that clouds of glittering foil were billowing out behind the falling ship. Like a great flower unfurling, the thousands of cubic yards of the balloon spread out across the sky, scooping up the thin gas until it was fully inflated. *Kon-Tiki*'s rate of fall dropped to a few miles an hour and remained constant. Now there was plenty of time; it would take him days to fall all the way down to the surface of Jupiter.

But he would get there eventually, even if he did nothing about it. The balloon overhead was merely acting as an efficient parachute. It was providing no lift; nor could it do so, while the gas inside and out was the same.

With its characteristic and rather disconcerting crack the fusion reactor started up, pouring torrents of heat into the envelope overhead. Within five minutes, the rate of fall had become zero; within six, the ship had started to rise. According to the radar altimeter, it had levelled out at about two hundred and sixty-seven miles above the surface – or whatever passed for a surface on Jupiter.

Only one kind of balloon will work in an atmosphere of hydrogen, which is the lightest of all gases – and that is a hot-hydrogen balloon. As long as the fuser kept ticking over, Falcon could remain aloft, drifting across a world that could hold a hundred Pacifics. After travelling over three hundred million miles, *Kon-Tiki* had at last begun to justify her name. She was an aerial raft, adrift upon the currents of the Jovian atmosphere.

Though a whole new world was lying around him, it was more than an hour before Falcon could examine the view. First he had to check all the capsule's systems and test its response to the controls. He had to learn how much extra heat was necessary to produce a desired rate of ascent, and how much gas he must vent in order to descend. Above all, there was the question of stability. He must adjust the length of the cables attaching his capsule to the huge, pear-shaped balloon, to damp out vibrations and get the smoothest possible ride. Thus far, he was lucky; at this level, the wind was steady, and the Doppler reading on the invisible surface gave him a ground speed of two hundred and seventeen and a half miles an hour. For Jupiter, that was modest; winds of up to a thousand had been observed. But mere speed was, of course, unimportant; the real danger was turbulence. If he ran into that, only skill and experience and swift reaction could save him – and these were not matters that could yet be programmed into a computer.

Not until he was satisfied that he had got the feel of his strange craft did Falcon pay any attention to Mission Control's pleadings. Then he deployed the booms carrying the instrumentation and the atmospheric samplers. The capsule now resembled a rather untidy Christmas tree, but still rode smoothly down the Jovian winds while it radioed its torrents of information to the records on the ship miles above. And now, at last, he could look around. . . .

His first impression was unexpected, and even a little disappointing. As far as the scale of things was concerned, he might have been ballooning over an ordinary cloudscape on Earth. The horizon seemed at a normal distance; there was no feeling at all that he was on a world eleven times the diameter of his own. Then he looked at the infrared radar, sounding the layers of atmosphere beneath him – and knew how badly his eyes had been deceived.

That layer of clouds apparently about three miles away was really more than thirty-seven miles below. And the horizon, whose distance he would have guessed at about one hundred and twenty-five, was actually eighteen hundred miles from the ship.

The crystalline clarity of the hydrohelium atmosphere and the enormous curvature of the planet had fooled him completely. It was even harder to judge distances here than on the Moon; everything he saw must be multiplied by at least ten.

It was a simple matter, and he should have been prepared for it. Yet somehow, it disturbed him profoundly. He did not feel that Jupiter was huge, but that *he* had shrunk – to a tenth of his normal size. Perhaps, with time, he would grow accustomed to the inhuman scale of this world; yet as he stared towards that unbelievably distant horizon, he felt as if a wind colder than the atmosphere around him was blowing through his soul. Despite all his arguments, this might never be a place for man. He could well be both the first and the last to descend through the clouds of Jupiter.

The sky above was almost black, except for a few wisps of ammonia cirrus perhaps twelve miles overhead. It was cold up there, on the fringes of space, but both pressure and temperature increased rapidly with depth. At the level where *Kon-Tiki* was drifting now, it was fifty below zero, and the pressure was five atmospheres. Sixty-five miles farther down, it would be as warm as equatorial Earth, and the pressure about the same as at the bottom of one of the shallower seas. Ideal conditions for life. . . .

A quarter of the brief Jovian day had already gone; the sun

was halfway up the sky, but the light on the unbroken cloud-scape below had a curious mellow quality. That extra three hundred million miles had robbed the Sun of all its power. Though the sky was clear, Falcon found himself continually thinking that it was a heavily overcast day. When night fell, the onset of darkness would be swift indeed; though it was still morning, there was a sense of autumnal twilight in the air. But autumn, of course, was something that never came to Jupiter. There were no seasons here.

Kon-Tiki had come down in the exact centre of the equatorial zone – the least colourful part of the planet. The sea of clouds that stretched out to the horizon was tinted a pale salmon; there were none of the yellows and pinks and even reds that banded Jupiter at higher altitudes. The Great Red Spot itself – most spectacular of all of the planet's features – lay thousands of miles to the south. It had been a temptation to descend there, but the south tropical disturbance was unusually active, with currents reaching over nine hundred miles an hour. It would have been asking for trouble to head into that maelstrom of unknown forces. The Great Red Spot and its mysteries would have to wait for future expeditions.

The Sun, moving across the sky twice as swiftly as it did on Earth, was now nearing the zenith and had become eclipsed by the great silver canopy of the balloon. *Kon-Tiki* was still drifting swiftly and smoothly westward at a steady two hundred and seventeen and a half, but only the radar gave any indication of this. Was it always as calm here? Falcon asked himself. The scientists who had talked learnedly of the Jovian doldrums, and had predicted that the equator would be the quietest place, seemed to know what they were talking about, after all. He had been profoundly sceptical of all such forecasts, and had agreed with one unusually modest researcher who had told him bluntly: 'There are *no* experts on Jupiter.' Well, there would be at least one by the end of this day.

If he managed to survive until then.

4. THE VOICE OF THE DEEP

That first day, the Father of the Gods smiled upon him. It was as calm and peaceful here on Jupiter as it had been, years ago, when he was drifting with Webster across the plains of northern India. Falcon had time to master his new skills, until *Kon-Tiki* seemed an extension of his own body. Such luck was more than he had dared to hope for, and he began to wonder what price he might have to pay for it.

The five hours of daylight were almost over; the clouds below were full of shadows, which gave them a massive solidity they had not possessed when the Sun was higher. Colour was swiftly draining from the sky, except in the west itself, where a band of deepening purple lay along the horizon. Above this band was the thin crescent of a closer moon, pale and bleached against the utter blackness beyond.

With a speed perceptible to the eye, the Sun went straight down over the edge of Jupiter, over eighteen hundred miles away. The stars came out in their legions – and there was the beautiful evening star of Earth, on the very frontier of twilight, reminding him how far he was from home. It followed the Sun down into the west. Man's first night on Jupiter had begun.

With the onset of darkness, *Kon-Tiki* started to sink. The balloon was no longer heated by the feeble sunlight and was losing a small part of its buoyancy. Falcon did nothing to increase lift; he had expected this and was planning to descend.

The invisible cloud deck was still over thirty miles below, and he would reach it about midnight. It showed up clearly on the infrared radar, which also reported that it contained a vast array of complex carbon compounds, as well as the usual hydrogen, helium, and ammonia. The chemists were dying for samples of that fluffy, pinkish stuff; though some atmospheric probes had already gathered a few grams, that had only whetted their appetites. Half the basic molecules of life were here, floating high above the surface of Jupiter. And where there was food, could life be far away? That was the question that, after more than a hundred years, no one had been able to answer.

The infrared was blocked by the clouds, but the microwave

radar sliced right through and showed layer after layer, all the way down to the hidden surface almost two hundred and fifty miles below. That was barred to him by enormous pressures and temperatures; not even robot probes had ever reached it intact. It lay in tantalizing inaccessibility at the bottom of the radar screen, slightly fuzzy, and showing a curious granular structure that his equipment could not resolve.

An hour after sunset, he dropped his first probe. It fell swiftly for about sixty miles, then began to float in the denser atmosphere, sending back torrents of radio signals, which he relayed to Mission Control. Then there was nothing else to do until sunrise, except to keep an eye on the rate of descent, monitor the instruments, and answer occasional queries. While she was drifting in this steady current, *Kon-Tiki* could look after herself.

Just before midnight, a woman controller came on watch and introduced herself with the usual pleasantries. Ten minutes later she called again, her voice at once serious and excited.

'Howard! Listen in on channel forty-six – high gain.'

Channel forty-six? There were so many telemetering circuits that he knew the numbers of only those that were critical; but as soon as he threw the switch, he recognized this one. He was plugged in to the microphone on the probe, floating more than eighty miles below him in an atmosphere now almost as dense as water.

At first, there was only a soft hiss of whatever strange winds stirred down in the darkness of that unimaginable world. And then, out of the background noise, there slowly emerged a booming vibration that grew louder and louder, like the beating of a gigantic drum. It was so low that it was felt as much as heard, and the beats steadily increased their tempo, though the pitch never changed. Now it was a swift, almost infrasonic throbbing. Then, suddenly, in mid-vibration, it stopped – so abruptly that the mind could not accept the silence, but memory continued to manufacture a ghostly echo in the deepest caverns of the brain.

It was the most extraordinary sound that Falcon had ever heard, even among the multitudinous noises of Earth. He could think of no natural phenomenon that could have caused it; nor was it like the cry of any animal, not even one of the great whales. . . .

It came again, following exactly the same pattern. Now that he was prepared for it, he estimated the length of the sequence; from first faint throb to final crescendo, it lasted just over ten seconds.

And this time there was a real echo, very faint and far away. Perhaps it came from one of the many reflecting layers, deeper in this stratified atmosphere; perhaps it was another, more distant source. Falcon waited for a second echo, but it never came.

Mission Control reacted quickly and asked him to drop another probe at once. With two microphones operating, it would be possible to find the approximate location of the sources. Oddly enough, none of *Kon-Tiki*'s own external mikes could detect anything except wind noises. The boomings, whatever they were, must have been trapped and channelled beneath an atmospheric reflecting layer far below.

They were coming, it was soon discovered, from a cluster of sources about twelve hundred miles away. The distance gave no indication of their power; in Earth's oceans, quite feeble sounds could travel equally far. And as for the obvious assumption that living creatures were responsible, the Chief Exobiologist quickly ruled that out.

'I'll be very disappointed,' said Dr. Brenner, 'if there are no micro-organisms or plants there. But nothing like animals, because there's no free oxygen. All biochemical reactions on Jupiter must be low-energy ones – there's just no way an active creature could generate enough power to function.'

Falcon wondered if this was true; he had heard the argument before, and reserved judgment.

'In any case,' continued Brenner, 'some of those sound waves are a hundred yards long! Even an animal as big as a whale couldn't produce them. They *must* have a natural origin.'

Yes, that seemed plausible, and probably the physicists would be able to come up with an explanation. What would a blind alien make, Falcon wondered, of the sounds he might hear when standing beside a stormy sea, or a geyser, or a volcano, or a waterfall? He might well attribute them to some huge beast.

About an hour before sunrise the voices of the deep died away, and Falcon began to busy himself with preparation for the dawn of his second day. *Kon-Tiki* was now only three miles above the nearest cloud layer; the external pressure had risen to ten atmospheres, and the temperature was a tropical thirty degrees. A man could be comfortable here with no more equipment than a breathing mask and the right grade of heliox mixture.

'We've some good news for you,' Mission Control reported, soon after dawn. 'The cloud layer's breaking up. You'll have partial clearing in an hour – but watch out for turbulence.'

'I've already noticed some,' Falcon answered. 'How far down will I be able to see?'

'At least twelve miles, down to the second thermocline. *That* cloud deck is solid – it never breaks.'

And it's out of my reach, Falcon told himself; the temperature down there must be over a hundred degrees. This was the first time that any balloonist had ever had to worry, not about his ceiling, but about his basement!

Ten minutes later he could see what Mission Control had already observed from its superior vantage point. There was a change in colour near the horizon, and the cloud layer had become ragged and humpy, as if something had torn it open. He turned up his little nuclear furnace and gave *Kon-Tiki* another three miles of altitude, so that he could get a better view.

The sky below was clearing rapidly, completely, as if something was dissolving the solid overcast. An abyss was opening before his eyes. A moment later he sailed out over the edge of a cloud canyon about twelve miles deep and six hundred miles wide.

A new world lay spread beneath him; Jupiter had stripped away one of its many veils. The second layer of clouds, unattainably far below, was much darker in colour than the first. It was almost salmon pink, and curiously mottled with little islands of brick red. They were all oval-shaped, with their long axes pointing east-west, in the direction of the prevailing wind. There were hundreds of them, all about the same size, and they reminded Falcon of puffy little cumulus clouds in the terrestrial sky.

He reduced buoyancy, and *Kon-Tiki* began to drop down the face of the dissolving cliff. It was then that he noticed the snow.

White flakes were forming in the air and drifting slowly downward. Yet it was much too warm for snow – and, in any event, there was scarcely a trace of water at this altitude. Moreover, there was no glitter or sparkle about these flakes as they went cascading down into the depths. When, presently, a few landed on an instrumental boom outside the main viewing port, he saw that they were a dull, opaque white – not crystalline at all – and quite large – several inches across. They looked like wax, and Falcon guessed that this was precisely what they were. Some chemical reaction was taking place in the atmosphere around him, condensing out the hydrocarbons floating in the Jovian air.

About sixty miles ahead, a disturbance was taking place in the cloud layer. The little red ovals were being jostled around, and were beginning to form a spiral – the familiar cyclonic pattern so common in the meteorology of Earth. The vortex was emerging with astonishing speed; if that was a storm ahead, Falcon told himself, he was in big trouble.

And then his concern changed to wonder – and to fear. What was developing in his line of flight was not a storm at all. Something enormous – something scores of miles across – was rising through the clouds.

The reassuring thought that it, too, might be a cloud – a thunderhead boiling up from the lower levels of the atmosphere – lasted only a few seconds. No; this was *solid*. It shouldered its way through the pink-and-salmon overcast like an iceberg rising from the deeps.

An *iceberg* floating on hydrogen? That was impossible, of course; but perhaps it was not too remote an analogy. As soon as he focused the telescope upon the enigma, Falcon saw that it was a whitish, crystalline mass, threaded with streaks of red and brown. It must be, he decided, the same stuff as the 'snowflakes' falling around him – a mountain range of wax. And it was not, he soon realized, as solid as he had thought; around the edges it was continually crumbling and re-forming. . . .

'I know what it is,' he radioed Mission Control, which for the last few minutes had been asking anxious questions. 'It's a mass of bubbles – some kind of foam. Hydrocarbon froth. Get the chemists working on . . . *Just a minute*!'

'What is it?' called Mission Control. 'What is it?'

He ignored the frantic pleas from space and concentrated all his mind upon the image in the telescope field. He had to be sure; if he made a mistake, he would be the laughingstock of the solar system.

Then he relaxed, glanced at the clock, and switched off the nagging voice from Jupiter V.

'Hello, Mission Control,' he said, very formally. 'This is Howard Falcon aboard *Kon-Tiki*. Ephemeris Time nineteen hours twenty-one minutes fifteen seconds. Latitude zero degrees five minutes North. Longitude one hundred and five degrees forty-two minutes, System One.

'Tell Dr. Brenner that there is life on Jupiter. And it's *big*. . . .'

5. THE WHEELS OF POSEIDON

'I'm very happy to be proved wrong,' Dr. Brenner radioed back cheerfully. 'Nature always has something up her sleeve. Keep the long-focus camera on target and give us the steadiest pictures you can.'

The things moving up and down those waxen slopes were still too far away for Falcon to make out many details, and they must have been very large to be visible at all at such a distance. Almost black, and shaped like arrowheads, they manoeuvred by slow undulations of their entire bodies, so that they looked rather like giant manta rays, swimming above some tropical reef.

Perhaps they were sky-borne cattle, browsing on the cloud pastures of Jupiter, for they seemed to be feeding along the dark, red-brown streaks that ran like dried-up river beds down the flanks of the floating cliffs. Occasionally, one of them would dive headlong into the mountains of foam and disappear completely from sight.

Kon-Tiki was moving only slowly with respect to the cloud layer below; it would be at least three hours before she was above those ephemeral hills. She was in a race with the Sun. Falcon hoped that darkness would not fall before he could get a good view of the mantas, as he had christened them, as well as the fragile landscape over which they flapped their way.

It was a long three hours. During the whole time, he kept the external microphones on full gain, wondering if here was the source of that booming in the night. The mantas were certainly large enough to have produced it; when he could get an accurate measurement, he discovered that they were almost a hundred yards across the wings. That was three times the length of the largest whale – though he doubted if they could weigh more than a few tons.

Half an hour before sunset, *Kon-Tiki* was almost above the 'mountains'.

'No,' said Falcon, answering Mission Control's repeated questions about the mantas, 'they're still showing no reaction to me. I don't think they're intelligent – they look like harmless vegetarians. And even if they try to chase me, I'm sure they can't reach my altitude.'

Yet he was a little disappointed when the mantas showed not the slightest interest in him as he sailed high above their feeding ground. Perhaps they had no way of detecting his presence. When he examined and photographed them through the telescope, he could see no signs of any sense organs. The creatures were simply huge black deltas, rippling over hills and valleys that, in reality, were little more substantial than the clouds of Earth. Though they looked solid, Falcon knew that anyone who stepped on those white mountains would go crashing through them as if they were made of tissue paper.

At close quarters he could see the myriads of cellules or bubbles from which they were formed. Some of these were quite large – a yard or so in diameter – and Falcon wondered in what witches' cauldron of hydrocarbons they had been brewed. There must be enough petrochemicals deep down in the atmosphere of Jupiter to supply all Earth's needs for a million years.

The short day had almost gone when he passed over the crest of the waxen hills, and the light was fading rapidly along their lower slopes. There were no mantas on this western side, and for some reason the topography was very different. The foam was sculptured into long, level terraces, like the interior of a lunar crater. He could almost imagine that they were gigantic steps leading down to the hidden surface of the planet.

And on the lowest of those steps, just clear of the swirling clouds that the mountain had displaced when it came surging skyward, was a roughly oval mass, one or two miles across. It was difficult to see, since it was only a little darker than the grey-white foam on which it rested. Falcon's first thought was that he was looking at a forest of pallid trees, like giant mushrooms that had never seen the Sun.

Yes, it must be a forest – he could see hundreds of thin trunks, springing from the white waxy froth in which they were rooted. But the trees were packed astonishingly close together; there was scarcely any space between them. Perhaps it was not a forest, after all, but a single enormous tree – like one of the giant multi-trunked banyans of the East. Once he had seen a banyan tree in Java that was over six hundred and fifty yards across; this monster was at least ten times that size.

The light had almost gone. The cloudscape had turned purple with refracted sunlight, and in a few seconds that, too, would have vanished. In the last light of his second day on Jupiter, Howard Falcon saw – or thought he saw – something that cast the gravest doubts on his interpretation of the white oval.

Unless the dim light had totally deceived him, those hundreds of thin trunks were beating back and forth, in perfect synchronism, like fronds of kelp rocking in the surge.

And the tree was no longer in the place where he had first seen it.

'Sorry about this,' said Mission Control, soon after sunset, 'but we think Source Beta is going to blow within the next hour. Probability seventy per cent.'

Falcon glanced quickly at the chart. Beta – Jupiter latitude one hundred and forty degrees – was over eighteen thousand six hundred miles away and well below his horizon. Even though major eruptions ran as high as ten megatons, he was much too far away for the shock wave to be a serious danger. The radio storm that it would trigger was, however, quite a different matter.

The decametre outbursts that sometimes made Jupiter the most powerful radio source in the whole sky had been discovered back in the 1950s, to the utter astonishment of the astronomers. Now, more than a century later, their real cause was still a mystery. Only the symptoms were understood; the explanation was completely unknown.

The 'volcano' theory had best stood the test of time, although no one imagined that this word had the same meaning on Jupiter as on Earth. At frequent intervals – often several times a day – titanic eruptions occurred in the lower depths of the atmosphere, probably on the hidden surface of the planet itself. A great column of gas, more than six hundred miles high, would start boiling upward as if determined to escape into space.

Against the most powerful gravitational field of all the planets, it had no chance. Yet some traces – a mere few million tons – usually managed to reach the Jovian ionosphere; and when they did, all hell broke loose.

The radiation belts surrounding Jupiter completely dwarf the feeble Van Allen belts of Earth. When they are short-circuited by an ascending column of gas, the result is an electrical discharge millions of times more powerful than any terrestrial flash of lightning; it sends a colossal thunderclap of radio noise flooding across the entire solar system and on out to the stars.

It had been discovered that these radio outbursts came from four main areas of the planet. Perhaps there were weaknesses there that allowed the fires of the interior to break out from time to time. The scientists on Ganymede, largest of Jupiter's many moons, now thought that they could predict the onset of a decametre storm; their accuracy was about as good as a weather forecaster's of the early 1900s.

Falcon did not know whether to welcome or to fear a radio storm; it would certainly add to the value of the mission – if he survived it. His course had been planned to keep as far as possible from the main centres of disturbance, especially the most active one, Source Alpha. As luck would have it, the threatening Beta was the closest to him. He hoped that the distance, almost three-fourths the circumference of Earth, was safe enough.

'Probability ninety per cent,' said Mission Control with a distinct note of urgency. 'And forget that hour. Ganymede says it may be any moment.'

The radio had scarcely fallen silent when the reading on the magnetic field-strength meter started to shoot upward. Before it could go off scale, it reversed and began to drop as rapidly as it had risen. Far away and thousands of miles below, something had given the planet's molten core a titanic jolt.

'There she blows!' called Mission Control.

'Thanks, I already know. When will the storm hit me?'

'You can expect onset in five minutes. Peak in ten.'

Far around the curve of Jupiter, a funnel of gas as wide as the Pacific Ocean was climbing spacewards at thousands of miles an hour. Already, the thunderstorms of the lower atmosphere would be raging around it – but they were nothing compared with the fury that would explode when the radiation belt was reached and began dumping its surplus electrons on to the planet. Falcon began to retract all the instrument booms that were extended out from the capsule. There were no other precautions he could take. It would be four hours before the atmospheric shock wave reached him – but the radio blast, travelling at the speed of light, would be here in a tenth of a second, once the discharge had been triggered.

The radio monitor, scanning back and forth across the spectrum, still showed nothing unusual, just the normal mush of background static. Then Falcon noticed that the noise level was slowly creeping upwards. The explosion was gathering its strength.

At such a distance he had never expected to *see* anything. But suddenly a flicker as of far-off lightning danced along the eastern horizon. Simultaneously, half the circuit breakers jumped out of the main switchboard, the lights failed, and all communications channels went dead.

He tried to move, but was completely unable to do so. The paralysis that gripped him was not merely psychological; he seemed to have lost all control of his limbs and could feel a painful tingling sensation over his entire body. It was impossible that the electric field could have penetrated this shielded cabin. Yet there was a flickering glow over the instrument board, and he could hear the unmistakable crackle of a brush discharge.

With a series of sharp bangs, the emergency systems went into operation, and the overloads reset themselves. The lights flickered on again. And Falcon's paralysis disappeared as swiftly as it had come.

After glancing at the board to make sure that all circuits were back to normal, he moved quickly to the viewing ports.

There was no need to switch on the inspection lamps – the cables supporting the capsule seemed to be on fire. Lines of light glowing an electric blue against the darkness stretched upwards from the main lift ring to the equator of the giant balloon; and rolling slowly along several of them were dazzling balls of fire.

The sight was so strange and so beautiful that it was hard to read any menace in it. Few people, Falcon knew, had ever seen ball lightning from such close quarters – and certainly none had survived if they were riding a hydrogen-filled balloon back in the atmosphere of Earth. He remembered the flaming death of the *Hindenburg*, destroyed by a stray spark when she docked at Lakehurst in 1937; as it had done so often in the past, the horrifying old newsreel film flashed through his mind. But at least that could not happen here, though there was more hydrogen above his head than had ever filled the last of the Zeppelins. It would be a few billion years yet, before anyone could light a fire in the atmosphere of Jupiter.

With a sound like briskly frying bacon, the speech circuit came back to life.

'Hello, *Kon-Tiki* – are you receiving? Are you receiving?'

The words were chopped and badly distorted, but intelligible. Falcon's spirits lifted; he had resumed contact with the world of men.

'I receive you,' he said. 'Quite an electrical display, but no damage – so far.'

'Thanks – thought we'd lost you. Please check telemetry channels three, seven, twenty-six. Also gain on camera two. And we don't quite believe the readings on the external ionization probes. . . .'

Reluctanctly Falcon tore his gaze away from the fascinating pyrotechnic display around *Kon-Tiki*, though from time to time he kept glancing out of the windows. The ball lightning disappeared first, the fiery globes slowly expanding until they reached a critical size, at which they vanished in a gentle explosion. But even an hour later, there were still faint glows around all the exposed metal on the outside of the capsule; and the radio circuits remained noisy until well after midnight.

The remaining hours of darkness were completely uneventful – until just before dawn. Because it came from the east, Falcon assumed that he was seeing the first faint hint of sunrise. Then he realized that it was twenty minutes too early for this – and the glow that had appeared along the horizon was moving towards him even as he watched. It swiftly detached itself from the arch of stars that marked the invisible edge of the planet, and he saw that it was a relatively narrow band, quite sharply defined. The beam of an enormous searchlight appeared to be swinging beneath the clouds.

Perhaps sixty miles behind the first racing bar of light came another, parallel to it and moving at the same speed. And beyond that another, and another – until all the sky flickered with alternating sheets of light and darkness.

By this time, Falcon thought, he had been inured to wonders, and it seemed impossible that this display of pure, soundless luminosity could present the slightest danger. But it was so astonishing, and so inexplicable, that he felt cold, naked fear gnawing at his self-control. No man could look upon such a sight without feeling like a helpless pygmy in the presence of forces beyond his comprehension. Was it possible that, after all, Jupiter carried not only life but also intelligence? And, perhaps, an intelligence that only now was beginning to react to his alien presence?

'Yes, we see it,' said Mission Control, in a voice that echoed his own awe. 'We've no idea what it is. Stand by, we're calling Ganymede.'

The display was slowly fading; the bands racing in from the far horizon were much fainter, as if the energies that powered them were becoming exhausted. In five minutes it was all over; the last faint pulse of light flickered along the western sky and then was gone. Its passing left Falcon with an overwhelming sense of relief. The sight was so hypnotic, and so disturbing, that it was not good for any man's peace of mind to contemplate it too long.

He was more shaken that he cared to admit. The electrical storm was something that he could understand; but *this* was totally incomprehensible.

Mission Control was still silent. He knew that the information banks up on Ganymede were now being searched as men and computers turned their minds to the problem. If no answer could be found there, it would be necessary to call Earth; that would mean a delay of almost an hour. The possibility that even Earth might be unable to help was one that Falcon did not care to contemplate.

He had never before been so glad to hear the voice of Mission Control as when Dr. Brenner finally came on the circuit. The biologist sounded relieved, yet subdued – like a man who has just come through some great intellectual crisis.

'Hello, *Kon-Tiki*. We've solved your problem, but we can still hardly believe it.

'What you've been seeing is bioluminescence, very similar

to that produced by micro-organisms in the tropical seas of Earth. Here they're in the atmosphere, not the ocean, but the principle is the same.'

'But the pattern,' protested Falcon, 'was so regular – so *artificial*. And it was hundreds of miles across!'

'It was even larger than you imagine; you observed only a small part of it. The whole pattern was over three thousand miles wide and looked like a revolving wheel. You merely saw the spokes, sweeping past you at about six-tenths of a mile a second. . . .'

'A *second*!' Falcon could not help interjecting. 'No animals could move that fast!'

'Of course not. Let me explain. What you saw was triggered by the shock wave from Source Beta, moving at the speed of sound.'

'But what about the pattern?' Falcon insisted.

'That's the surprising part. It's a very rare phenomenon, but identical wheels of light – except that they're a thousand times smaller – have been observed in the Persian Gulf and the Indian Ocean. Listen to this: British India Company's *Patna*, Persian Gulf, May 1880, 11.30 P.M. – "an enormous luminous wheel, whirling round, the spokes of which appeared to brush the ship along. The spokes were 200 or 300 yards long . . . each wheel contained about sixteen spokes. . . .' And here's one from the Gulf of Omar, dated May 23, 1906: "The intensely bright luminescence approached us rapidly, shooting sharply defined light rays to the west in rapid succession, like the beam from the searchlight of a warship. . . . To the left of us, a gigantic fiery wheel formed itself, with spokes that reached as far as one could see. The whole wheel whirled around for two or three minutes. . . ." The archive computer on Ganymede dug up about five hundred cases. It would have printed out the lot if we hadn't stopped it in time.'

'I'm convinced – but still baffled.'

'I don't blame you. The full explanation wasn't worked out until late in the twentieth century. It seems that these luminous wheels are the results of submarine earthquakes, and always occur in shallow waters where the shock waves can be reflected and cause standing wave patterns. Sometimes bars, sometimes rotating wheels – the "Wheels of Poseidon", they've been called. The theory was finally proved by making underwater explosions and photographing the results from a satellite. No wonder sailors used to be superstitious. Who would have believed a thing like *this*?'

So that was it, Falcon told himself. When Source Beta blew its top, it must have sent shock waves in all directions – through the compressed gas of the lower atmosphere, through the solid body of Jupiter itself. Meeting and crisscrossing, those waves must have cancelled here, reinforced there; the whole planet must have rung like a bell.

Yet the explanation did not destroy the sense of wonder and awe; he would never be able to forget those flickering bands of light, racing through the unattainable depths of the Jovian atmosphere. He felt that he was not merely on a strange planet, but in some magical realm between myth and reality.

This was a world where absolutely *anything* could happen, and no man could possibly guess what the future would bring.

And he still had a whole day to go.

6. MEDUSA

When the true dawn finally arrived, it brought a sudden change of weather. *Kon-Tiki* was moving through a blizzard; waxen snowflakes were falling so thickly that visibility was reduced to zero. Falcon began to worry about the weight that might be accumulating on the envelope. Then he noticed that any flakes settling outside the windows quickly disappeared; *Kon-Tiki*'s continual outpouring of heat was evaporating them as swiftly as they arrived.

If he had been ballooning on Earth, he would also have worried about the possibility of collision. At least that was no danger here; any Jovian mountains were several hundred miles below him. And as for the floating islands of foam, hitting them would probably be like ploughing into slightly hardened soap bubbles.

Nevertheless, he switched on the horizontal radar, which

until now had been completely useless; only the vertical beam, giving his distance from the invisible surface, had thus far been of any value. Then he had another surprise.

Scattered across a huge sector of the sky ahead were dozens of large and brilliant echoes. They were completely isolated from one another and apparently hung unsupported in space. Falcon remembered a phrase the earliest aviators had used to describe one of the hazards of their profession: 'clouds stuffed with rocks'. That was a perfect description of what seemed to lie in the track of *Kon-Tiki*.

It was a disconcerting sight; then Falcon again reminded himself that nothing *really* solid could possibly hover in this atmosphere. Perhaps it was some strange meteorological phenomenon. In any case, the nearest echo was about a hundred and twenty-five miles.

He reported to Mission Control, which could provide no explanation. But it gave the welcome news that he would be clear of the blizzard in another thirty minutes.

It did not warn him, however, of the violent cross wind that abruptly grabbed *Kon-Tiki* and swept it almost at right angles to its previous track. Falcon needed all his skill and the maximum use of what little control he had over his ungainly vehicle to prevent it from being capsized. Within minutes he was racing northward at over three hundred miles an hour. Then, as suddenly as it had started, the turbulence ceased; he was still moving at high speed, but in smooth air. He wondered if he had been caught in the Jovian equivalent of a jet stream.

The snow storm dissolved; and he saw what Jupiter had been preparing for him.

Kon-Tiki had entered the funnel of a gigantic whirlpool, some six hundred miles across. The balloon was being swept along a curving wall of cloud. Overhead, the sun was shining in a clear sky, but far beneath, this great hole in the atmosphere drilled down to unknown depths until it reached a misty floor where lightning flickered almost continuously.

Though the vessel was being dragged downwards so slowly that it was in no immediate danger, Falcon increased the flow of heat into the envelope until *Kon-Tiki* hovered at a constant altitude. Not until then did he abandon the fantastic spectacle outside and consider again the problem of the radar.

The nearest echo was now only about twenty-five miles away. All of them, he quickly realized, were distributed along the wall of the vortex, and were moving with it, apparently caught in the whirlpool like *Kon-Tiki* itself. He aimed the telescope along the radar bearing and found himself looking at a curious mottled cloud that almost filled the field of view.

It was not easy to see, being only a little darker than the whirling wall of mist that formed its background. Not until he had been staring for several minutes did Falcon realize that he had met it once before.

The first time it had been crawling across the drifting mountains of foam, and he had mistaken it for a giant, many-trunked tree. Now at last he could appreciate its real size and complexity and could give it a better name to fix its image in his mind. It did not resemble a tree at all, but a jellyfish – a medusa, such as might be met trailing its tentacles as it drifted along the warm eddies of the Gulf Stream.

This medusa was more than a mile across and its scores of dangling tentacles were hundreds of feet long. They swayed slowly back and forth in perfect unison, taking more than a minute for each complete undulation – almost as if the creature was clumsily rowing itself through the sky.

The other echoes were more distant medusae. Falcon focused the telescope on half a dozen and could see no variations in shape or size. They all seemed to be of the same species, and he wondered just why they were drifting lazily around in this six-hundred-mile orbit. Perhaps they were feeding upon the aerial plankton sucked in by the whirlpool, as *Kon-Tiki* itself had been.

'Do you realize, Howard,' said Dr. Brenner, when he had recovered from his initial astonishment, 'that this thing is about a hundred thousand times as large as the biggest whale? And even if it's only a gasbag, it must still weigh a million tons! I can't even guess at its metabolism. It must generate megawatts of heat to maintain its buoyancy.'

'But if it's just a gasbag, why is it such a damn good radar reflector?'

'I haven't the faintest idea. Can you get any closer?'

Brenner's question was not an idle one. If he changed altitude to take advantage of the different wind velocities, Falcon could approach the medusa as closely as he wished. At the móment, however, he preferred his present twenty-five miles and said so, firmly.

'I see what you mean,' Brenner answered, a little reluctantly. 'Let's stay where we are for the present.' That 'we' gave Falcon a certain wry amusement; an extra sixty thousand miles made a considerable difference in one's point of view.

For the next two hours *Kon-Tiki* drifted uneventfully in the gyre of the great whirlpool, while Falcon experimented with filters and camera contrast, trying to get a clear view of the medusa. He began to wonder if its elusive coloration was some kind of camouflage; perhaps, like many animals of Earth, it was trying to lose itself against its background. That was a trick used by both hunters and hunted.

In which category was the medusa? That was a question he could hardly expect to have answered in the short time that was left to him. Yet just before noon, without the slightest warning, the answer came. . . .

Like a squadron of antique jet fighters, five mantas came sweeping through the wall of mist that formed the funnel of the vortex. They were flying in a V formation directly towards the pallid grey cloud of the medusa; and there was no doubt, in Falcon's mind, that they were on the attack. He had been quite wrong to assume that they were harmless vegetarians.

Yet everything happened at such a leisurely pace that it was like watching a slow-motion film. The mantas undulated along at perhaps thirty miles an hour; it seemed ages before they reached the medusa, which continued to paddle imperturbably along at an even slower speed. Huge though they were, the mantas looked tiny beside the monster they were approaching. When they flapped down on its back, they appeared about as large as birds landing on a whale.

Could the medusa defend itself, Falcon wondered. He did not see how the attacking mantas could be in danger as long as they avoided those huge clumsy tentacles. And perhaps their host was not even aware of them; they could be insignificant parasites, tolerated as are fleas upon a dog.

But now it was obvious that the medusa was in distress. With agonizing slowness, it began to tip over like a capsizing ship. After ten minutes it had tilted forty-five degrees; it was also rapidly losing altitude. It was impossible not to feel a sense of pity for the beleaguered monster, and to Falcon the sight brought bitter memories. In a grotesque way, the fall of the medusa was almost a parody of the dying *Queen*'s last moments.

Yet he knew that his sympathies were on the wrong side. High intelligence could develop only among predators – not among the drifting browsers of either sea or air. The mantas were far closer to him than was this monstrous bag of gas. And anyway, who could *really* sympathize with a creature a hundred thousand times larger than a whale?

Then he noticed that the medusa's tactics seemed to be having some effect. The mantas had been disturbed by its slow roll and were flapping heavily away from its back – like gorged vultures interrupted at mealtime. But they did not move very far, continuing to hover a few yards from the still-capsizing monster.

There was a sudden, blinding flash of light synchronized with a crash of static over the radio. One of the mantas, slowly twisting end over end, was plummeting straight downwards. As it fell, a plume of black smoke trailed behind it. The resemblance to an aircraft going down in flames was quite uncanny.

In unison, the remaining mantas dived steeply away from the medusa, gaining speed by losing altitude. They had, within minutes, vanished back into the wall of cloud from which they had emerged. And the medusa, no longer falling, began to roll back towards the horizontal. Soon it was sailing along once more on an even keel, as if nothing had happened.

'Beautiful!' said Dr. Brenner, after a moment of stunned silence. 'It's developed electric defences, like some of our eels and rays. But that must have been about a million volts! Can you see any organs that might produce the discharge? Anything looking like electrodes?'

'No,' Falcon answered, after switching to the highest power of the telescope. 'But here's something odd. Do you see this pattern? Check back on the earlier images. I'm sure it wasn't there before.'

A broad, mottled band had appeared along the side of the medusa. It formed a startlingly regular checkerboard, each square of which was itself speckled in a complex subpattern of short horizontal lines. They were spaced at equal distances in a geometrically perfect array of rows and columns.

'You're right,' said Dr. Brenner, with something very much like awe in his voice. 'That's just appeared. And I'm afraid to tell you what I think it is.'

'Well, I have no reputation to lose – at least as a biologist. Shall I give my guess?'

'Go ahead.'

'That's a large metre-band radio array. The sort of thing they used back at the beginning of the twentieth century.'

'I was afraid you'd say that. Now we know why it gave such a massive echo.'

'But why has it just appeared?'

'Probably an aftereffect of the discharge.'

'I've just had another thought,' said Falcon, rather slowly. 'Do you suppose it's *listening* to us?'

'On this frequency? I doubt it. Those are metre – no, *decametre* antennas – judging by their size. Hmm . . . that's an idea!'

Dr. Brenner fell silent, obviously contemplating some new line of thought. Presently he continued: 'I bet they're tuned to the radio outbursts! That's something nature never got around to doing on Earth. . . . We have animals with sonar and even electric senses, but nothing ever developed a radio sense. Why bother where there was so much light?

'But it's different here. Jupiter is *drenched* with radio energy. It's worthwhile using it – maybe even tapping it. That thing could be a floating power plant!'

A new voice cut into the conversation.

'Mission Commander here. This is all very interesting, but

there's a much more important matter to settle. *Is it intelligent?* If so, we've got to consider the First Contact directives.'

'Until I came here,' said Dr. Brenner, somewhat ruefully, 'I would have sworn that anything that could make a short-wave antenna system *must* be intelligent. Now, I'm not sure. This could have evolved naturally. I suppose it's no more fantastic than the human eye.'

'Then we have to play safe and assume intelligence. For the present, therefore, this expedition comes under all the clauses of the Prime directive.'

There was a long silence while everyone on the radio circuit absorbed the implications of this. For the first time in the history of space flight, the rules that had been established through more than a century of argument might have to be applied. Man had – it was hoped – profited from his mistakes on Earth. Not only moral considerations, but also his own self-interest demanded that he should not repeat them among the planets. It could be disastrous to treat a superior intelligence as the American settlers had treated the Indians, or as almost everyone had treated the Africans. . . .

The first rule was: keep your distance. Make no attempt to approach, or even to communicate, until 'they' have had plenty of time to study you. Exactly what was meant by 'plenty of time', no one had ever been able to decide. It was left to the discretion of the man on the spot.

A responsibility of which he had never dreamed had descended upon Howard Falcon. In the few hours that remained to him on Jupiter, he might become the first ambassador of the human race.

And *that* was an irony so delicious that he almost wished the surgeons had restored to him the power of laughter.

7. PRIME DIRECTIVE

It was growing darker, but Falcon scarcely noticed as he strained his eyes towards that living cloud in the field of the telescope. The wind that was steadily sweeping *Kon-Tiki* around the funnel of the great whirlpool had now brought him within twelve miles of the creature. If he got much closer than six, he would take evasive action. Though he felt certain that the medusa's electric weapons were short ranged, he did not wish to put the matter to the test. That would be a problem for future explorers, and he wished them luck.

Now it was quite dark in the capsule. That was strange, because sunset was still hours away. Automatically, he glanced at the horizontally scanning radar, as he had done every few minutes. Apart from the medusa he was studying, there was no other object within about sixty miles of him.

Suddenly, with startling power, he heard the sound that had come booming out of the Jovian night – the throbbing beat that grew more and more rapid, then stopped in mid-crescendo. The whole capsule vibrated with it like a pea in a kettledrum.

Falcon realized two things almost simultaneously during the sudden, aching silence. *This* time the sound was not coming from thousands of miles away, over a radio circuit. It was in the very atmosphere around him.

The second thought was even more disturbing. He had quite forgotten – it was inexcusable, but there had been other apparently more important things on his mind – that most of the sky above him was completely blanked out by *Kon-Tiki*'s gasbag. Being lightly silvered to conserve its heat, the great balloon was an effective shield both to radar and to vision.

He had known this, of course; it had been a minor defect of the design, tolerated because it did not appear important. It seemed very important to Howard Falcon now – as he saw that fence of gigantic tentacles, thicker than the trunks of any tree, descending all around the capsule.

He heard Brenner yelling: 'Remember the Prime directive! Don't alarm it!' Before he could make an appropriate answer that overwhelming drumbeat started again and drowned all other sounds

The sign of a really skilled test pilot is how he reacts not to foreseeable emergencies, but to ones that nobody could have anticipated. Falcon did not hesitate for more than a second to analyse the situation. In a lightning-swift movement, he pulled the rip cord.

That word was an archaic survival from the days of the first hydrogen balloons; on *Kon-Tiki*, the rip cord did not tear open the gasbag but merely operated a set of louvres around the upper curve of the envelope. At once the hot gas started to rush out; *Kon-Tiki*, deprived of her lift, began to fall swiftly in this gravity field two and a half times as strong as Earth's.

Falcon had a momentary glimpse of great tentacles whipping upward and away. He had just time to note that they were studded with large bladders or sacs, presumably to give them buoyancy, and that they ended in multitudes of thin feelers like the roots of a plant. He half expected a bolt of lightning – but nothing happened.

His precipitous rate of descent was slackening as the atmosphere thickened and the deflated envelope acted as a parachute. When *Kon-Tiki* had dropped about two miles, he felt that it was safe to close the louvres again. By the time he had restored buoyancy and was in equilibrium once more, he had lost another mile of altitude and was getting dangerously near his safety limit

He peered anxiously through the overhead windows, though he did not expect to see anything except the obscuring bulk of the balloon. But he had sideslipped during his descent, and part of the medusa was just visible a couple of miles above him. It was much closer than he expected – and it was still coming down, faster than he would have believed possible.

Mission Control was calling anxiously. He shouted: 'I'm O.K. – but it's still coming after me. I can't go any deeper.'

That was not quite true. He could go a lot deeper – about one hundred and eighty miles. But it would be a one-way trip, and most of the journey would be of little interest to him.

Then, to his great relief, he saw that the medusa was levelling off, not quite a mile above him. Perhaps it had decided to approach this strange intruder with caution; or perhaps it, too, found this deeper layer uncomfortably hot. The temperature was over fifty degrees centigrade, and Falcon wondered how much longer his life-support system could handle matters.

Dr. Brenner was back on the circuit, still worrying about the Prime directive.

'Remember – it may only be inquisitive!' he cried, without much conviction. 'Try not to frighten it!'

Falcon was getting rather tired of this advice and recalled a TV discussion he had once seen between a space lawyer and an astronaut. After the full implications of the Prime directive had been carefully spelled out, the incredulous spacer had exclaimed: 'Then if there was no alternative, I must sit still and let myself be eaten?' The lawyer had not even cracked a smile when he answered: 'That's an *excellent* summing up.'

It had seemed funny at the time; it was not at all amusing now.

And then Falcon saw something that made him even more unhappy. The medusa was still hovering about a mile above him – but one of its tentacles was becoming incredibly elongated, and was stretching down towards *Kon-Tiki*, thinning out at the same time. As a boy he had once seen the funnel of a tornado descending from a storm cloud over the Kansas plains. The thing coming towards him now evoked vivid memories of that black, twisting snake in the sky.

'I'm rapidly running out of options,' he reported to Mission Control. 'I now have only a choice between frightening it – and giving it a bad stomach-ache. I don't think it will find *Kon-Tiki* very digestible, if that's what it has in mind.'

He waited for comments from Brenner, but the biologist remained silent.

'Very well. It's twenty-seven minutes ahead of time, but I'm starting the ignition sequencer. I hope I'll have enough reserve to correct my orbit later.'

He could no longer see the medusa; once more it was directly overhead. But he knew that the descending tentacle must now be very close to the balloon. It would take almost five minutes to bring the reactor up to full thrust. . . .

The fusor was primed. The orbit computer had not rejected the situation as wholly impossible. The air scoops were open, ready to gulp in tons of the surrounding hydrohelium on demand. Even under optimum conditions, this would have been the moment of truth – for there had been no way of testing how a nuclear ramjet would *really* work in the strange atmosphere of Jupiter.

Very gently something rocked *Kon-Tiki*. Falcon tried to ignore it.

Ignition had been planned at six miles higher, in an atmosphere of less than a quarter of the density and thirty degrees cooler. Too bad.

What was the shallowest dive he could get away with, for the air scoops to work? When the ram ignited, he'd be heading towards Jupiter with two and a half g's to help him get there. Could he possibly pull out in time?

A large, heavy hand patted the balloon. The whole vessel bobbed up and down, like one of the Yo-yos that had just become the craze on Earth.

Of course, Brenner *might* be perfectly right. Perhaps it was just trying to be friendly. Maybe he should try to talk to it over the radio. Which should it be: 'Pretty pussy'? 'Down, Fido'? Or 'Take me to your leader'?

The tritium-deuterium ratio was correct. He was ready to light the candle, with a hundred-million-degree match.

The thin tip of the tentacle came slithering around the edge of the balloon some sixty yards away. It was about the size of an elephant's trunk, and by the delicate way it was moving appeared to be almost as sensitive. There were little palps at its end, like questing mouths. He was sure that Dr. Brenner would be fascinated.

This seemed about as good a time as any. He gave a swift scan of the entire control board, started the final four-second ignition count, broke the safety seal, and pressed the JETTISON switch.

There was a sharp explosion and an instant loss of weight. *Kon-Tiki* was falling freely, nose down. Overhead, the discarded balloon was racing upward, dragging the inquisitive tentacle with it. Falcon had no time to see if the gasbag actually hit the medusa, because at that moment the ramjet fired and he had other matters to think about.

A roaring column of hot hydrohelium was pouring out of the reactor nozzles, swiftly building up thrust – but *towards* Jupiter, not away from it. He could not pull out yet, for vector control was too sluggish. Unless he could gain complete control and achieve horizontal flight within the next five seconds, the vehicle would dive too deeply into the atmosphere and would be destroyed.

With agonizing slowness – those five seconds seemed like fifty – he managed to flatten out, then pull the nose upward. He glanced back only once and caught a final glimpse of the medusa, many miles away. *Kon-Tiki*'s discarded gasbag had apparently escaped from its grasp for he could see no sign of it.

Now he was master once more – no longer drifting helplessly on the winds of Jupiter, but riding his own column of atomic fire back to the stars. He was confident that the ramjet would steadily give him velocity and altitude until he had reached near-orbital speed at the fringes of the atmosphere. Then, with a brief burst of pure rocket power, he would regain the freedom of space.

Halfway to orbit, he looked south and saw the tremendous enigma of the Great Red Spot – that floating island twice the size of Earth – coming up over the horizon. He stared into its mysterious beauty until the computer warned him that conversion to rocket thrust was only sixty seconds ahead. He tore his gaze reluctantly away.

'Some other time,' he murmured.

'What's that?' said Mission Control. 'What did you say?'

'It doesn't matter,' he replied.

8. BETWEEN TWO WORLDS

'You're a hero now, Howard,' said Webster, 'not just a celebrity. You've given them something to think about – injected some excitement into their lives. Not one in a million will actually travel to the Outer Giants, but the whole human race will go in imagination. And that's what counts.'

'I'm glad to have made your job a little easier.'

Webster was too old a friend to take offence at the note of irony. Yet it surprised him. And this was not the first change in Howard that he had noticed since the return from Jupiter.

The Administrator pointed to the famous sign on his desk, borrowed from an impresario of an earlier age: ASTONISH ME!

'I'm not ashamed of my job. New knowledge, new resources – they're all very well. But men also need novelty and excitement. Space travel has become routine; you've made it a great adventure once more. It will be a long, long time before we get Jupiter pigeonholed. And maybe longer still before we understand those medusae. I still think that one *knew* where your blind spot was. Anyway, have you decided on your next move? Saturn, Uranus, Neptune – you name it.'

'I don't know. I've thought about Saturn, but I'm not really needed there. It's only one gravity, not two and a half like Jupiter. So men can handle it.'

Men, thought Webster. He said 'men'. He's never done that before. And when did I last hear him use the word 'we'? He's changing, slipping away from us. . . .

'Well,' he said aloud, rising from his chair to conceal his slight uneasiness, 'let's get the conference started. The cameras are all set up and everyone's waiting. You'll meet a lot of old friends.'

He stressed the last word, but Howard showed no response. The leathery mask of his face was becoming more and more difficult to read. Instead, he rolled back from the Administrator's desk, unlocked his undercarriage so that it no longer formed a chair, and rose on his hydraulics to his full seven feet of height. It had been good psychology on the part of the surgeons to give him that extra twelve inches, to compensate somewhat for all that he had lost when the *Queen* had crashed.

Falcon waited until Webster had opened the door, then pivoted neatly on his balloon tyres and headed for it at a smooth and silent twenty miles an hour. The display of speed and precision was not flaunted arrogantly; rather, it had become quite unconscious.

Howard Falcon, who had once been a man and could still pass for one over a voice circuit, felt a calm sense of achievement – and, for the first time in years, something like peace of mind. Since his return from Jupiter, the nightmares had ceased. He had found his role at last.

He now knew why he had dreamed about that superchimp aboard the doomed *Queen Elizabeth*. Neither man nor beast, it was between two worlds; and so was he.

He alone could travel unprotected on the lunar surface. The life-support system inside the metal cylinder that had replaced his fragile body functioned equally well in space or under water. Gravity fields ten times that of Earth were an inconvenience, but nothing more. And no gravity was best of all. . . .

The human race was becoming more remote, the ties of kinship more tenuous. Perhaps these air-breathing, radiation-sensitive bundles of unstable carbon compounds had no right beyond the atmosphere; they should stick to their natural homes – Earth, Moon, Mars.

Some day the real masters of space would be machines, not men – and he was neither. Already conscious of his destiny, he took a sombre pride in his unique loneliness – the first immortal midway between two orders of creation.

He would, after all, be an ambassador; between the old and the new – between the creatures of carbon and the creatures of metal who must one day supersede them.

Both would have need of him in the troubled centuries that lay ahead.

SHAFFERY AMONG THE IMMORTALS

Fred Pohl, who is my age, and whose career in science fiction has paralleled my own, can write hard science fiction with the best. He is equipped with the necessary knowledge of science and has obtained it the hard way. Brought up during the Great Depression, circumstances prevented him from having science pounded into his head by great educational institutions (from which Clarke and I managed to profit.) So he did it on his own and ended up as expert as either of us. (More expert in some ways, but I hate to have to admit that.)

And he had this advantage, too, that he had had time to observe and understand people more than Clarke and I had a chance to do. (Did I say that science-fiction writers can write anything they choose? Fred has written a book on practical politics.)

In any case, none is better than Fred in demonstrating the function of science fiction as social satire. Here he does it in a combination of hard science and light heart that will have you snickering right down to almost the end.

SHAFFERY AMONG THE IMMORTALS

Frederik Pohl

Jeremy Shaffery had a mind a little bit like Einstein's, although maybe not in the ways that mattered most. When Einstein first realized that light carried mass, he sat down to write a friend about it and described the thought as 'amusing and infectious'. Shaffery would have thought that, too, although of course he would not likely have seen the implications of the Maxwell equations in the first place.

Shaffery looked a little bit like Einstein. He encouraged the resemblance, especially in the hair, until his hair began to run out. Since Einstein loved sailing, he kept a sixteen-foot trimaran tied up at the observatory dock. Seasickness kept him from using it much. Among the other things he envied Einstein for was the mirror-smooth Swiss lakes, so much nicer than the lower Caribbean in that respect. But after a day of poring over pairs of star photographs with a blink comparator or trying to discover previously unknown chemical compounds in interstellar space in a radio trace, he sometimes floated around the cove in his little yellow rubber raft. It was relaxing, and his wife never followed him there. To Shaffery that was important. She was a difficult woman, chronically p.o.'d because his career was so persistently pointed in the wrong direction. If she had ever been a proper helpmeet, she wasn't any more. Shaffery doubted she ever had, remembering that it was her unpleasant comments that had caused him to give up that other hallmark of the master, the violin.

At the stage in Shaffery's career at which he had become Director of the Carmine J. Nuccio Observatory, in the Lesser Antilles, he had begun to look less like Einstein and more like Edgar Kennedy. Nights when the seeing was good he remorsely scanned the heavens through the 22-inch reflector, hoping against hope for glory. Days when he was not sleeping he wandered through the home like a ghost, running his finger over desks for dust, filching preserved mushrooms from Mr. Nuccio's home-canned hoard, trying to persuade his two local assistants to remember to close the dome slit when it rained. They paid little attention. They knew where the muscle was, and that it wasn't with Shaffery. He had few friends. Most of the white residents couldn't stand his wife; some of them couldn't stand Shaffery very well, either. There was a nice old-lady drunk out from England in a tidy white house down the beach, a sort of hippie commune on the far side of the island, and a New York television talk-show operator who just flew down for weekends. When they were respectively sober, unstoned, and present, Shaffery sometimes talked to them. That wasn't often. The only one he really wanted to see much was the TV man, but there were obstacles. The big obstacle was that the TV man spent most of his waking time skin diving. The other obstacle was that Shaffery had discovered that the TV man occasionally laid Mrs. Shaffery. It wasn't the morality of the thing that bothered him; it was the feeling of doubt it raised in Shaffery's mind about the other's sanity. He never spoke to the TV man about it, partly because he wasn't sure what to say and partly because the man had half-way promised to have Shaffery on his show. Sometime or other.

One must be fair to Shaffery and say that he wasn't a bad man. Like Frank Morgan, his problem was that he wasn't a wizard. The big score always evaded him.

The Einstein method, which he had studied assiduously over many years, was to make a pretty theory and then see if, by any chance, observations of events in the real world seemed to confirm it. Shaffery greatly approved of that method. It just didn't seem to work out for him. At the Triple A-S meeting in Dallas he read an hour-long paper on his new Principle of Relevance Theory. That was a typical Einstein idea, he flattered himself. He had even worked out simple explanations for the lay public, like Einstein with his sitting on a hot stove or holding hands with a pretty girl. 'Relevance Theory,' he practised smiling to the little wavelets of the cove, 'only means

that observations that don't *relate* to anything don't *exist*. I'll
spare you the mathematics because –' self-deprecatory laugh
here – 'I can't even fill out my income tax without making a mistake.' Well, he had worked out the mathematics,
inventing signs and operators of his own, just like Einstein.
But he seemed to have made a mistake. Before the AAAS
audience, fidgeting and whispering to each other behind their
hands, he staked his scientific reputation on the prediction that
the spectrum of Mars at its next opposition would show a slight
but detectable displacement of some 150 angstroms towards
the violet. The son of a bitch didn't do anything of the kind.
One of the audience was a graduate student of Princeton, hard
up for a doctoral thesis subject, and he took a chance on
Shaffery and made the observations, and with angry satisfaction sent him the proof that Mars had remained obstinately
red.

The next year the International Astrophysical Union's
referees, after some discussion, finally allowed him twenty
minutes for a Brief Introduction into the General Consideration of Certain Electromagnetic Anomalies. He offered thirty-
one pages of calculations leading to the prediction that the
next lunar eclipse would be forty-two seconds late. It wasn't.
It was right on time. At the meeting of the World Space Science
Symposium they told him with great regret that overcommit-
ments of space and time had made it impossible for them to
schedule his no doubt valuable contribution, and by the time
of the next round of conferences they weren't even sending him
invitations any more.

Meanwhile all those other fellows were doing great. Shaffery
followed the careers of his contemporaries with rue. There was
Hoyle, still making a good thing out of the Steady State Hypothesis and Gamow's name, still reverenced for the Big Bang,
and new people like Dyson and Ehricke and Enzmann coming
along with all sorts of ideas that, if you looked at them objec-
tively, weren't any cleverer than his, Shaffery thought, except
for the detail that somehow or other they seemed lucky enough
to find supporting evidence from time to time. It did not strike
him as fair. Was he not a Mensa member? Was he not as well

educated as the successful ones, as honoured with degrees, as photogenic in the news-magazines and as colourfully entertaining on the talk shows? (Assuming Larry Nesbit ever gave him the chance on his show.) Why did they make out and he fall flat? His wife's theory he considered and rejected. 'Your trouble, Jeremy,' she would say to him, 'is you're a horse's ass.' But he knew that wasn't it. Who was to say Isaac Newton wasn't a horse's ass, too, if you looked closely enough at his freaky theology and his nervous breakdowns? And look where he got.

So Shaffery kept looking for the thing that would make him great. He looked all over. Sometimes he checked Kepler's analysis of the orbit of Mars with an adding machine, looking for mistakes in arithmetic. (He found half a dozen, but the damn things all cancelled each other out, which proves how hard it is to go wrong when your luck is in.) Sometimes he offered five-dollar prizes to the local kids for finding new stars that might turn out to be Shaffery's Nova, or anyway Shaffery's Comet. No luck. An ambitious scheme to describe stellar ballistics in terms of analogy with free-radical activity in the enzyme molecules fell apart when none of the biochemists he wrote to even answered his letters.

The file of failures grew. One whole drawer of a cabinet was filled with reappraisals of the great exploded theories of the past – *A New Look at Phlogiston*, incomplete because there didn't seem really to be anything to look at when you came down to it; a manuscript called *The Flat Earth Re-examined*, which no one would publish; three hundred sheets of drawings of increasingly tinier and increasingly quirkier circles to see if the Copernican epicycles could not somehow account for what the planet Mercury did that Einstein had considered a proof of relativity. From time to time he was drawn again to attempting to find a scientific basis for astrology and chiromancy, or predicting the paths of charged particles in a cloud chamber by means of yarrow stalks. It all came to nothing. When he was really despairing, he sometimes considered making his mark in industry rather than pure science, wherefore the sheaf of sketches for a nuclear-fuelled car, the experiments on smello-

vision that had permanently destroyed the nerves of his left
nostril, the attempt to preserve some of Mr. Nuccio's mushrooms by irradiation in his local dentist's X-ray room. He
knew that that sort of thing was not really worthy of a man
with all those graduate degrees, but in any event he did no
better there than anywhere else. Sometimes he dreamed of what
it would be like to run Mount Palomar or Jodrell Bank, with
fifty trained assistants to nail down his inspirations with evidence. He was not that fortunate. He had only Cyril and James.

It was not all bad, however, because he didn't have much
interference to worry about. The observatory where he was
employed, last and least of the string of eleven that had given
him a position since his final doctoral degree, didn't seem to
mind what he did, as long as he did it without bothering them.
On the other hand, they didn't give him much support, either.

Probably they just didn't know how. The observatory was
owned by something called the Lesser Antilles Vending
Machine Entertainment Co., Ltd., and, so Shaffery had been
told by the one old classmate who still kept up a sort of
friendship with him, was actually some sort of tax-evasion
scheme maintained by a Las Vegas gambling syndicate.
Shaffery didn't mind this, particularly, although from time
to time he got tired of being told that the only two astronomers
who mattered were Giovanni Schiaparelli and Galileo Galilei.
That was only a minor annoyance. The big cancerous agony
was that every year he got a year older and fame would not
come.

At his periodic low spots of despondency (he had even tried
linking them with the appositions of Jupiter, meteor showers,
and his wife's periods, but those didn't come to anything
either) he toyed with the notion of dropping it all and going
into some easier profession. Banking. Business. Law. 'President Shaffery' had the right kind of sound, if he entered
politics. But then he would drag his raft to the water, prop two
six-packs of Danish beer on his abdomen and float away, and by
the end of the first pack his courage would come flowing back,
and on the second he would be well into a scheme for detecting
gravity waves by statistical analysis of 40,000 acute gout suf-

ferers, telephoning the state of their twinges into a central computer facility.

On such a night he carried his little rubber raft to the shore of the cove, slipped off his sandals, rolled up his bell-bottoms, and launched himself. It was the beginning of the year, as close to winter as it ever got on the island, which meant mostly that the dark came earlier. It was a bad time of the year for him, because it was the night before the annual Board Meeting. The first year or two he had looked forward to the meetings as opportunities. He was no longer so hopeful. His objective for the present meeting was only to survive it, and there was some question of a nephew by marriage, an astronomy major at U.C.L.A., to darken even that hope.

Shaffery's vessel wasn't really a proper raft, only the sort of kid's toy that drowns a dozen or so nine-year-olds at the world's bathing beaches every year. It was less than five feet long. When he got himself twisted and wriggled into it, his back against the ribbed bottom, his head pillowed against one in-flated end, and his feet dangling into the water at the other, it was quite like floating in a still sea without the annoyance of getting wet. He opened the first beer and began to relax. The little waves rocked and turned him; the faint breeze competed with the tiny island tide, and the two of them combined to take him erratically away from the beach at the rate of maybe ten feet a minute. It didn't matter. He was still inside the cove, with islets, or low sandbanks, beaded across the mouth of it. If by any sudden meteorological miracle a storm should spring from that bright-lamped sky, the wind could take him nowhere but back to shore or near an island. And of course there would be no storm. He could paddle back whenever he chose, as easily as he could push his soap dish around his bathtub, as he routinely did while bathing, which in turn he did at least once a day, and when his wife was particularly difficult as often as six times. The bathroom was his other refuge. His wife never followed him there, being too well brought up to run the chance of inadvertently seeing him doing something filthy.

Up on the low hills he could see the corroded copper dome

of the observatory. A crescent of light showed that his assistant had opened the dome, but the light showed that he was not using it for any astronomical purpose. That was easy to un-riddle. Cyril had turned the lights on so that the cleaning woman could get the place spotless for the Board Meeting and had opened the dome because that proved the telescope was being used. Shaffery bent the empty beer can into a V, tucked it neatly beside him in the raft, and opened another. He was not yet tranquil, but he was not actively hurting anywhere. At least Cyril would not be using the telescope to study the windows of the Bon Repos Hotel across the cove, since the last time he'd done it he had jammed the elevating gears and it could no longer traverse anywhere near the horizon. Shaffery put aside an unwanted, fugitive vision of Idris, the senior and smartest cleaning lady, polishing the telescope mirror with Bon Ami, sipping his beer, thought nostalgically of Relevance Theory and how close he had come with the epicycles, and freed his mind for constructive thought.

The sun was wholly gone, except for a faint luminous purpling of the sky in the general direction of Venezuela. Almost directly overhead hung the three bright stars of Orion's Belt, slowly turning like the traffic signals on a railroad line, with Syrius and Procyon orbiting headlight bright around them. As his eyes dark-adapted he could make out the stars in Orion's sword, even the faint patch of light that was the great gas cloud. He was far enough from the shore so that sound could not carry, and he softly called out the great four-pointed pattern of first-magnitude stars that surrounded the constella-tion: 'Hey there, Betelguese. Hi, Bellatrix. What's new, Rigel? Nice to see you again, Saiph.' He glanced past red Aldebaran to the close-knit stars of the Pleiades, returned to Orion and, showing off now, called off the stars of the Belt: 'Hey, Alnitak! Yo, Alnilam! How goes it, Mintaka?'

The problem with drinking beer in the rubber raft was that your head was bent down towards your chest and it was diffi-cult to burp; but Shaffery arched his body up a little, getting in some water in the process but not caring, got rid of the burp, opened another beer, and gazed complacently at Orion. It was a satisfying constellation. It was satisfying that he knew so much about it. He thought briefly of the fact that the Arabs had called the Belt Stars by the name Jauzah, meaning the Golden Nuts; that the Chinese thought they looked like a weighing beam, and that Greenlanders called them Siktut, The Seal Hunters Lost at Sea. As he was going on to remember what the Australian aborigines had thought of them (they thought they resembled three young men dancing a corroboree), his mind flickered back to the lost seal hunters. Um, he thought. He raised his head and looked towards the shore.

It was now more than a hundred yards away. That was farther than he really wanted to be, and so he kicked the raft around, oriented himself by the stars and began to paddle back. It was easy and pleasant to do. He used a sort of splashy upside-down breast stroke of the old-fashioned angel's wing kind, but as all his weight was supported by the raft, he moved quickly across the water. He was rather enjoying the exercise, toes and fingers moving comfortably in the tepid sea, little ghosts of luminescence glowing where he splashed, until quite without warning the fingertips of one hand struck sharply and definitely against something that was resistantly massive and solid where there should have been only water, something that moved stubbornly, something that rasped them like a file. Oh, my God, thought Shaffery. What a lousy thing to happen. They so seldom came in this close to shore. He didn't even think about them. What a shame for a man who might have been Einstein to wind up, incomplete and unfulfilled, as shark shit.

He really was not a bad man, and it was the loss to science that was first on his mind, only a little later what it must feel like to be chopped and gulped.

Shaffery pulled his hands in and folded them on his chest, crossed his feet at the ankles, and rested them on the end of the boat, knees spread on the sides. There was now nothing trailing in the water that might strike a shark as bait. There was, on the other hand, no good way for him to get back to shore. He could yell, but the wind was the wrong way. He could wait till he drifted near one of the islets. But if he missed them, he would be out in the deep ocean before he knew it.

Shaffery was almost sure that sharks seldom attacked a boat, even a rubber one. Of course, he went on analytically, the available evidence didn't signify. They could flip a raft like this over easily enough. If this particular shark ate him off this particular half-shell, there would be no one to report it.

Still, there were some encouraging considerations. Say it was capable of tipping the boat or eating him boat and all. They were dull-witted creatures, and what was to keep one hanging around in the absence of blood, splashing, noise, trailing objects or any of the other things sharks were known to take an interest in? It might be a quarter mile away already. But it wasn't, because at that moment he heard the splash of some large object breaking the surface a foot from his head.

Shaffery could have turned to look, but he didn't; he remained quite motionless, listening to the gentle water noises, until they were punctuated by a sort of sucking sound and then a voice. A human voice. It said, 'Scared the piss out of you, didn't I? What do you say, Shaffery? Want a tow back to shore?'

It was not the first time Shaffery had encountered Larry Nesbit diving in the cove; it was only the first time it had happened at night. Shaffery twisted about in the raft and gazed at Nesbit's grinning face and its frame of wet strands of nape-length hair. It took a little time to make the transition in his mind from eighteen-foot shark to five-foot-eight TV star. 'Come on,' Nesbit went on, 'what do you say? Tell you what. I'll tow you in, and you give me some of old Nuccio's Scotch, and I'll listen to how you're going to invent antigravity while we get pissed.'

That Nesbit, he had a way with him. The upshot of it all was that Shaffery had a terrible hangover the next day; not the headache but the whole works, with trotting to the toilet and being able to tolerate only small sips of ginger ale and wishing, or almost wishing, he was dead. (Not, to be sure, before he did the one immortalizing thing. Whatever it was going to be.)

It was not altogether a disaster, the hangover. The next morning was very busy, and it was just as well that he was out of the way. When the Board of Directors convened to discuss

the astronomical events of the year, or whatever it is they did
discuss in the afternoon session to which Shaffery was definitely
not invited, it was always a busy time. They arrived separately,
each director with his pair of associates. One after another
40-foot cabin cruisers with fishing tops came up to the landing
and gave up cargoes of plump little men wearing crew cuts and
aloha shirts. The observatory car, not ever used by any of the
observatory personnel, was polished, fuelled and used for
round trips from the landing strip at Jubila, across the island,
to Coomray Hill and the observatory, Shaffery laid low in his
private retreat. He had never told his wife that he was not allowed in the observatory for the board meetings; so she didn't
look for him. He spent the morning in the tar-paper shack
where photographic material had once been kept, until he discovered that the damp peeled the emulsion away from the
backing. Now it was his home away from home. He had fitted
it with a desk, chair, icebox, coffeepot, and bed.

Shaffery paid no attention to the activity outside, not even
when the directors' assistants, methodically searching the
bushes and banana groves all around the observatory, came
to his shack, opened the door without knocking, and peered
in at him. They knew him from previous meetings, but they
studied him silently for a moment before the two in the doorway nodded to each other and left him again. They were not
well-mannered men, Shaffery thought, but no doubt they were
good at their jobs, whatever those jobs were. He resolutely did
not think about the Board Meeting, or about the frightening,
calumnious things Larry Nesbit had said to him the night
before, drinking the Board Chairman's Scotch and eating his
food, in that half-jocular, shafting, probing way he had.
Shaffery thought a little bit about the queasy state of his lower
abdomen, because he couldn't help it, but what he mostly
thought about was Fermat's Last Theorem.

A sort of picayune, derivative immortality was waiting there
for someone. Not much, but Shaffery was getting desperate.
It was one of those famous mathematical problems that grad
students played at for a month or two and amateurs assaulted
in vain all their lives. It looked easy enough to deal with. It

started with so elementary a proposition that every high-school boy mastered it about the time he learned to masturbate successfully. If you squared the sides of a right triangle, the sum of the squares of the two sides was equal to the square of the hypotenuse.

Well, that was all very well, and it was so easy to understand that it had been used to construct right angles by surveyors for centuries. A triangle whose sides were, say, 3 feet and 4 feet, and whose hypotenuse was 5 feet, had to make a right angle, because $3^2 + 4^2 = 5^2$; and it always had, since the time of Pythagoras, five hundred years B.C., $a^2 + b^2 = c^2$. The hitch was, if the exponent was anything but 2, you could never make the equation come out using whole numbers; $a^3 + b^3$ never equalled c^3, and $a^{27} + b^{27}$ did not add up to any c^{27}, no matter what numbers you used for a, b and c. Everybody knew that this was so. Nobody had ever proved that it *had* to be so, by mathematical proofs, except that Fermat had left a cryptic little note, found among his papers after his death claiming that he had found a 'truly wonderful' proof, only there wasn't enough room in the margin of the book he was writing on to put it all down.

Shaffery was no mathematician. But that morning, waking up to the revolution in his stomach and the thunder in his head, he had seen that that was actually a strength. One, all the mathematicians of three or four centuries had broken their heads against the problem; so obviously it couldn't be solved by any known mathematics anyway. Two, Einstein was weak in mathematics too and had disdained to worry about it, preferring to invent his own.

So he spent the morning, between hurried gallops across the parking lot to the staff toilet, filling paper with mathematical signs and operators of his own invention. It did not seem to be working out, to be sure. For a while he thought of an alternative scheme, to wit, inventing a 'truly wonderful' solution of his own and claiming he couldn't find room to write it down in the margin of, say, the latest issue of *Mathematical Abstracts*; but residual sanity persuaded him that perhaps no one would ever find it, or that if it was found it might well be laughed off, and

anyway that it would be purely posthumous celebrity and he
wanted to taste it while he was alive. So he broke for lunch,
came back feeling dizzy and ill and worried about the meeting
that was going on, and decided to take a nap before resuming
his labours.

When Cyril came looking for him to tell him the Directors
desired his presence, it was dark, and Shaffery felt like hell.

Coomray Hill was no taller than a small office building, but
it got the mirror away from most of the sea-level dampness.
The observatory sat on top of the hill like a mound of pistachio
ice cream, hemispheric green copper roof and circular walls of
green-painted plaster. Inside, the pedestal of the telescope
took up the centre of the floor. The instrument itself was traversed as low as it would go any more, clearing enough space
for the Directors and their gear. They were all there, looking at
him with silent distaste as he came in.

The inner sphere of the dome was painted (by Cyril's
talented half-sister) with a large map of Mars, showing Schiaparelli's famous canals in resolute detail; a view of the Bay of
Naples from the Vomero, with Vesuvius gently steaming in the
background; and an illuminated drawing of the constellation
Scorpius, which happened to be the sign of the constellation
under which the Chairman of the Board had been born. A
row of card tables had been lined up and covered with a green
cloth. There were six places set, each with ashtray, note pad,
three sharpened pencils, ice, glass, and bottle of John Begg.
Another row of tables against the wall held the antipasto,
replenished by Cyril after the depredations of the night before,
but now seriously depleted by the people for whom it was intended. Six cigars were going and a couple of others were
smouldering in the trays. Shaffery tried not to breathe Even
with the door open and the observing aperture in the dome
wide, the inside air was faintly blue. At one time Shaffery had
mentioned diffidently what the deposit of cigar smoke did to
the polished surface of the 22-inch mirror. That was at his
first annual meeting. The Chairman hadn't said a word, just
stared at him. Then he nodded to his right-hand man, a Mr.

DiFirenzo, who had taken a packet of Kleenex out of his pocket and tossed it to Shaffery. 'So wipe the goddamn thing off,' he had said. 'Then you could dump these ashtrays for us, okay?'

Shaffery did his best to smile at his Directors. Behind him he was conscious of the presence of their assistants, who were patrolling the outside of the observatory in loose elliptical orbits, perigeeing at the screen door to peer inside. They had studied Shaffery carefully as he came across the crunching shell of the parking lot, and under their scrutiny he had decided against detouring by way of the staff toilet, which he now regretted.

'Okay, Shaffery,' said Mr. DiFirenzo, after glancing at the Chairman of the Board. 'Now we come to you.'

Shaffery clasped his hands behind him in his Einstein pose and said brightly, 'Well, it has been a particularly productive year for the observatory. No doubt you've seen my reports on the Leonid meteriorite count and—'

'Right,' said Mr. DiFirenzo, 'but what we been talking about here is the space shots. Mr. Nuccio has expressed his views that this is a kind of strategic location, like how they shoot the rockets from Cape Kennedy. They have to go right over us, and we want a piece of that.'

Shaffery shifted his weight uneasily. 'I discussed that in my report last year—'

'No, Shaffery. This year, Shaffery. Why can't we get some of that federal money, like for tracking, for instance?'

'But the position hasn't changed, Mr. DiFirenzo. We don't have the equipment, and besides NASA has its own—'

'No good, Shaffery. You know how much you got out of us for equipment last year? I got the figures right here. And now you tell us you don't have what we need to make a couple of bucks?'

'Well, Mr. DiFirenzo, you see, the equipment we have is for purely scientific purposes. For this sort of work you need quite different instruments, and actually—'

'I don't want to hear.' DiFirenzo glanced at the Chairman and then went on. 'Next thing, what about that comet you said you were going to discover?'

Shaffery smiled forgivingly. 'Really, I can't be held account-
able for that. I didn't actually say we'd *find* one. I merely said
that the continuing *search* for comets was part of our basic
programme. Of course, I've done my very best to —'

'Not good enough, Shaffery. Besides your boy here told Mr.
Nuccio that if you did find a comet you wouldn't name it the
Mr. Carmine J. Nuccio Comet like Mr. Nuccio wanted.'

Shaffery was going all hollow inside, but he said bravely,
'It's not wholly up to me. There's an astronomical convention
that the discoverer's name goes on —'

'We don't like that convention, Shaffery. Three, now we
come to some really bad things, that I'm sorry to hear you've
got yourself into, Shaffery. We hear you been talking over the
private affairs of this institution and Mr. Nuccio with that
dick-head Nesbit. Shut, Shaffery,' the man said warningly as
Shaffery started to open his mouth. 'We know all about it. This
Nesbit is getting himself into big trouble. He has said some
very racist things about Mr. Nuccio on that sideshow of his on
the TV, which is going to cost him quite a bundle when Mr.
Nuccio's lawyers get through with him. That is very bad,
Shaffery, and also, four, there is this thing.'

He lifted up what had seemed like a crumpled napkin in
front of his place. It turned out that it was covering what
looked like a large transistor radio.

Shaffery identified it after a monent's thought; he had
seen it before, in Larry Nesbit's possession. 'It's a tape
recorder,' he said.

'Right on, Shaffery. Now the question is, who put it in here?
I don't mean just left it here like you could leave your rubbers
or something, Shaffery. I mean left it here with one of those
trick switches, so it was going when a couple of our associates
checked the place out and found it under the table.'

Shaffery swallowed very hard, but even so his voice sounded
unfamiliar to him when he was able to speak. 'I – I *assure* you,
Mr. DiFirenzo! I had nothing to do with it.'

'No, Shaffery, I know you didn't, because you are not that
smart. Mr. Nuccio was quite upset about this illegal bugging,
and he has already made some phone calls and talked to some

people, and we have a pretty good idea of who put it there, and he isn't going to have what he thinks he's going to have to play on his TV show. So here it is, Shaffery. Mr. Nuccio doesn't find your work satisfactory here, and he is letting you go. We got somebody else coming down to take over. We'd appreciate it if you could be out by tomorrow.'

There are situations in which there is not much scope for dignity. A man in his middle fifties who has just lost the worst job he ever had has few opportunities for making the sort of terminal remark that one would like to furnish one's biographers.

Shaffery discovered that he was worse off than that; he was frankly sick. The turmoil in his belly grew. The little saliva pumps under his tongue were flooding his mouth faster than he could swallow, and he knew that if he didn't get back to the staff toilet very quickly he would have another embarrassment to add to what was already an overwhelming load. He turned and walked away. Then marched. Then ran. When he had emptied himself of everything in belly, bladder and gut he sat on the edge of the toilet seat and thought of the things he could have said: 'Look Nuccio, you don't know anything about science.' 'Nuccio, Schiaparelli was all wrong about the canals on Mars.' It was too late to say them. It was too late to ask the questions that his wife would be sure to ask, about severance pay, pension, all the things that he had been putting off getting in writing. ('Don't worry about that stuff, Shaffery, Mr. Nuccio always takes care of his friends but he don't like to be aggravated.') He tried to make a plan for his future, and failed. He tried even to make a plan for his present. Surely he should at least call Larry Nesbit, to demand, to complain, and to warn ('Hist! The tape recorder has been discovered! All is lost! Flee!'), but he could not trust himself so far from the toilet. Not at that exact moment. And a moment later it was too late. Half an hour later, when one of the orbiting guards snapped the little lock and peered inside, the man who might have been Einstein was lying on the floor with his trousers around his knees, undignified, uncaring, and dead.

*

Ah, Shaffery! How disappointed he would have been in his *Times* obit, two paragraphs buried under the overhang of a pop singer's final notice. But afterwards. . . .

The first victim was Larry Nesbit, airsick in his Learjet all the way back to New York, overcome during the taping of his TV show, and dying the next day. The next victims were the Board of Directors, every man. They started home, by plane and boat. Some of them made it, but all of them died: en route or in Las Vegas, Detroit, Chicago, Los Angeles, New York, and Long Branch, New Jersey. Some of the 'assistants' died and some were spared. (Briefly.) The reason was not a mystery for very long. The source of the new plague was tracked down quickly enough to Mr. Nuccio's antipasto, and particularly to the preserved mushrooms that Shaffery had borrowed for his experiment.

The botulinus toxin was long recognized as the most deadly poison known to man. The mutated version that Shaffery and his dentist's X-rays had brought into being was not much more deadly, but it had another quality that was new and different. Old, established *Clostridium botulinum* is an organism with a feeble hold on life; expose it to light and air, and it dies. *B. shafferia* was more sturdy. It grew where it was. In anything. In Mr. Nuccio's antipasto, in a salad in a restaurant kitchen, in Mom's apple pie on a windowsill to cool, in the human digestive tract. There were nine deaths in the first five days, and then for a moment no more. The epidemiologists would not have bothered their heads about so short a casualty list if it had not been for the identities of some of the victims. But the bacteria was multiplying. The stain of vomit under the boardwalk at Long Branch dried; the bacteria turned into spores and were blown on the wind until they struck something damp and fertile. Whereupon they grew. The soiled Kleenex thrown from a Cadillac Fleetwood on the road leading from O'Hare to Evanston, the sneeze between flights at Miami, expectorations in a dozen places – all added to the score. From the urine and faeces of the afflicted men, from their sweat, even from their bed linen and discarded clothing, enspored bacteria leaped into the air and were inhaled, eaten, drunk, absorbed into cuts, in every way ingested into the waiting bodies of hundreds, then thousands, ultimately countless millions of human beings.

By the second week Detroit and Los Angeles were declared disaster areas. By the fourth the plague had struck every city in America and had leaped the oceans. If it had any merciful quality at all, it was that it was quick: an upset stomach, a sweat, a few pangs, and then death. None were immune. Few survived. Out of a hundred, three might outlive the disease. But then famine, riot, and lesser ills took their toll; and of the billions who lived on the Earth when Shaffery exposed his antipasto in the dentist's office, all but a few tens of millions died in the outbreak that the world will never forget of the disease called Shaffery's Syndrome.

PATRON OF THE ARTS

It is easy to set up dichotomies that don't exist, such as that between the scientist and the artist – as though there were no art in the work of the scientist, and no science in the work of the artist.

In the history of science there were advances that were directly due to artists who were interested in art. There were artists who studied anatomy, so that they could paint the human figure more accurately, and others who studied projective geometry, so they could present a three-dimensional effect on a two-dimensional surface with greater precision.

And conversely, whole new varieties of art have been made possible by advances in science and technology. Who knows what a marvellous photographer Michelangelo might have been had someone placed a camera in his hands; or what a motion picture Shakespeare might have written and directed if he and the film had come together across the gap of time.

So changing art-forms are a proper subject for science fiction, and Rotsler will show you a new art and its effect on people and the manner in which it raises new and fascinating questions about human emotion.

PATRON OF THE ARTS

William Rotsler

She stares out at you from her cube of near blackness, calm, quiet, breathing easily, just looking at you. She is naked to the hips where a jewelled girdle encircles her, and she sits regally on a pile of luxurious pillows. Her long white hair cascades down over her apricot-coloured shoulders and is made to shimmer slightly by some hidden light.

As you come closer to the life-size sensatron the vibrations get to you. The startling reality of the three-dimensional image cannot be overstated, for Michael Cilento's portrait of one of history's greatest society courtesans is a great work of art.

As you view the cube the image of Diana Snowdragon stops being quite so calm and in some subtle way becomes predatory, commanding, compelling. She is *naked*, not nude. The drifting bellsounds of melora musicians are heard . . . almost. The power of her unique personality is overwhelming, as it is in person, but in this artist's interpretation there are many other facets exposed.

Diana's sensatron cube portrait is universally hailed as a masterpiece. The subject was delighted.

The artist was disgusted and told me that the ego of the subject prevented her from seeing the reality he had constructed.

But it was this cube that gave Michael Benton Cilento the fame he wanted, needed, and hated. This was his first major sensatron cube and cubes were just then beginning to be used by artists, instead of scientists. It was becoming 'fashionable' to be working in sensations then and everywhere there was shop talk of electron brushes, cilli nets, and blankers.

Mike's portrait of society's most infamous – and richest – wanton made him famous overnight. Even the repro cubes you can buy today are impressive, but the original, with its original subtle circuits and focused broadcasts, is staggering.

A collector in Rome brought Cilento to my attention and when I had seen the Snowdragon cube I managed an introduction. We met at Santini's villa in Ostia and like most young artists he had heard of me.

We met by a pool and his first words were, 'You sponsored Wiesenthal for years, didn't you?' I nodded, wary now, for with every artist you help there are ten who demand it.

'His *Montezuma* opera was trash.'

I smiled. 'It was well received.'

'He did not understand that Aztec any more than he understood Cortez.' He looked at me with a challenge.

'I agree, but by the time I heard it, it was too late.'

He relaxed and kicked his foot in the water and squinted at two nearly nude daughters of a lunar mineral baron that were walking by. He seemed to have made his point and had nothing more to say.

Cilento intrigued me. In the course of a number of years of 'discovering' artists I had met all types, from the shy ones who hide to the burly ones who demand my patronage. And I had met the kind who seem indifferent to me, as Cilento seemed to be. But many others had acted that way and I had learned to disregard everything but finished work and the potential for work.

'Your Snowdragon cube was superb,' I said.

He nodded and squinted in another direction. 'Yeah,' he said. Then as an afterthought he added, 'Thank you.' We spoke for a moment of the cube and he told me what he thought of its subject.

'But it made you famous,' I said.

He squinted at me and after a moment he said, 'Is that what art is about?'

I laughed. 'Fame is very useful. It opens doors. It makes things possible. It makes it easier to be even more famous.'

'It gets you laid,' Cilento said with a smile.

'It can get you killed, too,' I added.

'It's a tool, Mr. Thorne, just like an integrated circuit or a knowledge of molecular electronics. But it can give you freedom. I want that freedom; every artist needs it.'

'That's why you picked Diana?'

He grinned and nodded. 'Besides, that female was a great challenge.'

'I imagine so,' I said and laughed, thinking of Diana at seventeen, beautiful and predatory, clawing her way up the monolithic walls of society.

We had a drink together, then shared a psychedelic in the ruins of a temple of Vesta, and became Mike and Brian to each other. We sat on old stones and leaned against the stub of a crumbling column and looked down at the lights of Santini's villa.

'An artist needs freedom,' Mike said, 'more than he needs paint or electricity or cube diagrams or stone. Or food. You can always get the materials, but the freedom to use them is precious. There is only so much time.'

'What about money? That's freedom, too,' I said.

'Sometimes. You can have money and no freedom, though. But usually fame brings money.' I nodded, thinking that in my case it was the other way around.

We looked out at the light of a half-moon on the Tyrrhenian Sea and had our thoughts. I thought of Madelon.

'There's someone I'd like you to do,' I said. 'A woman. A very special woman.'

'Not right now,' he said. 'Perhaps later. I have several commissions that I want to do.'

'Keep me in mind when you have time. She's a very un-usual woman.'

He glanced at me and tossed a pebble down the hill. 'I'm sure she is,' he said.

'You like to do women, don't you?' I asked.

He smiled in the moonlight and said, 'You figured that out from one cube?'

'No. I bought the three small ones you did before.'

He looked at me sharply. 'How did you know they even existed? I hadn't told anyone.'

'Something as good as the Snowdragon cube couldn't come out of nowhere. There had to be something earlier. I hunted down the owners and bought them.'

'The old lady is my grandmother,' he said. 'I'm a little sorry I sold it, but I needed money.' I made a mental note to have it sent back to him.

'Yes, I like doing women,' he said softly, leaning back against the pale column. 'Artists have always liked doing women. To . . . to capture that elusive shadow of a flicker of a glimpse of a moment . . . in paint, in stone, in clay, or in wood, or on film . . . or with molecular constructs.'

'Rubens saw them plump and gay,' I said. 'Lautrec saw them depraved and real.'

'To Da Vinci they were mysterious,' he said. 'Matisse saw them idle and voluptuous. Michelangelo hardly saw them at all. Picasso saw them in endless mad variety.'

'Gaugin . . . sensuality,' I commented. 'Henry Moore saw them as abstracts, a starting point for form. Van Gogh's women reflected his own mad genius brain.'

'Cezanne saw them as placid cows,' Mike laughed. 'Fellini saw them as multifaceted creatures that were part angel, part beast. In the photographs of Andre de Dienes the women are realistic fantasies, erotic and strange.'

'Tennessee Williams saw them as insane cannibals, fascinatingly repulsive. Sternberg's women were unreal, harsh, dramatic,' I said. 'Clayton's females were predatory fiends.'

'Jason sees them as angels, slightly confused,' Mike said, delighted with the little game. 'Marmon saw them as motherly monsters.'

'And you?' I asked.

He stopped and the smile faded. After a long moment he answered. 'As illusions, I suppose.'

He rolled a fragment of stone from the time of Caesar in his fingers and spoke softly, almost to himself.

'They . . . aren't quite real, somehow. The critics say I created a masterpiece of erotic realism, a milestone in figurative art. But . . . they're . . . wisps. They're incredibly real for only an instant . . . fantastically shadowy another. Women are never the same from moment to moment. Perhaps that's why they fascinate me.'

I didn't see Mike for some time after that, though we kept

in touch. He did a portrait of Princess Helga of the Netherlands, quite modestly clad, the cube filled with its famous dozen golden sculptures and the vibrations of love and peace.

Anything Mike chose to do was quickly bought and commissions came in from individuals, from companies, even from movements. What he did was a simple nude of his mistress of the moment that was erotic in pose but powerfully pornographic in vibrations. For his use of alpha, beta and gamma wave projectors, as well as integrated sonics, he was the subject of an entire issue of *Modern Electronics*. The young Shah of Iran bought the cube to install in his long-abuilding Gardens of Babylon.

For the monks at Redplanet Base on Mars Mike did a large cube of Christ, and it quickly became a tourist attraction. Although he did it for nothing the monks insisted he take a small percentage of the repro cube sales.

I met Mike again, at the opening of his 'Solar System' series in the Grand Museum in Athens. The ten cubes hung from the ceiling, each with its non-literal interpretation of the sun and planets, from the powerball of Sol to the hard, shiny ballbearing of Pluto.

Mike seemed caged, a tiger in a trap, but very happy to see me. He was a volunteer kidnappee as I spirited him away to my apartment in the old part of the town.

He sighed as we entered, tossed his jacket into a Life-style chair and strolled out on to the balcony. I picked up two glasses and a bottle of Cretan wine and joined him.

He sighed again, sank into the chair, and sipped the wine. I chuckled and said, 'Fame getting too much for you?'

He grunted at me. 'Why do they always want the artist at openings? The art speaks for itself.'

'Public relations. To touch the hem of creativity. Maybe some of it will rub off on them.' He grunted again, and we lapsed into comfortable silence, looking out at the Parthenon, high up and night-lit.

At last he spoke. 'Being an artist is all I ever wanted to be, like kids growing up to be astronauts or ball players. It's a honour to be able to do it, whatever *it* is. I've painted and I've sculpted. I've done light mosaics and glow dot patterns. I even tried air music for a while. None of them really seemed to be it. But I think molecular constructs are the closest.'

'Because of the extreme realism?'

'That's part of it. Abstraction, realism, expressionism – they're just labels. What matters is what *is*, the thoughts and emotions that you transmit. The sensatron units are fairly good tools. You can work almost directly on the emotions. When GE gets the new ones ready I think it will be possible to get even more subtle shadings with the alpha waves. And, of course, with more units you can get more complex.'

We lapsed into silence. The ancient city murmured at us. I thought about Madelon.

'I still want you to do that portrait of someone very close to me,' I reminded him.

'Soon. I want to do a cube on a girl I know first. But I must find a new place to work. They bother me there, now that they found where I was.'

I mentioned my villa on Sikinos, in the Aegean, and Mike seemed interested, so I offered it to him. 'There's an ancient grain storage there you could use as a studio. They have a controlled plasma fusion plant so there would be as much power as you need. There's a house, just the couple that take care of it, and a very small village nearby. I'd be honoured if you'd use it.'

He accepted the offer graciously and I talked of Sikinos and its history for a while.

'The very old civilizations interest me the most,' Mike said. 'Babylon, Assyria, Sumer, Egypt, the valley of the Euphrates. Crete seems like a newcomer to me. Everything was new then. There was everything to invent, to see, to believe. The gods were not parted into Christianity and all the others then. There was a god, a belief for everyone, big and small. It was not God and the Anti-gods. Life was simpler then.'

'Also more desperate,' I said. 'Despotic kings. Disease. Ignorance. Superstition. There was everything to invent, all right, because nothing much had been invented.'

'You're confusing technology with progress. They had clean

air, new lands, freshness. The world wasn't used up then.'

'You're a pioneer, Mike,' I said. 'You're working in a totally new medium.'

He laughed and took a gulp of wine. 'Not really. All art began as science and all science began as art. The engineers were using the sensatrons before the artists. Before that there were a dozen lines of thought and invention that crossed at one point to become sensatrons. The sensatrons just happen to be a better medium to say certain things. To say other things a pen drawing or a poem or a motion picture might be best. Or even not to say it at all.'

I laughed and said, 'The artist doesn't see things, he sees himself.'

Mike smiled and stared for a long time at the columned structure on the hill. 'Yes, he certainly does,' he said softly.

'Is that why you do women so well?' I asked. 'Do you see in them what you want to see, those facets of "you" that interest you?'

He turned his shaggy dark head and looked at me. 'I thought you were some kind of big businessman, Brian. You sound like an artist to me.'

'I am. Both. A businessman with a talent for money and an artist with no talent at all.'

'There are a lot of artists without talent. They used persistence instead.'

'I often wish they wouldn't,' I grumbled. 'Everyone thinks he's an artist. If I have any talent at all, it'd be to realize I have none. However, I am a first class appreciator. That's why I want you to do a cube of my friend.'

'Persistence, see?' He laughed. 'I'm going to do a very erotic nude while I'm on Sikinos. Afterwards, perhaps, I'll want to do something more calmly. Perhaps then I'll do your friend, if she interests me.'

'She might not be so calming. She's . . . an original.'

We left it at that and I told him to contact my office in Athens when he was ready to go to the island and that they would arrange everything.

I did not see Mike again for four months, although I

received a drawing from him of the view from the terrace at the villa, with a nude girl sunbathing. Then in late August I got a vidcall from him.

'I finished the cube on Sophia. I'm in Athens. Where are you? Your office was very secretive and insisted on patching me through to you.'

'That's their job. Part of my job is not letting certain people know where I am or what I'm doing. But I'm in New York. I'm going to Bombay Tuesday, but I could stop off there. I'm anxious to see the new cube. Who's Sophia?'

'A girl. She's gone now.'

'Is that good or bad?'

'Neither. I'm at Nikki's, so come on over. I'd like your opinion on the new one.'

I felt suddenly proud. 'Tuesday at Nikki's. Give her and Barry my love.'

I hung up and punched for Madelon.

Beautiful Madelon. Rich Madelon. Famous Madelon. Madelon of the superlatives. Madelon the Elusive. Madelon the Illusion.

I saw her at nineteen, slim yet voluptuous, standing at the centre of a semicircle of admiring men at a boring party in San Francisco. I wanted her, instantly, with that 'shock of recognition' they talk about.

She looked at me between the shoulders of a communications executive and a fossil fuels magnate. Her gaze was steady and her face quiet. I felt faintly foolish just staring and many of the automatic reflexes that rich men develop to save themselves money and heartbreak went into action. I started to turn away and she smiled.

I stopped, still looking at her, and she excused herself from the man speaking to her and leaned forward. 'Are you going now?' she asked.

I nodded, slightly confused. With great charm she excused herself from the reluctant semicircle and came over to me. 'I'm ready,' she said in that calm, certain way she had. I smiled, my protective circuits all activated and alert, but my ego was touched.

We went into the glass elevator that dropped down the outside of the Fairmont Tower Complex and looked out at the fog coming over the hills near Twin Peaks and flowing down into the city.

'Where are we going?' she asked.

'Where would you like to go?' I had met a thousand women that attached themselves to me with all the apparently natural lust, delight, and casualness possible between a poor girl and a rich man. Some had been bold, some subtle, some as subtle as it was possible for them to be. A few had frankly offered business arrangements. I had accepted some of each, in my time. But this one . . . this one was either different or subtler than most.

'You expect me to say "Wherever you are going", don't you?' she said with a smile.

'Yes. One way or another.' We left the elevator and went into the guarded garage directly. Entering your car on a public street is sometimes dangerous for a rich man.

'Well, where are we going?' She smiled at me as Bowie held the door open for us. The door clicked shut behind us like the safe door it nearly was.

'I had been contemplating two choices. My hotel and work on some papers . . . or Earth, Fire, Air, and Water.'

'Let's do both. I've never been to either place,' I picked up the intercom. 'Bowie, take us to Earth, Fire, Air, and Water.'

'Yessir; I'll report it to Control.'

The girl laughed and said, 'Is someone watching you?'

'Yes, my local Control. They must know where I am, even if I don't want to be found. It's the penalty for having businesses in different time zones. By the way, are we using names?'

'Sure, why not?' she smiled. 'You are Brian Thorne and I am Madelon Morgana. You're rich and I'm poor.'

I looked her over, from the casually tossed hair to the fragile sandals. 'No . . . I think you might be without money, but you are not poor.'

'Thank you, sir,' she said. San Francisco rolled by and Bowie blanked out the windows as we approached a small street riot, then turned off towards the waterfront. When it was safe, he brought the cityscape back to us as we rolled down a hill and up another.

When we arrived at Earth, Fire, Air, and Water, Bowie called me back apologetically as I was going through the door. I told Madelon to wait and went back to get the report on the interphone. When I joined Madelon inside she smiled at me and asked, 'How was my report?'

When I looked innocent she laughed. 'If Bowie didn't have a dossier on me from your Control or whatever it is I'd be very much surprised. Tell me, am I a dangerous type, an anarchist, or a blaster or something?'

I smiled, for I like perceptive people. 'It says you are the illegitimate daughter of Madame Chiang Kai-shek and Johnny Potseed with convictions for mopery, drudgery, and penury.'

'What's mopery?'

'I haven't the faintest. My omniscient staff tells me you are nineteen, a thick kid from Montana and a half-orphan who worked for eleven months in Great Falls in an office of the Blackfoot National Enterprises.'

Her eyes got big and she gasped. 'Found out at last! My desperate secrets revealed!' She took my arm and tugged me into the elevator that would drop us down to the cavern below. She looked up at me with big innocent eyes as we stood in the packed elevator. 'Gee, Mr. Thorne, when I agreed to baby-sit for you and Mrs. Thorne I never knew you'd be taking me out.'

I turned my head slowly and looked at her with a granite face, ignoring the curious and the grinning. 'The next time I catch you indulging in mopery with my Afghan I'm going to leave you home.'

Her eyes got all wet and sad. 'No, please, I promise to be good. You can whip me again when we get home.'

I raised my eyebrows. 'No, I think wearing the collar will be enough.' The door opened. 'Come, my dear. Excuse me, please.'

'Yes, master,' she said humbly.

The Earth part of the club was the raw ground under one of the many San Francisco hills, sprayed with a structural plastic so that it looked just like a raw-dug cave, yet quite strong. We went down the curving passage towards the maelstrom of noise that was a famous *quiver* group and came out into the huge hemispherical cave. Overhead a latticework of concrete supported a transparent swimming pool filled with nude and semi-nude swimmers, some guests, and some professional entertainers.

There was a waterfall at one end and torches burned in holders in the wall, while a flickering firelight was projected over everything. The *quiver* group blasted forth from a rough cave hacked into the dirt walls halfway up to the overhead swimming pool.

As I took her arm to guide her into the *quivering* mob on the dance floor I said, 'You know there is no Mrs. Thorne.'

She smiled at me with a serene confidence. 'That's right.'

The night swirled around us. Winds blew in, scented and warm, then cool and brisk. People crashed into the water over us with galaxies of bubbles around them. One *quiver* group gave way to another, tawny animals in pseudo-lion skins and shaggy hair, the women bare-breasted and wild.

Madelon was a hundred women in a hundred minutes, but seemingly without effort. They were all her, from sullen siren to goshwowing teenie. I confess to a helpless infatuation and cared not if she was laying a trap for me or not.

The elemental decor was a stimulant and I felt younger than I had in years. People joined us, laughed and drank and tripped, and left, and others came. Madelon was a magnet, attracting joy and delight, and I was very proud.

We came to the surface at dawn and I triggered a tagalong for Bowie. We drove out to watch sunup over the Bay, then went to my apartment. In the elevator I said, 'I'll have to make that up to Bowie, I don't often stay out like that.'

'Oh?' Her face was impish, then softened and we kissed outside my door. The night was long and beautiful and beautiful and satisfying and it changed my life.

Some have said that Madelon Morgana was a bitch, a Circe, a witch, a fortune-hunter, a corrupter. Some have said that she was misunderstood, an angel, a saint, a creature much

sinned against. I knew her very well and she was probably all
those things, at various times and places. I was the first, last
and only legal husband of Madelon Morgana.

I wanted her and I got her. I wanted her because she was
the most beautiful woman I had ever seen, and the least boring.
I got her because she was beautiful inside as well. Or to be
precise, I married her. I attracted her, our sex life was outstanding, and my wealth was exactly the convenience she
needed. My money was *her* freedom.

When we married, a few weeks after we met, she stopped
being Madelon Morgana and became, not Madelon Thorne,
but *Madelon Morgana*. At first I was a convenient and attrac-
tive aid, a refuge, a shoulder, a defender, an older and wiser
head. She liked what I was, then later, *who* I was. We became
friends. We fell in love. But I was not her only lover.

No one owned Madelon, not even I. Her other lovers were
infrequent, but real, but this distressed me only occasionally.
When she loved beneath her, as it were, it hurt me. Once in a
while a lover's ego outgrew his good sense and he bragged to
me that he was sleeping with the wife of the rich and famous
Brian Thorne. This always distressed Madelon and she invariably broke off the relationship immediately, something
that the lover rarely understood.

But Madelon and I were friends, as well as man and wife,
and one is not knowingly rude to friends. I frequently insult
people, but I am never rude to them. Madelon's taste was
excellent and these other relationships were usually fruitful
in learning and joy, so that the two or three that were dis-
tasteful to me were very much in the minority.

But Michael Cilento was different.

I talked to Madelon and then flew to see Mike at Nikki's.
Our meeting was warm. 'I can't thank you enough for the
villa,' he said, hugging me. 'It was so beautiful and Nikos
and Maria were so very nice to me. I did some drawings of
their daughter. But the island – ah! Beautiful . . . very peaceful, yet . . . exciting, somehow.'

'Where's the new cube?'

'At the Athena Gallery. They're having a one-man, one-cube show.'

'Well, let's go. I'm anxious to see it.' I turned to my man Stamos. 'Madelon will be along soon. Please meet her and take her directly to the Athena.' To Mike I said, 'Come – I'm excited.'

The cube was life-size, as were all of Mike's works. Sophia was olive-skinned and full-breasted, lying on a couch covered with deep fur, curled like a cat, yet fully displayed. There was a richness in the work, an opulence reminiscent of Matisse's odalisques. But the sheer animal eroticism of the girl over-powered everything.

She was the Earth Mother, Eve and Lilith together. She was the pagan princess, the high priestess of Ba'al, the great whore of Babylon. She was nude, but a sun ornament gleamed dully between her breasts. Beyond her, through an arch of ancient, worn stone, was a dawn world, lush and green beyond a high wall. There was a feeling of time here, a setting far back beyond recorded history, when myths were men and monsters perhaps real.

She lounged on animal furs, with the faint suggestion of a wanton sprawl, with no part of her hidden, and a half-eaten apple in her hand. The direct suggestion of Eve would have been ludicrous, except for the sheer raw power of the piece. Sud-denly the symbolism of the Biblical Eve and her apple of knowledge had a reality, a meaning.

Here, somewhere in Man's past, Michael Cilento seemed to be saying, there was a turning. From simplicity towards com-plexity, from innocence to knowledge and beyond, perhaps to wisdom. And always the intimate personal secret lusts of the body.

All this in one cube, from one face. I walked to the side. The girl did not change, except that I was now looking at her side, but the view through the arch had changed. It was the sea, stretching under heavy clouds to the unchanging horizon. The waves rolled in, oily and almost silent.

The back view was past the voluptuous girl towards what she looked at: a dim room, a corridor leading to it, lit with flickering torches, going back into darkness . . . into time?

Forward into time? The Earth Mother was waiting.

The fourth side was a solid stone wall beyond the waiting woman and on the wall was set a ring and from the ring hung a chain. Symbol? Decoration? But Mike was too much an artist to have something without meaning in his work, for decoration was just design without content.

I turned to Mike to speak, but he was looking at the door.

Madelon stood in the entrance, looking at the cube. Slowly she walked towards it, her eyes intent, secret, searching. I said nothing, but stepped aside. I glanced at Mike and my heart twisted. He was staring at her as intently as she looked at the sensatron cube.

As Madelon walked closer Mike stepped near me. 'Is this your friend?' he asked. I nodded. 'I'll do that cube you wanted,' he said softly.

We waited silently as Madelon walked slowly around the cube. I could see she was excited. She was tanned and fit, fresh from a submarine exploration of the Aegean with Markos. At last she turned away from the cube and came directly to me with a swirl of her skirt. We kissed and held each other a long time.

We looked into each other's eyes for a long time. 'You're well?' I asked her.

'Yes.' She looked at me a long moment more, a soft smile on her face, searching my eyes for any hurt she might have caused. In that shorthand, intimate language of old friends and old lovers she questioned me with her look.

'I'm fine,' I said, and meant it. I was always her friend but not so often her lover. But I still had more than most men, and I do not mean my millions. I had her love and respect, while others had usually just her interest.

She turned to Mike with a smile. 'You are Michael Cilento. Would you do my portrait, or use me as a subject?' She was perceptive enough to know that there was more than a subtle difference.

'Brian has already spoken to me about it,' he said.

'And?' She was not surprised.

'I always need to spend some time with my subject before

I can do a cube.' Except with the Christ cube, I thought with a smile.

'Whatever you need,' Madelon said.

Mike looked past her at me and raised his eyebrows. I made a gesture of acquiescence. Whatever was needed, I flatter myself that I understand the creative process better than most non-artists. What was needed was needed; what was not needed was unimportant. With Mike technology had ceased to be anything but a minimal hindrance between him and his art. Now he needed only intimacy and understanding of what he intended to do. And that meant time.

'Use the Transjet,' I said. 'Blake Mason has finished the house on Malagasy. Use that. Or roam around a while.'

People have said that I asked for it. But you cannot stop the tide; it comes in when it wants and it goes when it wants. Madelon was unlike any individual that I had ever known. She owned herself. Few people do. So many are mere reflections of others, mirrors of fame or power or personality. Many let others do their thinking for them. Some are not really people, but statistics.

But Madelon was unlike the others. She took and gave without regard for very many things, demanding only truth. She was hard on her friends, for even friends sometimes require a touch of non-truth to help them out.

She conformed to my own definition of friendship: a friend must interest, amuse, and protect you. He can do nothing more. Without interest there is no communication; without amusement there is no zest; without protection there is no intimacy, no truth, no security. Madelon was my friend.

It struck me that Michael Cilento was also unlike the others. He was an Original, on his way to being a Legend. At the bottom level there are people who are 'interesting' or 'different'. Those below that should not be allowed to waste your time. On the next step above is Unique. Then the Originals, and finally those rare Legends.

I might flatter myself and say that I was certainly different, possibly even Unique on a good day. Madelon was an undisputed Original. But I sensed that Michael Cilento had that something extra, the art, the drive, the vision, the talent that could make him a Legend. (Or destroy him.)

So they went off together. To Malagasy, off the African coast. To Capri. To New York. Then I heard they were in Algiers. I had my Control keep an extra special eye on them, even more than the usual protective surveillance I kept on Madelon. But I didn't check myself. It was their business.

A vidreport had them on Station One, dancing in the null gravity of the big ballroom balloon. Even without Control I was kept abreast of their actions and whereabouts by that host of people who found delight in telling me where my wife and her lover were. And what they were doing. How they looked. What they said. And so forth.

Somehow none of it surprised me. I knew Madelon and what she liked. I knew beautiful women. I knew that Mike's sensatron cubes were passports to immortality for many women.

Mike was not the only artist working in the medium, of course, for Leeward and Miflin were both exhibiting and Coe had already done his great 'Family'. But it was Mike the women wanted. Presidents and kings sought out Cinardo and Lisa Araminta. Vidstars thought Hampton fashionable. But Mike was the first choice for all the great beauties.

I was determined that Mike have the time and privacy to do a sensatron cube of Madelon and I made it mandatory at all my homes, offices, and branches that Mike and Madelon be isolated from the vidhacks and nuts and time wasters as much as possible.

It was the purest ego on my part, that lusting towards a sensatron portrait of Madelon. I suppose I wanted the world to know that she was 'mine' as much as she could belong to anyone. I realized that all my commissioning of art was, at the bottom, ego.

Make no mistake – I enjoyed the art I helped make possible, with a few mistakes that kept me alert. But I enjoyed many kinds and levels and degrees of art. I did not go by present popularity but preferred to find and encourage new artists.

You see, I am a businessman. A very rich one, a very

talented one, a very famous one, but no one will remember me beyond the memory of my few good friends. I would not even be a footnote in history, except for my association with the arts.

But the art I help create will make me live on. I am not unique in that. Some people endow colleges, or create scholarships or build stadiums. Some build great houses, or even cause laws to be passed. These are not always acts of pure egotism, but the ego often enters into it, I'm certain, and especially if it is tax-deductible.

Over the years I have commissioned Vardi to do the Fates for the Terrace Garden of the General Anomaly complex, my financial base and main corporation. I pressed for Darrin to do the Rocky Mountain sculptures for United Motors. I talked Willoughby into doing his golden beast series at my home in Arizona. Caruthers did his 'Man' series of cubes because of a commission from my Manpower company. The panels that are now in the Metropolitan were done for my Tahiti estate by Elinor Ellington. I gave the University of Pennsylvania the money to impregnate those hundreds of sandstone slab carvings on Mars and get them safely to Earth. I subsidized Eklundy for five years before he wrote his Martian Symphony. I sponsored the first air music concert at Sydney.

My ego has had a good working out.

I received a tape from Madelon the same day I had a call from the Pope, who wanted me to help him convince Mike to do his tomb sculptures. The new Reformed Church was once again involved in art patronage, a 2,500-year-old tradition.

But getting a tape from Madelon, instead of a call, where I could reply, hurt me. I suspected I had lost Madelon.

My armoured layers of sophistication told me glibly that I had asked for it, even had intrigued to achieve it. But my beast-gut told me that I had been a fool. This time I had out-smarted myself.

I dropped the tape in the playback. She was recording from a grove of rainbow trees in Trumpet Valley. I had given Tashura the grant that had made the transplants from Mars possible and the feathery splendour of the trees behind her seemed a suitable background for her beauty.

'Brian, he's fantastic. I've never met anyone like him.'

I died a little and was sad. Others had amused her, or pleased her golden body, or were momentarily mysterious to her, but this time . . . this time I knew it was different.

'He's going to start the cube next week. In Rome. I'm very excited.' I punched out the tape and got my secretary to track her down. She was in Rome, looking radiant.

'How much does he want to do it?' I asked. Sometimes my businessman's brain likes to keep things orderly and out front, before confusion and misunderstanding sets in. But this time I was abrupt, crass and rather brutal, though my words were delivered in a normal, light tone. But all I had to offer was the wherewithal that could pay for the sensatron cube.

'Nothing,' she said. 'He's doing it for nothing. Because he wants to, Brian.'

'Nonsense. I commissioned him. Cubes cost money to make. He's not that rich.'

'He told me to tell you he wants to do it without any money. He's out now, getting new cilli nets.'

I felt cheated. I had caused the series of events that would end in the creation of a sensatron portrait of Madelon, but I was going to be cheated of my only contribution, my only connection. I had to salvage something.

'It . . . it should be an extraordinary cube. Would Mike object if I built a structure just for it?'

'I thought you wanted to put it in the new house on Battle Mountain.'

'I do, but I thought I might make a special small dome of spraystone. On the point, perhaps. Something extra nice for a Cilento masterpiece.'

'It sounds like a shrine.' Her face was quiet, her eyes looking into me.

'Yes,' I answered slowly, 'perhaps it is.' Maybe people shouldn't get to know you so well that they can read your mind where you cannot. I changed the subject and we talked for a few minutes of various friends. Steve on the Venus probe. A fashionable *couturier* who was showing a line based on the new Martian tablet finds. A new sculptor working in magnaplastics. Blake Mason's designs for the Gardens of Babylon. A festival in Rio that Jules and Gina had invited us to. The Pope's desire for Mike to do his tomb. In short, all the gossip, trivia, and things of importance between friends.

I talked of everything except what I wanted to talk about.

When we parted Madelon told me with a sad, proud smile that she had never been so happy. I nodded and punched out, then stared sightlessly at the skyline. For a long moment I hated Michael Cilento and he was probably never so near death. But I loved Madelon and she loved Mike, so he must live and be protected. I knew that she loved me, too, but it was and had always been a different kind of love.

I went to a science board meeting at Tycho Base and looked at the green-brown-blue white-streaked Earth 'overhead' and only paid minimal attention to the speakers. I came down to a petroleum meeting at Hargesisa, in Somalia. I visited a mistress of mine in Samarkand, sold a company, bought an electro-snake for the Louvre, visited Armand in Nardonne, bought a company, commissioned a concerto from a new composer I liked in Ceylon, and donated an early Caruthers to the Prado.

I came, I went. I thought about Madelon. I thought about Mike. Then I went back to what I did best: making money, making work, getting things done, making time pass.

I had just come from a policy meeting of the North American Continent Ecology Council when Madelon called to say the cube was finished and would be installed in the Battle Mountain house by the end of the week.

'How is it?' I asked.

She smiled. 'See for yourself.'

'Smug bitch,' I grinned.

'It's his best one, Brian. The best sensatron in the world.'

'I'll see you Saturday.' I punched out and took the rest of the day off and had an early dinner with two Swedish blondes and did a little fleshly purging. It did not really help very much.

On Saturday I could see the two tiny figures waving at me from the causeway bridging the house with the tip of the spire of rock where the copter pad was. They were holding hands.

Madelon was tanned, fit, glowing, dressed in white with a necklace of Cartier Tempoimplant tattoos across her shoulders and breasts in glowing facets of liquid fire. She waved at Bowie as she came to me, squinting against the dust the copter blades were still swirling about.

Mike was there, dressed in black, looking haunted.

Getting to you, boy? I thought. There was a vicious thrill in thinking it and I shamed myself.

Madelon hugged me and we walked together back over the high causeway and directly to the new spraystone dome in the garden, at the edge of a five hundred foot cliff.

The cube was magnificent. There hadn't been anything like it, ever. Not ever.

It was the largest cube I'd seen. There have been bigger ones since but at the time it was quite large. None have been better. Its impact was stunning.

Madelon sat like a queen on what has come to be known as the Jewel Throne, a great solid thronelike block that seemed to be part temple, part jewel, part dream. It was immensely complex, set with faceted electronic patterns that gave it the effect of a superbly cut jewel that was somehow also liquid. Michael Cilento would have made his place in art history with that throne alone.

But on it sat Madelon. Nude. Her waist-long hair fell in a simple cascade. She looked right out at you, sitting erect, almost primly, with an almost triumphant expression.

It drew me from the doorway. Everyone, everything was forgotten, including the original and the creator with me. There was only the cube. The vibrations were getting to me and my pulse increased. Even knowing that pulse generators were working on my alpha waves and broadcast projectors were doing this and sonics were doing that and my own alpha waves was being synchronized and reprojected did not affect me. Only the cube affected me. All else was forgotten.

There was just the cube and me, with Madelon in it, more real than the reality.

I walked to stand before it. The cube was slightly raised so that she sat well above the floor, as a queen should. Behind her, beyond the dark violet eyes, beyond the incredible *presence* of the woman, there was a dark, misty background that may or may not have been moving and changing.

I stood there a long time, just looking, experiencing. 'It's incredible,' I whispered.

'Walk around it,' Madelon said. I felt the note of pride in her voice. I moved to the right and it was as if Madelon followed me with her eyes without moving them, following me by sensing me, alert, alive, ready for me. Already, the electronic image within the cilli nets was *real*.

The figure of Madelon sat there, proudly naked, breathing normally with that fantastically lifelike movement possible to the skilled molecular constructors. The figure had none of the flamboyance that Caruthers or Raeburn brought to their figures, so delighted in their ability to bring 'life' to their work that they saw nothing else.

But Mike had restraint. He had *power* in his work, understatement, demanding that the viewer put something of himself into it.

I walked around to the back. Madelon was no longer sitting on the throne. It was empty, and beyond it, stretching to the horizon, was an ocean and above the toppling waves, stars. New constellations glowed. A meteor flashed. I stepped back to the side. The throne was unchanged but Madelon was back. She sat there, a queen, waiting.

I walked around the cube. She was on the other side, waiting, breathing, *being*. But in back she was gone.

But to where?

I looked long into the eyes of the figure in the cube. She stared back at me, into me. I seemed to feel her thoughts. Her face changed, seemed about to smile, grew sad, drew back into queenliness.

I drew back into myself. I went to Mike to congratulate him. 'I'm stunned. There are no words.'

He seemed relieved at my approval. 'It's yours,' he said. I nodded. There was nothing to say. It was the greatest work of art I knew. It was more than Madelon or the sum of all the Madelons that I knew existed. It was Woman as well as a specific woman. I felt humble in the presence of such great art. It was 'mine' only in that I could house it. I could not contain it. It had to belong to the world.

I looked at the two of them. There was something else. I sensed what it was and I died some more. A flicker of hate for both of them flashed across my mind and was gone, leaving only emptiness.

'Madelon is coming with me,' Mike said.

I looked at her. She made a slight nod, looking at me gravely, with deep concern in her eyes. 'I'm sorry, Brian.'

I nodded, my throat constricted suddenly. It was almost a business deal: the greatest work of art for Madelon, even trade. I turned back to look at the sensatron again and this time the image-Madelon seemed sad, yet compassionate. My eyes were wet and the cube shimmered. I heard them leave and long after the throb of the copter had faded away I stood there, looking into the cube, into Madelon, into myself.

They went to Athens, I heard, then to Russia for a while. When they went to India so that Mike might do his Holy Men series I called off the discreet monitors Control had put on them.

I bought companies. I made things. I commissioned art. I sold companies. I went places. I changed mistresses. I made money. I fought stock control fights. Some I lost. I ruined people. I made others happy and rich. I was alone a lot.

I return often to Battle Mountain. That is where the cube is.

The greatness of it never bores me; it is different each time I see it, for I am different each time. But then Madelon never bored me either, unlike all other women, who sooner or later revealed either their shallowness or my inability to find anything deeper.

I look at the work of Michael Cilento and I know that he is an artist of his time, yet like many artists, *not* of his time. He uses the technology of his time, the attitude of an alien, and the same basic subject matter that generations of fascinated artists have used.

Michael Cilento is an artist of women. Many have said he is

the artist who caught women as they were, as they wanted to be, and as *he* saw them, all in one work of art.

When I look at my sensatron cube, and at all the other Cilentos I have acquired, I am proud to have helped cause the creation of such art. But when I look at the Madelon that is in my favourite cube I sometimes wonder if the trade was worth it.

The cube is more than Madelon or the sum of the sum of all the Madelons who ever existed. But the reality of art is not the reality of reality.

WHEN IT CHANGED

One of the values of science fiction is the freedom it gives the writers. There were always fewer taboos in science fiction than in other forms of literature.

The taboo against the 'sad ending' was less important in science fiction than elsewhere, for instance, and the science-fiction reader was always aware that in any given story the whole world, even the whole universe, *might* be destroyed. Science-fiction stories, dealing with other societies, could easily mock any aspect of our own society, and make a villain of even mother love.

In one respect, though, science fiction was rather behind most forms of literature. It was more male chauvinist than most. Most of the writers and most of the readers were male, and if any female intruded in the stories, she was there chiefly to be captured by some alien monster and then rescued. Her conversation consisted largely of screaming.

Well, times have changed. There are more women writing and reading science fiction and there are more characters in the stories who are people as well as women. And if science fiction can bring itself to do this, it can go all the way as no other type of fiction can. Joanna Russ here gives us the description, and tragedy, of a society that is entirely female in a way no society outside science fiction could possibly be.

WHEN IT CHANGED

Joanna Russ

Katy drives like a maniac; we must have been doing over 120 km/hr on those turns. She's good, though, extremely good, and I've seen her take the whole car apart and put it together again in a day. My birthplace on Whileaway was largely given to farm machinery and I refuse to wrestle with a five-gear shift at unholy speeds, not having been brought up to it, but even on those terms in the middle of the night, on a country road as bad as only our district can make them, Katy's driving didn't scare me. The funny thing about my wife, though: she will not handle guns. She has even gone hiking in the forests above the 48th parallel without firearms, for days at a time. And that *does* scare me.

Katy and I have three children between us, one of hers and two of mine. Yuriko, my eldest, was asleep in the back seat, dreaming twelve-year-old dreams of love and war: running away to sea, hunting in the North, dreams of strangely beautiful people in strangely beautiful places, all the wonderful guff you think up when you're turning twelve and the glands start going. Some day soon, like all of them, she will disappear for weeks on end to come back grimy and proud, having knifed her first cougar or shot her first bear, dragging some abominably dangerous dead beastie behind her, which I will never forgive for what it might have done to my daughter. Yuriko says Katy's driving puts her to sleep.

For someone who has fought three duels, I am afraid of far, far too much. I'm getting old. I told this to my wife.

'You're thirty-four,' she said. Laconic to the point of silence, that one. She flipped the lights on, on the dash – three km

Nebula Award, Best Short Story 1972

to go and the road getting worse all the time. Far out in the country. Electric-green trees rushed into our headlights and around the car. I reached down next to me where we bolt the carrier panel to the door and eased my rifle into my lap. Yuriko stirred in the back. My height but Katy's eyes, Katy's face. The car engine is so quiet, Katy says, that you can hear breathing in the back seat. Yuki had been alone in the car when the message came, enthusiastically decoding her dot-dashes (silly to mount a wide-frequency transceiver near an I.C. engine, but most of Whileaway is on steam). She had thrown herself out of the car, my gangly and gaudy offspring, shouting at the top of her lungs, so of course she had had to come along. We've been intellectually prepared for this ever since the Colony was founded, ever since it was abandoned, but this is different. This is awful.

'Men!' Yuki had screamed, leaping over the car door. 'They've come back! Real Earth men!'

We met them in the kitchen of the farmhouse near the place where they had landed; the windows were open, the night air very mild. We had passed all sorts of transportation when we parked outside, steam tractors, trucks, an I.C. flat-bed, even a bicycle. Lydia, the district biologist, had come out of her Northern taciturnity long enough to take blood and urine samples and was sitting in a corner of the kitchen shaking her head in astonishment over the results; she even forced herself (very big, very fair, very shy, always painfully blushing) to dig up the old language manuals – though I can talk the old tongues in my sleep. And do. Lydia is uneasy with us; we're Southerners and too flamboyant. I counted twenty people in that kitchen, all the brains of North Continent. Phyllis Spet, I think, had come in by glider. Yuki was the only child there.

Then I saw the four of them.

They are bigger than we are. They are bigger and broader. Two were taller than me, and I am extremely tall, 1m 80cm in my bare feet. They are obviously of our species but *off*, inde-scribably off, and as my eyes could not and still cannot quite comprehend the lines of those alien bodies, I could not, then, bring myself to touch them, though the one who spoke Russian – what voices they have! – wanted to 'shake hands', a custom from the past, I imagine. I can only say they were apes with human faces. He seemed to mean well, but I found myself shuddering back almost the length of the kitchen – and then I laughed apologetically – and then to set a good example (*interstellar amity*, I thought) did 'shake hands' finally. A hard, hard hand. They are heavy as draft horses. Blurred, deep voices. Yuriko had sneaked in between the adults and was gazing at *the men* with her mouth open.

He turned *his* head – those words have not been in our language for six hundred years – and said, in bad Russian:

'Who's that?'

'My daughter,' I said, and added (with that irrational attention to good manners we sometimes employ in moments of insanity), 'My daughter, Yuriko Janetson. We use the patronymic. You would say matronymic.'

He laughed, involuntarily. Yuki exclaimed, 'I thought they would be *good-looking*!' greatly disappointed at this reception of herself. Phyllis Helgason Spet, whom someday I shall kill, gave me across the room a cold, level, venomous look, as if to say: *Watch what you say. You know what I can do.* It's true that I have little formal status, but Madam President will get herself in serious trouble with both me and her own staff if she continues to consider industrial espionage good clean fun. Wars and rumours of wars, as it says in one of our ancestors' books. I translated Yuki's words into *the man*'s dog-Russian, once our *lingua franca*, and *the man* laughed again.

'Where are all your people?' he said conversationally.

I translated again and watched the faces around the room; Lydia embarrassed (as usual), Spet narrowing her eyes with some damned scheme, Katy very pale.

'This is Whileaway,' I said.

He continued to look unenlightened.

'Whileaway,' I said. 'Do you remember? Do you have records? There was a plague on Whileaway.'

He looked moderately interested. Heads turned in the back

of the room, and I caught a glimpse of the local professions-parliament delegate; by morning every town meeting, every district caucus, would be in full session.

'Plague?' he said. 'That's most unfortunate.'

'Yes,' I said. 'Most unfortunate. We lost half our population in one generation.'

He looked properly impressed.

'Whileaway was lucky,' I said. 'We had a big initial gene pool, we had been chosen for extreme intelligence, we had a high technology and a large remaining population in which every adult was two-or-three experts in one. The soil is good. The climate is blessedly easy. There are thirty millions of us now. Things are beginning to snowball in industry – do you understand? – give us seventy years and we'll have more than one real city, more than a few industrial centres, full-time professions, full-time radio operators, full-time machinists, give us seventy years and not everyone will have to spend three quarters of a lifetime on the farm.' And I tried to explain how hard it is when artists can practise full-time only in old age, when there are so few, so very few who can be free, like Katy and myself. I tried also to outline our government, the two houses, the one by professions and the geographic one; I told him the district caucases handled problems too big for the individual towns. And that population control was not a political issue, not yet, though give us time and it would be. This was a delicate point in our history; give us time. There was no need to sacrifice the quality of life for an insane rush into industrialization. Let us go our own pace. Give us time.

'Where are all the people?' said that monomaniac.

I realized then that he did not mean people, he meant *men*, and he was giving the word the meaning it had not had on Whileaway for six centuries.

'They died,' I said. 'Thirty generations ago.'

I thought we had poleaxed him. He caught his breath. He made as if to get out of the chair he was sitting in; he put his hand to his chest; he looked around at us with the strangest blend of awe and sentimental tenderness. Then he said, solemnly and earnestly:

'A great tragedy.'

I waited, not quite understanding.

'Yes,' he said, catching his breath again with that queer smile, that adult-to-child smile that tells you something is being hidden and will be presently produced with cries of encouragement and joy, 'a great tragedy. But it's over.' And again he looked around at all of us with the strangest deference. As if we were invalids.

'You've adapted amazingly,' he said.

'To what?' I said. He looked embarrassed. He looked inane. Finally he said, 'Where I come from, the women don't dress so plainly.'

'Like you?' I said. 'Like a bride?' for the men were wearing silver from head to foot. I had never seen anything so gaudy. He made as if to answer and then apparently thought better of it; he laughed at me again. With an odd exhilaration – as if we were something childish and something wonderful, as if he were doing us an enormous favour – he took one shaky breath and said, 'Well, we're here.'

I looked at Spet, Spet looked at Lydia, Lydia looked at Amalia, who is the head of the local town meeting, Amalia looked at I don't know who. My throat was raw. I cannot stand local beer, which the farmers swill as if their stomachs had iridium linings, but I took it anyway, from Amalia (it was her bicycle we had seen outside as we parked), and swallowed it all. This was going to take a long time. I said, 'Yes, here you are,' and smiled (feeling like a fool), and wondered seriously if male Earth people's minds worked so very differently from female Earth people's minds, but that couldn't be so or the race would have died out long ago. The radio network had got the news around-planet by now and we had another Russian speaker, flown in from Varna; I decided to cut out when *the man* passed around pictures of his wife, who looked like the priestess of some arcane cult. He proposed to question Yuki, so I barrelled her into a back room in spite of her furious protests, and went out on the front porch. As I left, Lydia was explaining the difference between parthenogenesis (which is so easy that anyone can practise it) and what we do, which is the merging of ova. That is why Katy's baby looks like me. Lydia went on to the Ansky Process and Katy Ansky, our one full-polymath genius and the great-great-I don't know how many times great-greatmother of my own Katharina.

A dot-dash transmitter in one of the outbuildings chattered faintly to itself: operators flirting and passing jokes down the line.

There was a man on the porch. The other tall man. I watched him for a few minutes – I can move very quietly when I want to – and when I allowed him to see me, he stopped talking into the little machine hung around his neck. Then he said calmly, in excellent Russian, 'Did you know that sexual equality has been re-established on Earth?'

'You're the real one,' I said, 'aren't you? The other one's for show.' It was a great relief to get things cleared up. He nodded affably.

'As a people, we are not very bright,' he said. 'There's been too much genetic damage in the last few centuries. Radiation. Drugs. We can use Whileaway's genes, Janet.' Strangers do not call strangers by the first name.

'You can have cells enough to drown in,' I said. 'Breed your own.'

He smiled. 'That's not the way we want to do it.' Behind him I saw Katy come into the square of light that was the screened-in door. He went on, low and urbane, not mocking me, I think, but with the self-confidence of someone who has always had money and strength to spare, who doesn't know what it is to be second-class or provincial. Which is very odd, because the day before, I would have said that was an exact description of me.

'I'm talking to you, Janet,' he said, 'because I suspect you have more popular influence than anyone else here. You know as well as I do that parthenogenetic culture has all sorts of inherent defects, and we do not – if we can help it – mean to use you for anything of the sort. Pardon me; I should not have said "use". But surely you can see that this kind of society is un-natural.'

'Humanity is unnatural,' said Katy. She had my rifle under

her left arm. The top of that silky head does not quite come up to my collar-bone, but she is as tough as steel; he began to move, again with that queer smiling deference (which his fellow had shown to me but he had not) and the gun slid into Katy's grip as if she had shot with it all her life.

'I agree,' said the man. 'Humanity is unnatural. I should know. I have metal in my teeth and metal pins here.' He touched his shoulder. 'Seals are harem animals,' he added, 'and so are men; apes are promiscuous and so are men; doves are monogamous and so are men; there are even celibate men and homosexual men. There are homosexual cows, I believe. But Whileaway is still missing something.' He gave a dry chuckle. I will give him the credit of believing that it had something to do with nerves.

'I miss nothing,' said Katy, 'except that life isn't endless.'

'You are –?' said the man, nodding from me to her.

'Wives,' said Katy. 'We're married.' Again the dry chuckle.

'A good economic arrangement,' he said, 'for working and taking care of the children. And as good an arrangement as any for randomizing heredity, if your reproduction is made to follow the same pattern. But think, Katharina Michaelason, if there isn't something better that you might secure for your daughters. I believe in instincts, even in Man, and I can't think that the two of you – a machinist, are you? and I gather you are some sort of chief of police – don't feel somehow what even you must miss. You know it intellectually, of course. There is only half a species here. Men must come back to Whileaway.'

Katy said nothing.

'I should think, Katharina Michaelason,' said the man gently, 'that you, of all people, would benefit most from such a change,' and he walked past Katy's rifle into the square of light coming from the door. I think it was then that he noticed my scar, which really does not show unless the light is from the side: a fine line that runs from temple to chin. Most people don't even know about it.

'Where did you get that?' he said, and I answered with an involuntary grin, 'In my last duel.' We stood there bristling at each other for several seconds (this is absurd but true) until he went inside and shut the screen door behind him. Katy said in a brittle voice, 'You damned fool, don't you know when we've been insulted?' and swung up the rifle to shoot him through the screen, but I got to her before she could fire and knocked the rifle out of aim; it burned a hole through the porch floor. Katy was shaking. She kept whispering over and over, 'That's why I never touched it, because I knew I'd kill some-one, I knew I'd kill someone.' The first man – the one I'd spoken with first – was still talking inside the house, something about the grand movement to re-colonize and re-discover all that Earth had lost. He stressed the advantages to Whileaway: trade, exchange of ideas, education. He too said that sexual equality had been re-established on Earth.

Katy was right, of course; we should have burned them down where they stood. Men are coming to Whileaway. When one culture has the big guns and the other has none, there is a certain predictability about the outcome. Maybe men would have come eventually in any case. I like to think that a hundred years from now my great-grandchildren could have stood them off or fought them to a standstill, but even that's no odds; I will remember all my life those four people I first met who were muscled like bulls and who made me – if only for a moment – feel small. A neurotic reaction, Katy says. I re-member everything that happened that night; I remember Yuki's excitement in the car, I remember Katy's sobbing when we got home as if her heart would break, I remember her lovemaking, a little peremptory as always, but wonderfully soothing and comforting. I remember prowling restlessly around the house after Katy fell asleep with one bare arm flung into a patch of light from the hall. The muscles of her forearms are like metal bars from all that driving and testing of her machines. Sometimes I dream about Katy's arms. I remember wandering into the nursery and picking up my wife's baby, dozing for a while with the poignant, amazing warmth of an infant in my lap, and finally returning to the kitchen to find Yuriko fixing herself a late snack. My daughter eats like a Great Dane.

'Yuki,' I said, 'do you think you could fall in love with a man?' and she whooped derisively. 'With a ten-foot toad!' said my tactful child.

But men are coming to Whileaway. Lately I sit up nights and worry about the men who will come to this planet, about my two daughters and Betta Katharinason, about what will happen to Katy, to me, to my life. Our ancestors' journals are one long cry of pain and I suppose I ought to be glad now but one can't throw away six centuries, or even (as I have lately discovered) thirty-four years. Sometimes I laugh at the question those four men hedged about all evening and never quite dared to ask, looking at the lot of us, hicks in overalls, farmers in canvas pants and plain shirts: *Which of you plays the role of the man?* As if we had to produce a carbon copy of their mistakes! I doubt very much that sexual equality has been re-established on Earth. I do not like to think of myself mocked, of Katy deferred to as if she were weak, of Yuki made to feel unimportant or silly, of my other children cheated of their full humanity or turned into strangers. And I'm afraid that my own achievements will dwindle from what they were – or what I thought they were – to the not-very-interesting curiosa of the human race, the oddities you read about in the back of the books, things to laugh at sometimes because they are so exotic, quaint but not impressive, charming but not useful. I find this more painful than I can say. You will agree that for a woman who has fought three duels, all of them kills, indulging in such fears is ludicrous. But what's around the corner now is a duel so big that I don't think I have the guts for it; in Faust's words: *Verweile doch, du bist so schoen!* Keep it as it is. Don't change.

Sometimes at night I remember the original name of this planet, changed by the first generation of our ancestors, those curious women for whom, I suppose, the real name was too painful a reminder after the men died. I find it amusing, in a grim way, to see it all so completely turned around. This too shall pass. All good things must come to an end.

Take my life but don't take away the meaning of my life.
For-A-While.

ON THE DOWNHILL SIDE

Science fiction is not fantasy, but the two fields are closely allied and much effort and time has been wasted in trying to differentiate the two. It is not enough to say that science deals with the possible and fantasy with the impossible. Many of the common gimmicks of science fiction (anti-gravity, time-travel, faster-than-light velocity) are impossible by modern physical theory; while some of the staples of fantasy may prove to be not so impossible once science extends itself into the inner realms of consciousness.

Perhaps it is a difference in attitude. In science fiction, you strive to make the not-so seem plausible; you demonstrate a knowledge of what the rules of science are before you break them. In fantasy, however, you are not concerned with plausibility; you merely accept.

Not all science-fiction writers can write good fantasy; nor all good fantasy writers turn out good science fiction. In general, a writer of hard science fiction is out of sympathy with fantasy, while those writers who are out of sympathy with science find themselves drawn to fantasy.

I myself sometimes envy the fantasy writers. I write fantasies sometimes but not often and am inhibited by my desire for plausibility even then. Which means that in my attempts to work out something physiologically reasonable, I could never even dream of creating anything as tantalizingly lovely as Ellison's unicorn.

ON THE DOWNHILL SIDE

Harlan Ellison

'In love, there is always one who kisses and one who offers the cheek.'

FRENCH PROVERB

I knew she was a virgin because she was able to ruffle the silken mane of my unicorn. Named Lizette, she was a Grecian temple in which no sacrifice had ever been made. Vestal virgin of New Orleans, found walking without shadow in the thankgod coolness of cockroach-crawling Louisiana night. My unicorn whinnied, inclined his head, and she stroked the ivory spiral of his horn.

Much of this took place in what is called the Irish Channel, a strip of street in old New Orleans where the lace curtain micks had settled decades before; now the Irish were gone and the Cubans had taken over the Channel. Now the Cubans were sleeping, recovering from the muggy today that held within its hours the *déjà vu* of muggy yesterday, the *déjà rêvé* of intolerable tomorrow. Now the crippled bricks of side streets off Magazine had given up their nightly ghosts, and one such phantom had come to me, calling my unicorn to her – thus, clearly, a virgin – and I stood waiting.

Had it been Sutton Place, had it been a Manhattan evening, and had we met, she would have kneeled to pet my dog. And I would have waited. Had it been Puerto Vallarta, had it been 20° 36' N, 105° 13' W, and had we met, she would have crouched to run her fingertips over the oil-slick hide of my iguana. And I would have waited. Meeting in streets requires ritual. One must wait and not breathe too loud, if one is to enjoy the congress of the nightly ghosts.

She looked across the fine head of my unicorn and smiled at me. Her eyes were a shade of grey between onyx and miscalculation. 'Is it a bit chilly for you?' I asked.

'When I was thirteen,' she said, linking my arm, taking a tentative two steps that led me with her, up the street, 'or perhaps I was twelve, well no matter, when I was that approximate age, I had a marvellous shawl of Belgian lace. I could look through it and see the mysteries of the sun and the other stars unriddled. I'm sure someone important and very nice has purchased that shawl from an antique dealer, and paid handsomely for it.'

It seemed not a terribly responsive reply to a simple question.

'A queen of the Mardi Gras Ball doesn't get chilly,' she added, unasked. I walked along beside her, the cool evasiveness of her arm binding us, my mind a welter of answer choices, none satisfactory.

Behind us, my unicorn followed silently. Well, not entirely silently. His platinum hooves clattered on the bricks. I'm afraid I felt a straight pin of jealousy. Perfection does that to me.

'When were you queen of the Ball?'

The date she gave was one hundred and thirteen years before.

It must have been brutally cold down in the stones.

There is a little book they sell, a guide to manners and dining in New Orleans: I've looked: nowhere in the book do they indicate the proper responses to a ghost. But then, it says nothing about the wonderful cemeteries of New Orleans's West Bank, or Metairie. Or the gourmet dining at such locations. One seeks, in vain, through the mutable, mercurial universe, for the compleat guide. To everything. And failing in the search, one makes do the best one can. And suffers the frustration, suffers the ennui.

Perfection does that to me.

We walked for some time, and grew to know each other, as best we'd allow. These are some of the high points. They lack continuity. I don't apologize, I merely point it out, adding with some truth, I feel, that *most* liaisons lack continuity. We find ourselves in odd places at various times, and for a brief span we link our lives to others – even as Lizette had linked her arm with mine – and then, our time elapsed, we move apart.

Through a haze of pain occasionally; usually through a veil of memory that clings then passes; sometimes as though we have never touched.

'My name is Paul Ordahl,' I told her. 'And the most awful thing that ever happened to me was my first wife, Bernice. I don't know how else to put it – even if it sounds melodramatic, it's simply what happened – she went insane, and I divorced her, and her mother had her committed to a private mental home.'

'When I was eighteen,' Lizette said, 'my family gave me my coming-out party. We were living in the Garden District, on Prytania Street. The house was a lovely white Plantation – they call them antebellum now – with Grecian pillars. We had a persimmon-green gazebo in the rear gardens, directly beside a weeping willow. It was six-sided. Octagonal. Or is that hexagonal? It was the loveliest party. And while it was going on, I sneaked away with a boy . . . I don't remember his name . . . and we went into the gazebo, and I let him touch my breasts. I don't remember his name.'

We were on Decatur Street, walking towards the French Quarter; the Mississippi was on our right, dark but making its presence known.

'Her mother was the one had her committed, you see. I only heard from them twice after the divorce. It had been four stinking years and I really didn't want any more of it. Once, after I'd started making some money, the mother called and said Bernice had to be put in the state asylum. There wasn't enough money to pay for the private home any more. I sent a little; not much. I suppose I could have sent more, but I was remarried, there was a child from her previous marriage. I didn't want to send any more. I told the mother not to call me again. There was only once after that . . . it was the most terrible thing that ever happened to me.'

We walked around Jackson Square, looking in at the very black grass, reading the plaques bolted to the spear-topped fence, plaques telling how New Orleans had once belonged to the French. We sat on one of the benches in the street. The street had been closed to traffic, and we sat on one of the benches.

'Our name was Charbonnet. Can you say that?'

I said it, with a good accent.

'I married a very wealthy man. He was in real estate. At one time he owned the entire block were the *Vieux Carré* now stands, on Bourbon Street. He admired me greatly. He came and sought my hand, and my *maman* had to strike the bargain because my father was too weak to do it; he drank. I can admit that now. But it didn't matter, I'd already found out how my suitor was set financially. He wasn't common, but he wasn't quality, either. But he was wealthy and I married him. He gave me presents. I did what I had to do. But I refused to let him make love to me after he became friends with that awful Jew who built the Metairie Cemetery over the race track because they wouldn't let him race his Jew horses. My husband's name was Dunbar. Claude Dunbar, you may have heard the name? Our parties were *de rigueur*.'

'Would you like some coffee and *beignets* at Du Monde?'

She stared at me for a moment, as though she wanted me to say something more, then she nodded and smiled.

We walked around the Square. My unicorn was waiting at the kerb. I scratched his rainbow flank and he struck a spark off the cobblestones with his right front hoof. 'I know,' I said to him, 'we'll soon start the downhill side. But not just yet. Be patient. I won't forget you.'

Lizette and I went inside the Café du Monde and I ordered two coffees with warm milk and two orders of *beignets* from a waiter who was originally from New Jersey, but had lived most of his life only a few miles from College Station, Texas.

There was a coolness coming off the levee.

'I was in New York,' I said. 'I was receiving an award at an architects' convention – did I mention I was an architect – yes, that's what I was at the time, an architect – and I did a television interview. The mother saw me on the programme, and checked the newspapers to find out what hotel we were using for the convention, and she got my room number and called me. I had been out quite late after the banquet where I'd got my award, quite late. I was sitting on the side of the bed,

taking off my shoes, my tuxedo tie hanging from my unbut-
toned collar, getting ready to just throw clothes on the floor
and sink away, when the phone rang. It was the mother. She
was a terrible person, one of the worst I ever knew, a shrike, a
terrible, just a terrible person. She started telling me about
Bernice in the asylum. How they had her in this little room and
how she stared out of the window most of the time. She'd
reverted to childhood, and most of the time she couldn't even
recognize the mother; but when she did, she'd say something
like, "Don't let them hurt me, Mommy, don't let them hurt
me." So I asked her what she wanted me to do, did she want
money for Bernice or what . . . did she want me to go see her
since I was in New York . . . and she said God no. And then
she did an awful thing to me. She said the last time she'd been
to see Bernice, my ex-wife had turned around and put her finger
to her lips and said, "Shhh, we have to be very quiet. Paul is
working." And I swear, a snake uncoiled in my stomach. It
was the most terrible thing I'd ever heard. No matter how
secure you are that you honest to God had *not* sent someone
to a madhouse, there's always that little core of doubt, and
saying what she'd said just burned out my head. I couldn't
even think about it, couldn't even really *hear* it, or it would have
collapsed me. So down came these iron walls and I just kept
on talking, and after a while she hung up.

'It wasn't till two years later that I allowed myself to think
about it, and then I cried; it had been a long time since I'd
cried. Oh, not because I believed that nonsense about a man
isn't supposed to cry, but just because I guess there hadn't been
anything that important to cry *about*. But when I let myself
hear what she'd said, I started crying, and just went on and on
till I finally went in and looked into the bathroom mirror and
I asked myself face-to-face if I'd done that, if I'd ever made her
be quiet so I could work on blue-prints or drawings . . .

'And after a while I saw myself shaking my head no, and
it was easier. That was perhaps three years before I died.'

She licked the powdered sugar from the *beignets* off her
fingers, and launched into a long story about a lover she had
taken. She didn't remember his name.

It was some time after midnight. I'd thought midnight would signal the start of the downhill side, but the hour had passed, and we were still together, and she didn't seem ready to vanish. We left the Café Du Monde and walked into the Quarter.

I despise Bourbon Street. The strip joints, with the pasties over nipples, the smell of need, the dwarfed souls of men attuned only to flesh. The noise.

We walked through it like art connoisseurs at a showing of motel room paintings. She continued to talk about her life, about the men she had known, about the way they had loved her, the ways in which she had spurned them, and about the trivia of her past existence. I continued to talk about my loves, about all the women I had held dear in my heart for however long each had been linked with me. We talked across each other, our conversation at right angles, only meeting in the intersections of silence at story's end.

She wanted a Julep and I took her to the Royal Orleans Hotel and we sat in silence as she drank. I watched her, studying that phantom face, seeking for even the smallest flicker of light off the ice in her eyes, hoping for an indication that glacial melting could be forthcoming. But there was nothing, and I burned to say correct words that might cause heat. She drank and reminisced about evenings with young men in similar hotels, a hundred years before.

We went to a night club where a Flamenco dancer and his two-woman troupe performed on a stage of unpolished woods, their star-shining black shoes setting up resonances in me that I chose to ignore.

Then I realized there were only three couples in the club, and that the extremely pretty Flamenco dancer was playing to Lizette. He gripped the lapels of his bolero jacket and clattered his heels against the stage like a man driving nails. She watched him, and her tongue made a wholly flirtatious trip around the rim of her liquor glass. There was a two-drink minimum, and as I have never liked the taste of alcohol, she was more than willing to prevent waste by drinking mine as well as her own. Whether she was getting drunk or simply indulging herself, I do not know. It didn't matter. I became blind with jealousy, and dragons took possession of my eyes.

When the dancer was finished, when his half hour show was concluded, he came to our table. His suit was skin tight and the colour of Arctic lakes. His hair was curly and moist from his exertions, and his prettiness infuriated me. There was a scene. He asked her name, I interposed a comment, he tried to be polite sensing my ugly mood, she overrode my comment, he tried again in Castilian, *th*-ing his *esses*, she answered, I rose and shoved him, there was a scuffle. We were asked to leave.

Once outside, she walked away from me.

My unicorn was at the kerb, eating from a porcelain *Sèvres* soup plate filled with *flan*. I watched her walk unsteadily up the street towards Jackson Square. I scratched my unicorn's neck and he stopped eating the egg custard. He looked at me for a long moment. Ice crystals were sparkling in his mane. We were on the downhill side. 'Soon, old friend,' I said.

He dipped his elegant head towards the plate. 'I see you've been to the Las Americas. When you return the plate, give my best to *Señor* Pena.'

I followed her up the street. She was walking rapidly towards the Square. I called to her, but she wouldn't stop. She began dragging her left hand along the steel bars of the fence enclosing the Square. Her fingertips thudded softly from bar to bar, and once I heard the chitinous *clak* of a manicured nail.

'Lizette!'

She walked faster, dragging her hand across the dark metal bars.

'Lizette! Damn it!'

I was reluctant to run after her; it was somehow terribly demeaning. But she was getting farther and farther away. There were bums in the Square, sitting slouched on the benches, their arms out along the backs. Itinerants, kids with beards and knapsacks. I was suddenly frightened for her. Impossible. She had been dead for a hundred years. There's no reason to it . . . I was afraid for her!

I started running, the sound of my footsteps echoing up and around the Square. I caught her at the corner and dragged her around. She tried to slap me, and I caught her hand. She kept trying to hit me, to scratch my face with the manicured nails. I held her and swung her away from me, swung her around, and around, dizzyingly, trying to keep her off-balance. She swung wildly, crying out and saying things inarticulately. Finally, she stumbled and I pulled her in to me and held her tight against my body.

'Stop it! Stop, Lizette! I . . . *stop it*!' She went limp against me and I felt her crying against my chest. I took her into the shadows and my unicorn came down Decatur Street and stood under a street lamp, waiting.

The chimera winds rose. I heard them, and knew we were well on the downhill side, that time was growing short. I held her close and smelled the woodsmoke scent of her hair. 'Listen to me,' I said, softly, close to her. 'Listen to me, Lizette. Our time's almost gone. This is our last chance. You've lived in stone for a hundred years; I've heard you cry. I've come there, to that place, night after night, and I've heard you cry. You've paid enough, God knows. So have I. We can do it. We've got one more chance, and we can make it, if you'll try. That's all I ask. Try.'

She pushed away from me, tossing her head so the auburn hair swirled away from her face. Her eyes were dry. Ghosts can do that. Cry without making tears. Tears are denied us. Other things; I won't talk of them here.

'I lied to you,' she said.

I touched the side of her face. The high cheekbone just at the hairline. 'I know. My unicorn would never have let you touch him if you weren't pure. I'm not, but he has no choice with me. He was assigned to me. He's my familiar and he puts up with me. We're friends.'

'No. Other lies. My life was a lie. I've told them all to you. We can't make it. You have to let me go.'

I didn't know exactly where, but I knew how it would happen. I argued with her, trying to convince her there was a way for us. But she couldn't believe it, hadn't the strength or the will or the faith. Finally, I let her go.

She put her arms around my neck, and drew my face down

to hers, and she held me that way for a few moments. Then the winds rose, and there were sounds in the night, the sounds of calling, and she left me there, in the shadows.

I sat down on the kerb and thought about the years since I'd died. Years without much music. Light leached out. Wandering. Nothing to pace me but memories and the unicorn. How sad I was for *him*; assigned to me till I got my chance. And now it had come and I'd taken my best go, and failed.

Lizette and I were the two sides of the same coin; devalued and impossible to spend. Legal tender of nations long since vanished, no longer even names on the cracked papyrus of cartographers' maps. We had been snatched away from final rest, had been set adrift to roam for our crimes, and only once between death and eternity would we receive a chance. This night . . . this nothing special night . . . this was our chance.

My unicorn came to me, then, and brushed his muzzle against my shoulder. I reached up and scratched around the base of his spiral horn, his favourite place. He gave a long, silvery sigh, and in that sound I heard the sentence I was serving on him, as well as myself. We had been linked, too. Assigned to one another by the one who had ordained this night's chance. But if I lost out, so did my unicorn; he who had wandered with me through all the soundless, lightless years.

I stood up. I was by no means ready to do battle, but at least I could stay in for the full ride . . . all the way on the downhill side. 'Do you know where they are?'

My unicorn started off down the street.

I followed, hopelessness warring with frustration. Dusk to dawn is the full ride, the final chance. After midnight is the downhill side. Time was short, and when time ran out there would be nothing for Lizette or me or my unicorn *but* time. Forever.

When we passed the Royal Orleans Hotel I knew where we were going. The sound of the Quarter had already faded. It was getting on towards dawn. The human lice had finally crawled into their flesh-mounds to sleep off the night of revelry.

Though I had never experienced directly the New Orleans in which Lizette had grown up, I longed for the power to blot out the cancerous blight that Bourbon Street and the Quarter had become, with its tourist filth and screaming neon, to restore it to the colourful, yet healthy state in which it had thrived a hundred years before. But I was only a ghost, not one of the gods with such powers, and at that moment I was almost at the end of the line held by one of those gods.

My unicorn turned down dark streets, heading always in the same general direction, and when I saw the first black shapes of the tombstones against the night sky, the *lightening* night sky, I knew I'd been correct in my assumption of destination.

The Saint Louis Cemetery.

Oh, how I sorrow for anyone who has never seen the world famous Saint Louis Cemetery in New Orleans. It is the perfect graveyard, the complete graveyard, the finest graveyard in the universe. (There is a perfection in some designs that informs the function totally. There are Danish chairs that could be nothing *but* chairs, are so totally and completely *chair* that if the world as we know it ended, and a billion years from now the New Orleans horsy cockroaches became the dominant species, and they dug down through the alluvial layers, and found one of those chairs, even if they themselves did not use chairs, were not constructed physically for the use of chairs, had never seen a chair, *still* they would know it for what it had been made to be: a chair. Because it would be the essence of *chairness*. And from it, they could reconstruct the human race in replica. *That* is the kind of graveyard one means when one refers to the world famous Saint Louis Cemetery.)

The Saint Louis Cemetery is ancient. It sighs with shadows and the comfortable bones and their after-images of deaths that became great merely because those who died went to be interred in the Saint Louis Cemetery. The water table lies just eighteen inches below New Orleans – there are no graves in the earth for that reason. Bodies are entombed aboveground in crypts, in sepulchres, vaults, mausoleums. The gravestones are all different, no two alike, each one a testament to the stone-cutter's art. Only secondarily testaments to those who lie beneath the markers.

We had reached the moment of final nightness. That ultimate moment before day began. Dawn had yet to fill the eastern sky, yet there was a warming of tone to the night; it was
the last of the downhill side of my chance. Of Lizette's chance.

We approached the cemetery, my unicorn and I. From
deep in the centre of the skyline of stones beyond the fence I
could see the ice-chill glow of a pulsing blue light. The light
one finds in a refrigerator, cold and flat and brittle.

I mounted my unicorn, leaned close along his neck, clinging
to his mane with both hands, knees tight to his silken sides,
now rippling with light and colour, and I gave a little hiss of
approval, a little sound of go.

My unicorn sailed over the fence, into the world famous Saint
Louis Cemetery.

I dismounted and thanked him. We began threading our
way between the tombstones, the sepulchres, the crypts.

The blue glow grew more distinct. And now I could hear the
chimera winds rising, whirling, coming in off alien seas. The
pulsing of the light, the wail of the winds, the night dying. My
unicorn stayed close. Even we of the spirit world know when
to be afraid.

After all, I was only operating off a chance; I was under no
god's protection. Naked, even in death.

There is no fog in New Orleans.

Mist began to form around us.

Except sometimes in the winter, there is no fog in New
Orleans.

I remembered the daybreak of the night I'd died. There had
been mist. I had been a suicide.

My third wife had left me. She had gone away during the
night, while I'd been at a business meeting with a client; I
had been engaged to design a church in Baton Rouge. All
that day I'd steamed the old wallpaper off the apartment we'd
rented. It was to have been our first home together, paid for
by the commission. I'd done the steaming myself, with a tall
ladder and a steam condenser and two flat pans with steam
holes. Up near the ceiling the heat had been so awful I'd al-

most fainted. She'd brought me lemonade, freshly-squeezed. Then I'd showered and changed and gone to my meeting. When I'd returned, she was gone. No note.

Lizette and I were two sides of the same coin, cast off after death for the opposite extremes of the same crime. She had never loved. I had loved too much. Overindulgence in something as delicate as love is to be found monstrously offensive in the eyes of the God of Love. And some of us – who have never understood the salvation in the Golden Mean – some of us are cast adrift with but one chance. It can happen.

Mist formed around us, and my unicorn crept close to me, somehow smaller, almost timid. We were moving into realms he did not understand, where his limited magics were useless. These were realms of potency so utterly beyond even the limbo creatures – such as my unicorn – so completely alien to even the intermediary zone wanderers – Lizette and myself – that we were as helpless and without understanding as those who live. We had only one advantage over living, breathing, as yet undead humans: we *knew* for certain that the realms on the other side existed.

Above, beyond, deeper: where the gods live. Where the one who had given me my chance, had given Lizette *her* chance, where He lived. Undoubtedly watching.

The mist swirled up around us, as chill and final as the dust of pharaohs' tombs.

We moved through it, towards the pulsing heart of blue light. And as we came into the penultimate circle, we stopped. We were in the outer ring of potency, and we saw the claiming things that had come for Lizette. She lay on an altar of crystal, naked and trembling. They stood around her, enormously tall and transparent. Man shapes without faces. Within their transparent forms a strange, silvery fog swirled, like smoke from holy censers. Where eyes should have been on a man or a ghost, there were only dull flickering firefly glowings, inside, hanging in the smoke, moving, changing shape and position. No eyes at all. And tall, very tall, towering over Lizette and the altar.

For me, over committed to love, when dawn came without salvation, there was only an eternity of wandering, with my unicorn as sole companion. Ghost for evermore. Incense chimera viewed as dust-devil on the horizon, chilling as I passed in city streets, forever gone, invisible, lost, empty, helpless, wandering.

But for her, empty vessel, the fate was something else entirely. The God of Love had allowed her the time of wanderings, trapped by day in stones, freed at night to wander. He had allowed her the final chance. And having failed to take it, her fate was with these claiming creatures, gods themselves . . . of another order . . . higher or lower I had no idea. But terrible.

'*Lagniappe*!' I screamed the word. The old French word they use in New Orleans when they want a little extra; a bonus of *croissants*, a few additional carrots dumped into the shopping bag, a larger portion of clams or crabs or shrimp. '*Lagniappe*! Lizette, take a little more! Try for the extra! Try . . . demand it . . . there's time . . . you have it coming to you . . . you've paid . . . I've paid . . . it's ours . . . *try*!'

She sat up, her naked body lit by lambent fires of chill blue cold from the other side. She sat up and looked across the inner circle to me, and I stood there with my arms out, trying desperately to break through the outer circle to her. But it was solid and I could not pass. Only virgins could pass.

And they would not let her go. They had been promised a feed, and they were there to claim. I began to cry, as I had cried when I finally heard what the mother had said, when I finally came home to the empty apartment and knew I had spent my life loving too much, demanding too much, myself a feeder at a board that *could* be depleted and emptied and serve up no more. She wanted to come to me, I could *see* she wanted to come to me. But they would have their meal.

Then I felt the muzzle of my unicorn at my neck, and in a step he had moved through the barrier that was impenetrable to me, and he moved across the circle and stood waiting. Lizette leaped from the altar and ran to me.

It all happened at the same time. I felt Lizette's body anchor in to mine, and *we* saw my unicorn standing over there on the other side, and for a moment *we* could not summon up the necessary reactions, the correct sounds. We knew for the first time in either our lives or our deaths what it was to be paralysed. Then reactions began washing over me, we, us in wave after wave: cascading joy that Lizette had come to . . . us; utter love for this Paul ghost creature; realization that instinctively part of us was falling into the same pattern again; fear that part would love too much at this mystic juncture; resolve to temper our love; and then anguish at the sight of our unicorn standing there, waiting to be claimed. . . .

We called to him . . . using his secret name, one we had never spoken aloud. We could barely speak. Weight pulled at his throat, our throats. 'Old friend . . .' We took a step towards him but could not pass the barrier. Lizette clung to me, Paul held me tight as I trembled with terror and the cold of that inner circle still frosting my flesh.

The great transparent claimers stood silently, watching, waiting, as if content to allow us our moments of final decision. But there impatience could be felt in the air, a soft purring, like the death rattle always in the throat of a cat. 'Come back! Not for me . . . don't do it for me . . . it's not fair!'

Paul's unicorn turned his head and looked at us.

My friend of starless nights, when we had gone sailing together through the darkness. My friend who had walked with me on endless tours of empty places. My friend of gentle nature and constant companionship. Until Lizette, my friend, my only friend, my familiar assigned to an onerous task, who had come to love me and to whom I had belonged, even as he had belonged to me.

I could not bear the hurt that grew in my chest, in my stomach; my head was on fire, my eyes burned from tears first for Paul, and now for the sweetest creature a god had ever sent to temper a man's anguish . . . and for myself. I could not bear the hurt of never knowing – as Paul had known it – the silent company of that gentle, magical beast.

But he turned back, and moved to them, and they took that as final decision, and the great transparent claimers moved in around him, and their quickglass hands reached down to touch him, and for an instant they seemed to hesitate, and I called out, 'Don't be afraid . . .' and my unicorn turned his head to look across the mist of potency for the last time, and I saw he *was* afraid, but not as much as he would have been if I had not been there.

Then the first of them touched his smooth, silvery flank and he gave a trembling sigh of pain. A ripple ran down his hide. Not the quick flesh movement of ridding himself of a fly, but a completely alien, unnatural tremor – containing in its swiftness all the agony and loss of eternities. A sigh went out from Paul's unicorn, though he had not uttered it.

We could feel the pain, the loneliness. My unicorn with no time left to him. Ending. All was now a final ending; he had stayed with me, walked with me, and had grown to care for me, until that time when he would be released from his duty by that special god; but now freedom was to be denied him; an ending.

The great transparent claimers all touched him, their ice fingers caressing his warm hide as we watched, helpless, Lizette's face buried in Paul's chest. Colours surged across my unicorn's body, as if by becoming more intense the chill touch of the claimers could be beaten off. Pulsing waves of rainbow colour that lived in his hide for moments, then dimmed, brightened again and were bled off. Then the colours leaked away one by one, chroma weakening: purple-blue, manganese violet, discord, cobalt blue, doubt, affection, chrome green, chrome yellow, raw sienna, contemplation, alizarin crimson, irony, silver, severity, compassion, cadmium red, white.

They emptied him . . . he did not fight them . . . going colder and colder . . . flickers of yellow, a whisper of blue, pale as white . . . the tremors blending into one constant shudder . . . the wonderful golden eyes rolled in torment, went flat, brightness dulled, flat metal . . . the platinum hoofs caked with rust . . . and he stood, did not try to escape, gave himself for us . . . and he was emptied. Of everything. Then, like the claimers, we could see through him. Vapours swirled within the transparent husk, a fogged glass, shimmering . . . then nothing. And then they absorbed even the husk.

The chill blue light faded, and the claimers grew indistinct in our sight. The smoke within them seemed thicker, moved more slowly, horribly, as though they had fed and were sluggish and would go away, back across the line to that dark place where they waited, always waited, till their hunger was aroused again. And my unicorn was gone. I was alone with Lizette. I was alone with Paul. The mist died away, and the claimers were gone, and once more it was merely a cemetery as the first rays of the morning sun came easing through the tumble and disarray of headstones.

We stood together as one, naked body white and virginal in my weary arms; and as the light of the sun struck us we began to fade, to merge, to mingle our bodies and our wandering spirits one into the other, forming one spirit that would neither love too much, nor too little, having taken out chance on the downhill side.

We faded and were lifted invisibly on the scented breath of that good God who had owned us, and were taken away from there. To be born again as one spirit, in some other human form, man or woman we did not know which. Nor would we remember. Nor did it matter.

This time, love would not destroy us. This time out, we would have luck.

The luck of silken mane and rainbow colours and platinum hooves and spiral horn.

THE FIFTH HEAD OF CERBERUS

Not all branches of science are equally useful in science fiction. The science that is science-fictional *par excellence* is, of course, astronomy. What is so intrinsically wonderful as the vast reaches of empty space, and the existence of different worlds with properties almost unimaginable? What can supply the writer with so naturally different a society as one that is on a different world, one without an atmosphere, one with six suns, one with alien intelligences?

Science fiction writers, following the line of least resistance, chose astronomical plots and let the wonder of the background make less necessary the development of character in the foreground.

At the other extreme is biology, far more difficult in detail than astronomy, far more man-centred, and, indeed, sure to involve human beings intimately. Except for the introduction of extra-terrestrial creatures (by their nature not involving human beings) biology rarely intruded into science fiction in earlier decades.

It is different now that molecular biology has become the most dramatic of the branches of science. It is interesting that of the two stories that ended in a virtual tie in the novella category, one, 'A Meeting with Medusa' by Clarke, which won by a hair, is intricately astronomical in nature, while the other, 'The Fifth Head of Cerberus' by Gene Wolfe, which lost by a hair, is as intimately biological.

Come and see what the world of the new biology can be like.

THE FIFTH HEAD OF CERBERUS

Gene Wolfe

> When the ivy-tod is heavy with snow,
> And the owlet whoops to the wolf below,
> That eats the she-wolf's young.
>
> Samuel Taylor Coleridge
> *The Rime of the Ancient Mariner*

When I was a boy my brother David and I had to go to bed early whether we were sleepy or not. In summer particularly, bedtime often came before sunset; and because our dormitory was in the east wing of the house, with a broad window facing the central courtyard and thus looking west, the hard, pinkish light sometimes streamed in for hours while we lay staring out at my father's crippled monkey perched on a flaking parapet, or telling stories, one bed to another, with soundless gestures.

Our dormitory was on the uppermost floor of the house, and our window had a shutter of twisted iron which we were forbidden to open. I suppose the theory was that a burglar might, on some rainy morning (this being the only time he could hope to find the roof garden deserted), let down a rope and so enter our room unless the shutter was closed.

The object of this hypothetical and very courageous thief would not, of course, be merely to steal us. Children, whether boys or girls, were extraordinarily cheap in Port-Mimizon; and indeed I was once told that my father, who had formerly traded in them, no longer did so because of the poor market. Whether or not this was true, everyone – or nearly everyone – knew of some professional who would furnish what was wanted, within reason, at a low price. These men made the children of the poor and the careless their study, and should you want, say, a brown-skinned, red-haired little girl, or one who was plump, or who lisped, a blond boy like David, or a pale, brown-haired, brown-eyed boy such as I, they could provide one in a few hours.

Neither, in all probability, would the imaginary burglar seek to hold us for ransom, though my father was thought in some quarters to be immensely rich. There were several reasons for this. Those few people who knew that my brother and I existed knew also, or at least had been led to believe, that me father cared nothing at all for us. Whether this was true or not I cannot say; certainly I believed it, and my father never gave me the least reason to doubt it, though at the time the thought of killing him had never occurred to me.

And if these reasons were not sufficiently convincing, anyone with an understanding of the stratum in which he had become perhaps the most permanent feature would realize that for him, who was already forced to give large bribes to the secret police, to disgorge money once in that way would leave him open to a thousand ruinous attacks; and this may have been – this and the fear in which he was held – the real reason we were never stolen.

The iron shutter is (for I am writing now in my old dormitory room) hammered to resemble in a stiff and oversymmetrical way the boughs of a willow. In my boyhood it was overgrown by a silvertrumpet vine (since dug up) which had scrambled up the wall from the court below, and I used to wish that it would close the window entirely and thus shut out the sun when we were trying to sleep; but David, whose bed was under the window, was for ever reaching up to snap off branches so that he could whistle through the hollow stems, making a sort of Panpipe of four or five. The piping, of course, growing louder as David grew bolder, would in time attract the attention of Mr. Million, our tutor. Mr. Million would enter the room in perfect silence, his wide wheels gliding across the uneven floor while David pretended sleep. The Panpipe might by this time be concealed under his pillow, in the sheet, or even under the mattress, but Mr. Million would find it.

What he did with those little musical instruments after confiscating them from David I had forgotten until yesterday; although in prison, when we were kept in by storms or heavy snow, I often occupied myself by trying to recall it. To have broken them, or dropped them through the shutter into the patio below would have been completely unlike him; Mr. Million never broke anything intentionally, and never wasted anything. I could visualize perfectly the half-sorrowing expression with which he drew the tiny pipes out (the face which seemed to float behind his screen was much like my father's) and the way in which he turned and glided from the room. But what became of them?

Yesterday, as I said (this is the sort of thing that gives me confidence), I remembered. He had been talking to me here while I worked, and when he left it seemed to me – as my glance idly followed his smooth motion through the doorway – that something, a sort of flourish I recalled from my earliest days, was missing. I closed my eyes and tried to remember what the appearance had been, eliminating any scepticism, any attempt to guess in advance what I 'must' have seen; and I found that the missing element was a brief flash, the glint of metal, over Mr. Million's head.

Once I had established this I knew that it must have come from a swift upward motion of his arm, like a salute, as he left our room. For an hour or more I could not guess the reason for that gesture, and could only suppose it, whatever it had been, to have been destroyed by time. I tried to recall if the corridor outside our dormitory had, in that really not so distant past, held some object now vanished: a curtain or a windowshade, an appliance to be activated, anything that might account for it. There was nothing.

I went into the corridor and examined the floor minutely for marks indicating furniture. I looked for hooks or nails driven into the walls, pushing aside the coarse old tapestries. Craning my neck, I looked at the door itself and saw what I had not seen in the thousands of times I had passed through it: that like all the doors in this house, which is very old, it had a massive frame of wooden slabs, and that one of these, forming the lintel, protruded enough from the wall to make a narrow shelf above the door.

I pushed my chair into the hall and stood on the seat. The

shelf was thick with dust, in which lay forty-seven of my brother's pipes and a wonderful miscellany of other small objects. Objects many of which I recalled, but some of which still fail to summon any flicker of response from the recesses of my mind —

The small blue egg of a songbird, speckled with brown. I suppose the bird must have nested in the vine outside our window, and that David or I despoiled the nest only to be robbed ourselves by Mr. Million. But I do not recall the incident.

And there is a (broken) puzzle made of the bronzed viscera of some small animal, and – wonderfully evocative – one of those large and fancifully decorated keys, sold annually, which during the year of its currency will admit the possessor to certain rooms of the city library after hours. Mr. Million, I suppose, must have confiscated it when, after expiration, he found it doing duty as a toy; but what memories!

My father had his own library, now in my possession; but we were forbidden to go there. I have a dim memory of standing – at how early an age I cannot say – before that huge, carved door. Of seeing it swing back, and the crippled monkey on my father's shoulder pressing itself against his hawk face, with the black scarf and scarlet dressing gown beneath and the rows and rows of shabby books and notebooks behind them, and the sick-sweet smell of formaldehyde coming from the laboratories beyond the sliding mirror.

I do not remember what he said, or whether it had been I or another who had knocked, but I do recall that after the door had closed again a woman in pink whom I thought very pretty stooped to bring her face to the level of my own and assured me that my father had written all the books I had just seen, and that I doubted it not at all.

My brother and I, as I have said, were forbidden this room; but when we were a little older Mr. Million used to take us, about twice a week, on expeditions to the city library. These were very nearly the only times we were allowed to leave the house, and since our tutor disliked curling the jointed length of his metal modules into a hirecart, and no sedan chair would have withstood his weight or contained his bulk, these forays were made on foot.

For a long time this route to the library was the only part of the city I knew. Three blocks down Saltimbanque Street where our house stood, right at the Rue d'Asticot to the slave market and a block beyond that to the library. A child, not knowing what is extraordinary and what commonplace, usually lights midway between the two, finds interest in incidents adults consider beneath notice and calmly accepts the most improbable occurrences. My brother and I were fascinated by the spurious antiques and bad bargains of the Rue d'Asticot, but often bored when Mr. Million insisted on stopping for an hour at the slave market.

It was not a large one, Port-Mimizon not being a centre of the trade, and the auctioneers and their merchandise were frequently on a most friendly basis – having met several times previously as a succession of owners discovered the same faults. Mr. Million never bid, but watched the bidding, motionless, while we kicked our heels and munched the fried bread he had bought at a stall for us. There were sedan chairmen, their legs knotted with muscle, and simpering bath attendants; fighting slaves in chains, with eyes dulled by drugs or blazing with imbecile ferocity; cooks, house servants, a hundred others – yet David and I used to beg to be allowed to proceed alone to the library.

This library was a wastefully large building which had held government offices in the old French-speaking days. The park in which it had once stood had died of petty corruption, and the library now rose from a clutter of shops and tenements. A narrow thoroughfare led to the main doors, and once we were inside the squalor of the neighbourhood vanished, replaced by a kind of peeling grandeur. The main desk was directly beneath the dome, and this dome, drawing up with it a spiralling walkway lined with the library's main collection, floated five hundred feet in the air: a stony sky whose least chip falling might kill one of the librarians on the spot.

While Mr. Million browsed his way majestically up the

helix, David and I raced ahead until we were several full turns in advance and could do what we liked. When I was still quite young it would often occur to me that, since my father had written (on the testimony of the lady in pink) a roomful of books, some of them should be here; and I would climb resolutely until I had almost reached the dome, and there rummage. Because the librarians were very lax about reshelving, there seemed always a possibility of finding what I had failed to find before. The shelves towered far above my head, but when I felt myself unobserved I climbed them like ladders, stepping on books when there was no room on the shelves themselves for the square toes of my small brown shoes, and occasionally kicking books to the floor where they remained until our next visit and beyond, evidence of the staff's reluctance to climb that long, coiled slope.

The upper shelves were, if anything, in worse disorder than those more conveniently located, and one glorious day when I attained the highest of all I found occupying that lofty, dusty position only a lorn copy of *Monday or Tuesday* leaning against a book about the assassination of Trotsky.

I never found any books of my father's, but I did not regret the long climbs to the top of the dome. If David had come with me we raced up together, up and down the sloping floor – or peered over the rail at Mr. Million's slow progress while we debated the feasibility of putting an end to him with one cast of some ponderous work. If David preferred to pursue interests of his own farther down I ascended to the very top where the cap of the dome curved right over my head; and there, from a rusted iron catwalk not much wider than one of the shelves I had been climbing (and I suspect not nearly so strong) opened in turn each of a circle of tiny piercings – piercings in a wall of iron, but so shallow a wall that when I had slid the corroded cover plates out of the way I could thrust my head through and feel myself truly outside, with the wind and the circling birds and the lime-spotted expanse of the dome curving away beneath me.

To the west, since it was taller than the surrounding houses and marked by the orange trees on the roof, I could make out our house. To the south, the masts of the ships in the harbour, and in clear weather – if it was the right time of day – the whitecaps of the tidal race Sainte Anne drew between the peninsulas called First Finger and Thumb (And once, as I very well recall, while looking south I saw the great geyser of sunlit water when a star-crosser splashed down.) To east and north spread the city proper, the citadel and the grand market and the forests and mountains beyond.

But sooner or later, whether David had accompanied me or gone off on his own, Mr. Million summoned us. Then we were forced to go with him to one of the wings to visit this or that science collection. This meant books for lessons. My father insisted that we learn biology, anatomy, and chemistry thoroughly, and under Mr. Million's tutelage learn them we did – he never considering a subject mastered until we could discuss every topic mentioned in every book catalogued under the heading. The life sciences were my own favourites, but David preferred languages, literature, and law; for we got a smattering of these as well as anthropology, cybernetics, and psychology.

When he had selected the books that would form our study for the next few days and urged us to choose more for ourselves, Mr. Million would retire with us to some quiet corner of one of the science reading rooms, where there were chairs and a table and room sufficient for him to curl the jointed length of his body or align it against a wall or bookcase in a way that left the aisles clear. To designate the formal beginning of our class he used to begin by calling roll, my own name always coming first.

I would say, 'Here', to show that he had my attention.

'And David.'

'Here.' (David has an illustrated *Tales from the Odyssey* open on his lap where Mr. Million cannot see it, but he looks at Mr. Million with bright, feigned interest. Sunshine slants down to the table from a high window, and shows the air aswarm with dust.)

'I wonder if either of you noticed the stone implements in the room through which we passed a few moments ago?'

We nod, each hoping the other will speak.

'Were they made on Earth, or here on our own planet?'

This is a trick question, but an easy one. David says, 'Neither one. They're plastic.' And we giggle.

Mr. Million says patiently, 'Yes, they're plastic reproductions, but from where did the originals come?' His face, so similar to my father's, but which I thought of at this time as belonging only to him, so that it seemed a frightening reversal of nature to see it on a living man instead of his screen, was neither interested, nor angry, nor bored; but coolly remote.

David answers, 'From Sainte Anne.' Sainte Anne is the sister planet to our own, revolving with us about a common centre as we swing around the sun. 'The sign said so, and the aboriginals there made them – there weren't any abos here.'

Mr. Million nods, and turns his impalpable face towards me. 'Do you feel these stone implements occupied a central place in the lives of their makers? Say no.'

'No.'

'Why not?'

I think frantically, not helped by David, who is kicking my shins under the table. A glimmering comes.

'Talk. Answer at once.'

'It's obvious, isn't it?' (Always a good thing to say when you're not even sure 'it' is even possible.) 'In the first place, they can't have been very good tools, so why would the abos have relied on them? You might say they needed those obsidian arrowheads and bone fishhooks for getting food, but that's not true. They could poison the water with the juices of certain plants, and for primitive people the most effective way to fish is probably with weirs, or with nets of rawhide or vegetable fibre. Just the same way, trapping or driving animals with fire would be more effective than hunting; and anyway stone tools wouldn't be needed at all for gathering berries and the shoots of edible plants and things like that, which were probably their most important foods – those stone things got in the glass case here because the snares and nets rotted away and they're all that's left, so the people that make their livings that way pretend they were important.'

'Good. David? Be original, please. Don't repeat what you've just heard.'

David looks up from his book, his blue eyes scornful of both of us. 'If you could have asked them they would have told you that their magic and their religion, the songs they sang and the traditions of their people were what were important. They killed their sacrificial animals with flails of sea shells that cut like razors, and they didn't let their men father children until they had stood enough fire to cripple them for life. They mated with trees and drowned the children to honour their rivers. That was what was important.'

With no neck, Mr. Million's face nodded. 'Now we will debate the humanity of those aborigines. David negative and first.'

(I kick him, but he has pulled his hard, freckled legs up beneath him, or hidden them behind the legs of his chair, which is cheating.) 'Humanity,' he says in his most objectionable voice, 'in the history of human thought implies descent from what we may conveniently call *Adam*; that is, the original Terrestrial stock, and if the two of you don't see that you're idiots.'

I wait for him to continue, but he is finished. To give myself time to think I say, 'Mr. Million, it's not fair to let him call me names in a debate. Tell him that's not debating, it's *fighting*, isn't it?'

Mr. Million says, 'No personalities, David.' (David is already peeking at Polyphemus the Cyclops and Ulysses, hoping I'll go on for a long time. I feel challenged and decide to do so.)

I begin, 'The argument which holds descent from Terrestrial stock privotal is neither valid nor conclusive. Not conclusive because it is distinctly possible that the aborigines of Sainte Anne were descendants of some earlier wave of human expansion – one, perhaps, even predating *the Homeric Greeks*.'

Mr. Million says mildly, 'I would confine myself to arguments of higher probability if I were you.'

I nevertheless gloss upon the Etruscans, Atlantis, and the tenacity and expansionist tendencies of a hypothetical technological culture occupying Gondwanaland. When I have finished Mr. Million says, 'Now reverse. David, affirmative without repeating.'

My brother, of course, has been looking at his book instead of listening, and I kick him with enthusiasm expecting him to be stuck; but he says, 'The abos are human because they're all dead.'

'Explain.'

'If they were alive it would be dangerous to let them be human because they'd ask for things, but with them dead it makes it more interesting if they were, and the settlers killed them all.'

And so it goes. The spot of sunlight travels across the black-streaked red of the tabletop – travelled across it a hundred times. We would leave through one of the side doors and walk through a neglected areaway between two wings. There would be empty bottles there and wind-scattered papers of all kinds, and once a dead man in bright rags over whose legs we boys skipped while Mr. Million rolled silently around him. As we left the areaway for a narrow street the bugles of the garrison at the citadel (sounding so far away) would call the troopers to their evening mess. In the Rue d'Asticot the lamplighter would be at work, and the shops shut behind their iron grilles. The sidewalks magically clear of old furniture would seem broad and bare.

Our own Saltimbanque Street would be very different, with the first revellers arriving. White-haired hearty men guiding very young men and boys, men and boys handsome and muscular but a shade overfed; young men who made diffident jokes and smiled with excellent teeth. These were always the early ones, and when I was a little older I sometimes wondered if they were early only because the white-haired men wished to have their pleasure and get a good night's sleep as well, or if it was because they knew the young men they were introducing to my father's establishment would be drowsy and irritable after midnight, like children who have been kept up too late.

Because Mr. Million did not want us to use the alleys after dark we came in the front entrance with the white-haired men and their nephews and sons. There was a garden there, not much bigger than a small room and recessed into the window-less front of the house. In it were beds of ferns the size of graves; a little fountain whose water fell upon rods of glass to make a continual tinkling, and which had to be protected from the street boys; and, with his feet firmly planted, indeed almost buried in moss, an iron statue of a dog with three heads.

It was this statue, I suppose, that gave our house its popular name of La Maison du Chien, though there may have been a reference to our surname as well. The three heads were sleekly powerful, with pointed muzzles and ears. One was snarling and one, the centre head, regarded the world of garden and street with a look of tolerant interest. The third, the one nearest the brick path that led to our door, was – there is no other term for it – frankly grinning; and it was the custom for my father's patrons to pat this head between the ears as they came up the path. Their fingers had polished the spot to the consistency of black glass.

This, then, was my world at seven of our world's long years, and perhaps for half a year beyond. Most of my days were spent in the little classroom over which Mr. Million presided, and my evenings in the dormitory where David and I played and fought in total silence. They were varied by the trips to the library I have described or, very rarely, elsewhere. I pushed aside the leaves of the silvertrumpet vine occasionally to watch the girls and their benefactors in the court below, or heard their talk drifting down from the roof garden, but the things they did and talked of were of no interest to me. I knew that the tall, hatchet-faced man who ruled our house and was called Maître by the girls and servants was my father. I had known for as long as I could remember that there was somewhere a fearsome woman – the servants were in terror of her – called Madame, but that she was neither my mother nor David's, nor my father's wife.

That life and my childhood, or at least my infancy, ended one evening after David and I, worn out with wrestling and silent arguments, had gone to sleep. Someone shook me by the shoulder and called me, and it was not Mr. Million but one of

the servants, a hunched little man in a shabby red jacket. 'He
wants you,' this summoner informed me. 'Get up.'

I did, and he saw that I was wearing nightclothes. This I
think had not been covered in his instructions, and for a
moment during which I stood and yawned he debated with
himself. 'Get dressed,' he said at last. 'Comb your hair.'

I obeyed, putting on the black velvet trousers I had worn
the day before, but (guided by some instinct) a new, clean
shirt. The room to which he then conducted me (through tortu-
ous corridors now emptied of the last patrons; and others,
musty, filthy with the excrement of rats, to which patrons
were never admitted) was my father's library – the room with
the great carved door before which I had received the whispered confidences of the woman in pink. I had never been inside it, but when my guide rapped discreetly on the door it
swung back, and I found myself within almost before I
realized what had happened.

My father, who had opened the door, closed it behind me,
and leaving me standing where I was, walked to the most
distant end of that long room and threw himself down in a
huge chair. He was wearing the red dressing gown and black
scarf in which I had most often seen him, and his long, sparse
hair was brushed straight back. He stared at me, and I remember that my lip trembled as I tried to keep from breaking
into sobs.

'Well,' he said, after we had looked at one another for a
long time, 'and there you are. What am I going to call you?'

I told him my name, but he shook his head. 'Not that.
You must have another name for me – a private name. You
may choose it yourself if you like.'

I said nothing. It seemed to me quite impossible that I
should have any name other than the two words which were,
in some mystic sense I only respected without understanding,
my name.

'I'll choose for you then,' my father said. 'You are Number
Five. Come here, Number Five.'

I came, and when I was standing in front of him he told me,
'Now we are going to play a game. I am going to show you

some pictures, do you understand? And all the time you are watching them you must talk. Talk about the pictures. If you talk you win, but if you stop, even for just a second, I do. Understand?'

I said I did.

'Good. I know you're a bright boy. As a matter of fact Mr. Million has sent me all the examinations he has given you, and the tapes he makes when he talks with you, did you know that? Did you ever wonder what he did with them?'

I said, 'I thought he threw them away,' and my father, I noticed, leaned forward as I spoke, a circumstance I found flattering at the time.

'No, I have them here.' He pressed a switch. 'Now remember, you must not stop talking.'

But for the first few moments I was much too interested to talk.

There had appeared in the room, as though by magic, a boy considerably younger than I, and a painted wooden soldier almost as large as I was myself, which when I reached out to touch them proved as insubstantial as air. 'Say something,' my father said. 'What are you thinking about, Number Five?'

I was thinking about the soldier, of course, and so was the younger boy, who appeared to be about three. He toddled through my arm like mist and attempted to knock it over.

They were holographs – three-dimensional images formed by the interference of two wave fronts of light – things which had seemed very dull when I had seen them illustrated by flat pictures of chessmen in my physics book; but it was some time before I connected those chessmen with the phantoms who walked in my father's library at night! All this time my father was saying, 'Talk! Say something! What do you think the little boy is feeling?'

'Well, the little boy likes the big soldier, but he wants to knock him down if he can because the soldier's only a toy, really, but it's bigger than he is . . . ' And so I talked, and for a long time, hours I suppose, continued. The scene changed and changed again. The giant soldier was replaced by a pony, a rabbit, a meal of soup and crackers. But the three-year-old boy remained the central figure. When the hunched man in the shabby coat came again, yawning, to take me back to my bed, my voice had worn to a husky whisper and my throat ached. In my dreams that night I saw the little boy scampering from one activity to another, his personality in some way confused with my own and my father's so that I was at once observer, observed, and a third presence observing both.

The next night I fell asleep almost at the moment Mr. Million sent us up to bed, retaining consciousness only long enough to congratulate myself on so doing. I woke when the hunched man entered the room, but it was not me whom he roused from the sheets but David. Quietly, pretending I still slept (for it had occurred to me, and seemed quite reasonable at the time, that if he were to see I was awake he might take both of us), I watched as my brother dressed and struggled to impart some sort of order to his fair tangle. When he returned I was sound asleep, and had no opportunity to question him until Mr. Million left us alone, as he sometimes did, to eat our breakfast. I had told him my own experiences as a matter of course, and what he had to tell me was simply that he had had an evening very similar to mine. He had seen holographic pictures, and apparently the same pictures: the wooden soldier, the pony. He had been forced to talk constantly, as Mr. Million had so often made us do in debates and verbal examinations. The only way in which this interview with our father had differed from mine, as nearly as I could determine, appeared when I asked him by what name he had been called.

He looked at me blankly, a piece of toast half raised to his mouth.

I asked again, 'What name did he call you by when he talked to you?'

'He called me David. What did you think?'

With the beginning of these interviews the pattern of my life changed, the adjustments I assumed to be temporary becoming imperceptibly permanent, settling into a new shape of which neither David nor I was consciously aware. Our games and stories after bedtime stopped, and David less and less

often made his Panpipes of the silvertrumpet vine. Mr.
Million allowed us to sleep later and we were in some subtle
way acknowledged to be more adult. At about this time too he
began to take us to a park where there was an archery range
and provision for various games. This little park, which was
not far from our house, was bordered on one side by a canal.
And there, while David shot arrows at a goose stuffed with
straw or played tennis, I often sat staring at the quiet, only
slightly dirty water; or waiting for one of the white ships –
great ships with bows as sharp as the scalpel-bills of king-
fishers and four, five, or even seven masts – which were, in-
frequently, towed up from the harbour by ten or twelve spans
of oxen.

In the summer of my eleventh or twelfth year – I think the
twelfth – we were permitted for the first time to stay after
sundown in the park, sitting on the grassy, sloped margin of
the canal to watch a fireworks display. The first preliminary
flight of rockets had no sooner exhausted itself half a mile
above the city than David became ill. He rushed to the water
and vomited, plunging his hands half up to the elbows in mud
while the red and white stars burned in glory above him. Mr.
Million took him up in his arms and when poor David had
emptied himself we hurried home.

His disease proved not much more lasting than the tainted
sandwich that had occasioned it, but while our tutor was
putting him to bed I decided not to be cheated of the re-
mainder of the display, parts of which I had glimpsed between
the intervening houses as we made our way home; I was forbidden the roof after dark, but I knew very well where the
nearest stair was. The thrill I felt in penetrating that prohibited
world of leaf and shadows while fireflowers of purple and gold
and blazing scarlet overtopped it affected me like the aftermath
of a fever, leaving me short of breath, shaking, and cold in the
midst of summer.

There were a great many more people on the roof than I had
anticipated, the men without cloaks, hats or sticks, (all of which
they had left in my father's checkrooms) and the girls, my

father's employees, in costumes that displayed their rouged breasts in enclosures of twisted wire like birdcages, or gave them the appearance of great height (dissolved only when someone stood very close to them), or gowns whose skirts reflected their wearer's faces and busts as still water does the trees standing near it, so that they appeared, in the intermittent coloured flashes, like the queens of strange suits in a tarot deck.

I was seen of course, since I was much too excited to conceal myself effectively; but no one ordered me back, and I suppose they assumed I had been permitted to come up to see the fireworks.

These continued for a long time. I remember one patron, a heavy, square-faced, stupid-looking man who seemed to be someone of importance, who was so eager to enjoy the company of his protégé – who did not want to go in until the display was over – that, since he insisted on privacy, twenty or thirty bushes and small trees had to be rearranged on the parterre to make a little grove around them. I helped the waiters carry some of the smaller tubs and pots, and managed to duck into the structure as it was completed. Here I could still watch the exploding rockets and 'aerial bombs' through the branches, and at the same time the patron and his protégé, who was watching them a good deal more intently than I.

My motive, as well as I can remember, was not prurience but simple curiosity. I was at that age when we are passionately interested, but the passion is one of science. Mine was nearly satisfied when I was grasped by the shirt by someone behind me and drawn out of the shrubbery.

When I was clear of the leaves I was released, and I turned expecting to see Mr. Million, but it was not he. My captor was a little grey-haired woman in a black dress whose skirt, as I noticed even at the time, fell straight from her waist to the ground. I suppose I bowed to her, since she was clearly no servant, but she returned no salutation at all, staring intently into my face in a way that made me think she could see as well in the intervals between the bursting glories as she could by their light. At last, in what must have been the finale of the display, a great rocket rose screaming on a river of flame, and for an instant she consented to look up. Then, when it had exploded in a mauve orchid of unbelievable size and brilliance, this formidable little woman grabbed me again and led me firmly towards the stairs.

While we were on the level stone pavement of the roof garden she did not, as nearly as I could see, walk at all, but rather seemed to glide across the surface like an onyx chessman on a polished board; and that, in spite of all that has happened since, is the way I still remember her: as the Black Queen, a chess queen neither sinister nor beneficent, and black only as distinguished from some White Queen I was never fated to encounter.

When we reached the stairs, however, this smooth gliding became a fluid bobbing that brought two inches or more of the hem of her black skirt into contact with each step, as if her torso were descending each step as a small boat might a rapids – now rushing, now pausing, now almost backing in the crosscurrents of turbulence.

She steadied herself on these steps not only by holding on to me, but by grasping the arm of a maid who had been waiting for us at the stairhead and who assisted her from the other side. I had supposed, while we were crossing the roof garden, that her gliding motion had been the result, merely, of a marvellously controlled walk and good posture, but I now understood her to be in some way handicapped; and I had the impression that without the help the maid and I gave her she might have fallen headfirst.

Once we had reached the bottom of the steps her smooth progress was resumed. She dismissed the maid with a nod and led me down the corridor in the direction opposite to that in which our dormitory and classroom lay until we reached a stairwell far towards the back of the house, a corkscrew, seldom-used flight, very steep, with only a low iron bannister between the steps and a six-storey drop into the cellars. Here she released me and told me crisply to go down. I went down several steps, then turned to see if she was having any difficulty.

She was not, but neither was she using the stairs. With her

long skirt hanging as straight as a curtain she was floating, suspended, watching me, in the centre of the stairwell. I was so startled that I stopped (which made her jerk her head angrily), then began to run. As I fled around and around the spiral she revolved with me, turning towards me always a face extraordinarily like my father's, one hand always on the railing. When we had descended to the second floor she swooped down and caught me as easily as a cat takes charge of an errant kitten, and led me through rooms and passages where I had never been permitted to go until I was as confused as I might have been in a strange building. At last we stopped before a door in no way different from any other. She opened it with an old-fashioned brass key with an edge like a saw and motioned for me to go in.

The room was brightly lit, and I was able to see clearly what I had only sensed on the roof and in the corridors: that the hem of her skirt hung two inches above the floor no matter how she moved, and that there was nothing between the hem and the floor at all. She waved me to a little footstool covered with needlepoint and said, 'Sit down,' and when I had done so she glided across to a wingbacked rocker and sat facing me. After a moment she asked, 'What's your name?' and when I told her she cocked an eyebrow at me and started the chair in motion by pushing gently with her fingers at a floor lamp that stood beside it. After a long time she said, 'And what does he call you?'

'He?' I was stupid, I suppose, with lack of sleep.

She pursed her lips. 'My brother.'

I relaxed a little. 'Oh,' I said, 'you're my aunt then. I thought you looked like my father. He calls me Number Five.'

For a moment she continued to stare, the corners of her mouth drawing down as my father's often did. Then she said, 'That number's either far too low or too high. Living, there are he and I, and I suppose he's counting the simulator. Have you a sister, Number Five?'

Mr. Million had been having us read *David Copperfield*, and when she said this she reminded me so strikingly and un-

expectedly of Aunt Betsy Trotwood that I shouted with
laughter.

'There's nothing absurd about it. Your father had a sister –
why shouldn't you? You have none?'

'No, ma'am, but I have a brother. His name is David.'

'Call me Aunt Jeannine. Does David look like you, Number
Five?'

I shook my head. 'His hair is curly and blond instead of like
mine. Maybe he looks a little like me, but not a lot.'

'I suppose,' my aunt said under her breath, 'he used one of
my girls.'

'Ma'am?'

'Do you know who David's mother was, Number Five?'

'We're brothers, so I guess she would be the same as mine,
but Mr. Million says she went away a long time ago.'

'Not the same as yours,' my aunt said. 'No. I could show
you a picture of your own. Would you like to see it?' She rang
a bell, and a maid came curtseying from some room beyond;
my aunt whispered to her and she went out again. My aunt
asked, 'And what do you do all day, Number Five, besides
run up to the roof when you shouldn't? Are you taught?'

I told her about my experiments (I was stimulating un-
fertilized frog's eggs to asexual development and then doubling
the chromosomes by a chemical treatment so that a further
asexual generation could be produced) and the dissections Mr.
Million was by then encouraging me to do, and while I talked
I happened to drop some remark about how interesting it would
be to perform a biopsy on one of the aborigines of Sainte Anne
if any were still in existence, since the first explorers' descrip-
tions differed so widely and some pioneers there had claimed
the abos could change their shapes.

'Ah,' my aunt said, 'you know about them. Let me test you
Number Five. What is Veil's Hypothesis?'

We had learned that several years before, so I said, 'Veil's
Hypothesis supposes the abos to have possessed the ability to
mimic men perfectly. Veil thought that when the ships came
from Earth, the abos killed everyone and took their places
and the ships, so they're not dead at all, we are.'

'You mean the Earth people are,' my aunt said. 'The human beings.'

'Ma'am?'

'If Veil was correct, then you and I are abos from Sainte Anne, at least in origin; which I suppose is what you meant. Do you think he was right?'

'I don't think it makes any difference. He said the imitation would have to be perfect, and if it is, they're the same as we were anyway,' I thought I was being clever, but my aunt smiled, rocking more vigorously. It was very warm in the close, bright little room.

'Number Five, you're too young for semantics, and I'm afraid you've been led astray by that word *perfectly*. Dr. Veil, I'm certain, meant to use it loosely rather than as precisely as you seem to think. The imitation could hardly have been exact, since human beings don't possess that talent and to imitate them *perfectly* the abos would have to lose it.'

'Couldn't they?'

'My dear child, abilities of every sort must evolve. And when they do they must be utilized or they atrophy. If the abos had been able to mimic so well as to lose the power to do so that would have been the end of them, and no doubt it would have come long before the first ships reached them. Of course there's not the slightest evidence they could do anything of the sort. They simply died off before they could be thoroughly studied, and Veil, who wants a dramatic explanation for the cruelty and irrationality he sees around him, has hung fifty pounds of theory on nothing.'

This last remark, especially as my aunt seemed so friendly, appeared to me to offer an ideal opportunity for a question about her remarkable means of locomotion, but as I was about to frame it we were interrupted, almost simultaneously from two directions. The maid returned carrying a large book bound in tooled leather, and she had no sooner handed it to my aunt than there was a tap at the door. My aunt said absently, 'Get that,' and since the remark might as easily have been addressed to me as to the maid I satisfied my curiosity in another form by racing her to answer the knock.

Two of my father's girls, costumed and painted until they seemed more alien than any abos, stately as Lombardy poplars and inhuman as spectres, with green and yellow eyes made to look the size of eggs and inflated breasts pushed almost shoulder-high, were waiting in the hall; and though they maintained an inculcated composure I was pleasantly aware that they were startled to find me in the doorway. I bowed them in, but as the maid closed the door behind them my aunt said absently, 'In a moment, girls. I want to show the boy here something, then he's going to leave.'

The 'something' was a photograph utilizing, as I supposed, some novelty technique which washed away all colour save a light brown. It was small, and from its general appearance and crumbling edges very old. It showed a girl of twenty-five or so, thin and as nearly as I could judge rather tall, standing beside a stocky young man on a paved walkway and holding a baby. The walkway ran along the front of a remarkable house, a very long wooden house only a storey in height, with a porch or veranda that changed its architectural style every twenty or thirty feet so as to give almost the impression of a number of exceedingly narrow houses constructed with their side walls in contact. I mention this detail, which I hardly noticed at the time, because I have so often since my release from prison tried to find some trace of this house. When I was first shown the picture I was much more interested in the girl's face, and the baby's. The latter was in fact scarcely visible, he being nearly smothered in white wool blankets. The girl had large features and a brilliant smile which held a suggestion of that rarely seen charm which is at once careless, poetic, and sly. Gypsy, was my first thought, but her complexion was surely too fair for that. Since on this world we are all descended from a relatively small group of colonists, we are rather a uniform population, but my studies had given me some familiarity with the original Terrestrial races, and my second guess, almost a certainty, was Celtic. 'Wales,' I said aloud. 'Or Scotland. Or Ireland.'

'What?' my aunt said. One of the girls giggled; they were seated on the divan now, their long, gleaming legs crossed before them like the varnished staffs of flags.

'It doesn't matter.'

My aunt looked at me acutely and said, 'You're right. I'll send for you and we'll talk about this when we've both more leisure. For the present my maid will take you to your room.'

I remember nothing of the long walk the maid and I must have had back to the dormitory, or what excuses I gave Mr. Million for my unauthorized absence. Whatever they were I suppose he penetrated them, or discovered the truth by questioning the servants, because no summons to return to my aunt's apartment came, although I expected it daily for weeks afterwards.

That night – I am reasonably sure it was the same night – I dreamed of the abos of Sainte Anne, abos dancing with plumes of fresh grass on their heads and arms and ankles, abos shaking their shields of woven rushes and their nephrite-tipped spears until the motion affected my bed and became, in shabby red cloth, the arms of my father's valet come to summon me, as he did almost every night, to his library.

That night, and this time I am quite certain it was the same night – that is, the night I first dreamed of the abos – the pattern of my hours with him, which had come over the four or five years past to have a predictable sequence of conversation, holographs, free association, and dismissal – a sequence I had come to think unalterable – changed. Following the preliminary talk designed, I feel sure, to put me at ease (at which it failed, as it always did), I was told to roll up a sleeve and lie down upon an old examining table in a corner of the room. My father then made me look at the wall, which meant at the shelves heaped with ragged notebooks. I felt a needle being thrust into the inner part of my arm, but my head was held down and my face turned away, so that I could neither sit up nor look at what he was doing. Then the needle was withdrawn and I was told to lie quietly.

After what seemed a very long time, during which my father occasionally took my pulse or spread my eyelids to look at my eyes, someone in a distant part of the room began to tell a very long and confusingly involved story. My father made notes of what was said, and occasionally stopped to ask questions I found it unnecessary to answer, since the storyteller did it for me.

The drug he had given me did not, as I had imagined it would, lessen its hold on me as the hours passed. Instead it seemed to carry me progressively farther from reality and the mode of consciousness best suited to preserving the individuality of thought. The peeling leather of the examination table vanished under me, and was now the deck of a ship, now the wing of a dove beating far above the world; and whether the voice I heard reciting was my own or my father's I no longer cared. It was pitched sometimes higher, sometimes lower, but then I felt myself at times to be speaking from the depths of a chest larger than my own; and his voice, identified as such by the soft rustling of the pages of his notebook, might seem the high, treble cries of the racing children in the streets as I heard them in summer when I thrust my head through the windows at the base of the library dome.

With that night my life changed again. The drugs – for there seemed to be several, and although the effect I have described was the usual one, there were also times when I found it impossible to lie still, but ran up and down for hours as I talked, or sank into blissful or indescribably frightening dreams – affected my health. I often wakened in the morning with a headache that kept me in agony all day, and I became subject to periods of extreme nervousness and apprehension. Most frightening of all, whole sections of days sometimes disappeared, so that I found myself awake and dressed, reading, walking, and even talking, with no memory at all of anything that had happened since I had lain muttering to the ceiling in my father's library the night before.

The lessons I had had with David did not cease, but in some sense Mr. Million's role and mine were now reversed. It was I, now, who insisted on holding our classes when they were held at all; and it was I who chose the subject matter and, in most cases, questioned David and Mr. Million about it. But often when they were at the library or the park I remained in bed reading, and I believe there were many times when I read and studied from the time I found myself conscious in my bed until my father's valet came for me again.

David's interviews with our father, I should note here, suffered the same changes as my own and at the same time; but since they were less frequent – and they became less and less frequent as the hundred days of summer wore away to autumn and at last to the long winter – and he seemed on the whole to have less adverse reactions to the drugs, the effect on him was not nearly as great.

If at any single time, it was during this winter that I came to the end of childhood. My new ill health forced me away from childish activities, and encouraged the experiments I was carrying out on small animals, and my dissections of the bodies Mr. Million supplied in an unending stream of open mouths and staring eyes. Too, I studied or read, as I have said, for hours on end; or simply lay with my hands behind my head while I struggled to recall, perhaps for whole days together, the narratives I had heard myself give my father. Neither David nor I could ever remember enough even to build a coherent theory of the nature of the questions asked us, but I have still certain tableaux fixed in my memory which I am sure I have never seen, and I believe these are my visualizations of suggestions whispered while I bobbed and dived through those altered states of consciousness.

My aunt, who had previously been so remote, now spoke to me in the corridors and even visited our room. I learned that she controlled the internal arrangements of our house, and through her I was able to have a small laboratory of my own set up in the same wing. But I spent the winter, as I have described, mostly at my enamel dissecting table or in bed. The white snow drifted half up the glass of the window, clinging to the bare stems of the silvertrumpet vine. My father's patrons, on the rare occasions when I saw them, came in with wet boots, the snow on their shoulders and their hats, puffing and red-faced as they beat their coats in the foyer. The orange trees were gone, the roof garden no longer used, and the courtyard under our window only late at night when

half a dozen patrons and their protégés, whooping with hilarity
and wine, fought with snowballs – an activity invariably concluded by stripping the girls and tumbling them naked in the
snow.

Spring surprised me, as she always does those of us who
remain most of our lives indoors. One day, while I still thought,
if I thought about the weather at all, in terms of winter, David
threw open the window and insisted that I go with him to the
park – and it was April. Mr. Million went with us, and I remember that as we stepped out of the front door into the little
garden that opened into the street, a garden I had last seen
banked with the snow shovelled from the path, but which was
now bright with early bulbs and the chiming of the fountain,
David tapped the iron dog on its grinning muzzle and recited:

"And thence the dog
    With fourfold head brought to these realms of light."

I made some trivial remark about his having miscounted.
'Oh, no. Old Cerberus has four heads, don't you know that?
The fourth's her maidenhead, and she's such a bitch no dog
can take it from her.' Even Mr. Million chuckled, but I
thought afterwards, looking at David's ruddy good health and
the foreshadowing of manhood already apparent in the set of
his shoulders, that if, as I had always thought of them, the
three heads represented Maître, Madame, and Mr. Million,
that is, my father, my aunt (David's *maidenhead*, I suppose),
and my tutor, then indeed a fourth would have to be welded
in place soon for David himself.

The park must have been a paradise for him, but in my
poor health I found it bleak enough and spent most of the
morning huddled on a bench, watching David play squash.
Towards noon I was joined, not on my own bench, but on
another close enough for there to be a feeling of proximity,
by a dark-haired girl with one ankle in a cast. She was brought
there, on crutches, by a sort of nurse or governess who seated
herself, I felt sure deliberately, between the girl and me. This

unpleasant woman was, however, too straightbacked for her chaperonage to succeed completely. She sat on the edge of the bench, while the girl, with her injured leg thrust out before her, slumped back and thus gave me a good view of her profile, which was beautiful; and occasionally, when she turned to make some remark to the creature beside her, I could study her full face – carmine lips and violet eyes, a round rather than an oval face, with a broad point of black hair dividing the forehead; archly delicate black eyebrows and long, curling lashes. When a vendor, an old woman, came selling Cantonese egg rolls (longer than your hand, and still so hot from the boiling fat that they needed to be eaten with great caution as though they were in some way alive) I made her my messenger and, buying one for myself, sent her with two scalding delicacies to the girl and her attendant monster.

The monster, of course, refused; the girl, I was charmed to see, pleaded, her huge eyes and bright cheeks eloquently proclaiming arguments I was just too far away to hear but could follow in pantomime: it would be a gratuitous insult to a blameless stranger to refuse; she was hungry and had intended to buy an egg roll in any event – how thriftless to object when what she had wished for was tendered free! The vending woman, who clearly delighted in her role as go-between, announced herself on the point of weeping at the thought of being forced to refund my gold (actually a bill of small denomination nearly as greasy as the paper in which her rolls were wrapped, and considerably dirtier), and eventually their voices grew loud enough for me to hear the girl's, which was a clear and very pleasing contralto. In the end, of course, they accepted; the monster conceded me a frigid nod, and the girl winked at me behind her back.

Half an hour later when David and Mr. Million, who had been watching him from the edge of the court, asked if I wanted lunch, I told them I did, thinking that when we returned I could take a seat closer to the girl without being brazen about it. We ate, I (at least so I fear) very impatiently, in a clean little café close to the flower market; but when we came back to the park the girl and her governess were gone.

We returned to the house, and about an hour afterwards my father sent for me. I went with some trepidation, since it was much earlier than was customary for our interview – before the first patrons had arrived, in fact, while I usually saw him only after the last had gone. I need not have feared. He began by asking about my health, and when I said it seemed better than it had been during most of the winter he began, in a self-conscious and even pompous way, as different from his usual fatigued incisiveness as could be imagined, to talk about his business and the need a young man had to prepare himself to earn a living. He said, 'You are a scientific scholar, I believe.'

I said I hoped I was in a small way, and braced myself for the usual attack upon the uselessness of studying chemistry or biophysics on a world like ours where the industrial base was so small: of no help at the civil service examinations, does not even prepare one for trade, and so on. He said instead, 'I'm glad to hear it. To be frank, I asked Mr. Million to encourage you in that way as much as he could. He would have done it anyway, I'm sure; he did with me. These studies will not only be of great satisfaction to you, but will' – he paused, cleared his throat, and massaged his face and scalp with his hands – 'be valuable in all sorts of ways. And they are, as you might say, a family tradition.'

I said, and indeed felt, that I was very happy to hear that.

'Have you seen my lab? Behind the big mirror there?'

I hadn't, though I had known that such a suite of rooms existed beyond the sliding mirror in the library, and the servants occasionally spoke of his 'dispensary' where he compounded doses for them, examined monthly the girls we employed, and occasionally prescribed treatment for 'friends' of patrons, men recklessly imprudent who had failed (as the wise patrons had not) to confine their custom to our establishment exclusively. I told him I should very much like to see it.

He smiled. 'But we are wandering from our topic. Science is of great value; but you will find, as I have, that it consumes more money than it produces. You will want apparatus and books and many other things, as well as a livelihood for yourself. We have a not unprofitable business here, and though I hope to live a long time – thanks in part to science – you are the heir and it will be yours in the end.'

(So I was older than David!)

'. . . every phase of what we do. None of them, believe me, are unimportant.'

I had been so surprised, and in fact elated, by my discovery, that I had missed a part of what he said. I nodded, which seemed safe.

'Good. I want you to begin by answering the front door. One of the maids has been doing it, and for the first month or so she'll stay with you, since there's more to be learned there than you think. I'll tell Mr. Million, and he can make the arrangements.'

I thanked him, and he indicated that the interview was over by opening the door of the library. I could hardly believe, as I went out, that he was the same man who devoured my life in the early hours of almost every morning.

I did not connect this sudden elevation in status with the events in the park. I now realize that Mr. Million, who has, quite literally, eyes in the back of his head, must have reported to my father that I had reached the age at which desires in childhood subliminally fastened to parental figures begin, half consciously, to grope beyond the family.

In any event, that same evening I took up my new duties and became what Mr. Million called the 'greeter' and David (explaining that the original sense of the word was related to *portal*) the 'porter' of our house – thus assuming in a practical way the functions symbolically executed by the iron dog in our front garden. The maid who had previously carried them out, a girl named Nerissa who had been selected because she was not only one of the prettiest but one of the tallest and strongest of the maids as well, a large-boned, long-faced, smiling girl with shoulders broader than most men's, remained, as my father had promised, to help. Our duties were not onerous, since my father's patrons were all men of some position and wealth, not given to brawling or loud arguments except under unusual circumstances of intoxication; and for the most part they had visited our house already dozens, and in a few cases even hundreds of times. We called them by nicknames that were used only here (of which Nerissa informed me *sotto voce* as they came up the walk), hung up their coats, and directed them – or if necessary conducted them – to the various parts of the establishment. Nerissa flounced (a formidable sight, as I observed, to all but the most heroically proportioned patrons), allowed herself to be pinched, took tips, and talked to me afterwards, during slack periods, of the times she had been 'called upstairs' at the request of some connoisseur of scale, and the money she had made that night. I laughed at jokes and refused tips in such a way as to make the patrons aware that I was a part of the management. Most patrons did not need the reminder, and I was often told that I strikingly resembled my father.

When I had been serving as a receptionist in this way for only a short time, I think on only the third or fourth night, we had an unusual visitor. He came early one evening, but it was the evening of so dark a day, one of the last really wintry days, that the garden lamps had been lit for an hour or more and the occasional carriages that passed on the street beyond, though they could be heard, could not be seen. I answered the door when he knocked, and as we always did with strangers, asked him politely what he wished.

He said, 'I should like to speak to Dr. Aubrey Veil.'

I am afraid I looked blank.

"This is Six Sixty-six Saltimbanque?'

It was, of course; and the name of Dr. Veil, although I could not place it, touched a chime of memory. I supposed that one of our patrons had used my father's house as an *adresse de convenance*, and since this visitor was clearly legitimate, and it was not desirable to keep anyone arguing in the doorway despite the partial shelter afforded by the garden, I asked him in; then I sent Nerissa for coffee so that we might have a few moments of private talk in a receiving room that opened off the foyer. It was a room very seldom used, and the maids had been remiss in dusting it, as I saw as soon as I opened the door. I made a mental note to speak to my aunt about it, and as I did so, I recalled where it was that I had heard Dr. Veil mentioned. My aunt, on the first occasion when I had spoken to her, had referred to his theory that we might in fact be the natives of Sainte Anne, having murdered the original Terrestrial colonists and displaced them so thoroughly as to forget our own past.

The stranger had seated himself in one of the musty, gilded armchairs. He wore a beard, very black and more full than the current style, and would have been a handsome man if the skin of his face – what could be seen of it – had not been of so colourless a white as almost to constitute a disfigurement. His dark clothing seemed abnormally heavy, like felt, and I recalled having heard from some patron that a star-crosser from Sainte Anne had splashed down in the bay yesterday; I asked if he had perhaps been on board it. He looked startled for a moment, then laughed. 'You're a wit, I see. And living with Dr. Veil you'd be familiar with his theory. No, I'm from Earth. My name is Marsch.' He gave me his card, and I read it twice before the meaning of the delicately embossed abbreviation registered in my mind. My visitor was a scientist, a doctor of philosophy in anthropology, from Earth.

I said, 'I wasn't trying to be witty. I thought you might really have come from Sainte Anne. Here most of us have a kind of planetary face, except for the gypsies and criminal tribes, and you don't seem to fit the pattern.'

He said, 'I've noticed what you mean; you seem to have it yourself.'

'I'm supposed to look a great deal like my father.'

'Ah,' he said. He stared at me. Then, 'Are you cloned?'

'Cloned?' I had read the term, but only in conjunction with botany, and as has happened to me often when I have especially wanted to impress someone with my intelligence, nothing came. I felt like a stupid child.

'Parthenogenetically reproduced, so that the new individual – or individuals, you can have a thousand if you want – will have a genetic structure identical to the parent. It's anti-evolutionary, so it's illegal on Earth, but I don't suppose things are as closely watched out here.'

'You're talking about human beings?'

He nodded.

'I've never heard of it. Really I doubt if you'd find the necessary technology here; we're quite backward compared to Earth. Of course, my father might be able to arrange something for you.'

'I don't want to have it done.'

Nerissa came in with the coffee then, effectively cutting off anything further Dr. Marsch might have said. Actually, I had added the suggestion about my father more from force of habit than anything else, and thought it was unlikely that he could pull off any such biochemical tour de force, but there was always the possibility, particularly if a large sum was offered. As it was we fell silent while Nerissa arranged the cups and poured, and when she had gone Marsch said appreciatively, 'Quite an unusual girl.' His eyes, I noticed, were a bright green, without the brown tones most green eyes have.

I was wild to ask him about Earth and the new developments there, and it had already occurred to me that the girls might be an effective way of keeping him here, or at least of bringing him back. I said, 'You should see some of them. My father has wonderful taste.'

'I'd rather see Dr. Veil. Or is Dr. Veil your father?'

'Oh, no.'

'This is his address, or at least the address I was given. Number Six Sixty-six Saltimbanque Street, Port-Mimizon, Département de la Main, Sainte Croix.'

He appeared quite serious, and it seemed possible that if I told him flatly that he was mistaken he would leave. I said, 'I learned about Veil's Hypothesis from my aunt. She seemed quite conversant with it. Perhaps later this evening you'd like to talk to her about it.'

'Couldn't I see her now?'

'My aunt sees very few visitors. To be frank, I'm told she quarrelled with my father before I was born, and she seldom leaves her own apartments. The housekeepers report to her there and she manages what I suppose I must call our domestic economy, but it's very rare to see Madame outside her rooms, or for any stranger to be let in.'

'And why are you telling me this?'

'So that you'll understand that with the best will in the world it may not be possible for me to arrange an interview for you. At least, not this evening.'

'You could simply ask her if she knows Dr. Veil's present address, and if so what it is.'

'I'm trying to help you, Dr. Marsch. Really I am.'

'But you don't think that's the best way to go about it?'

'No.'

'In other words if your aunt were simply asked, without being given a chance to form her own judgment of me, she wouldn't give me information even if she had it?'

'It would help if we were to talk a bit first. There are a great many things I'd like to learn about Earth.'

For an instant I thought I saw a sour smile under the black beard. He said, 'Suppose I ask you first –'

He was interrupted – again – by Nerissa, I suppose because she wanted to see if we required anything further from the kitchen. I could have strangled her when Dr. Marsch halted in midsentence and said instead, 'Couldn't this girl ask your aunt if she would see me?'

I had to think quickly. I had been planning to go myself and, after a suitable wait, return and say that my aunt would receive Dr. Marsch later, which would have given me an additional opportunity to question him while he waited. But there was at least a possibility (no doubt magnified in my eyes by my eagerness to hear of new discoveries from Earth) that he would not wait – or that, when and if he did eventually see my aunt, he might mention the incident. If I sent Nerissa I would at least have him to myself while she ran her errand, and there was an excellent chance – or at least so I imagined – that my aunt would in fact have some business which she would want to conclude before seeing a stranger. I told Nerissa to go, and Dr. Marsch gave her one of his cards after writing a few words on the back.

'Now,' I said, 'what was it you were about to ask me?'

'Why, this house, on a planet that has been inhabited less

than two hundred years, seems so absurdly old.'

'It was built a hundred and forty years ago, but you must have many on Earth that are far older.'

'I suppose so. Hundreds. But for every one of them there are ten thousand that have been up less than a year. Here, almost every building I see seems nearly as old as this one.'

'We've never been crowded here, and we haven't had to tear down; that's what Mr. Million says. And there are less people here now than there were fifty years ago.'

'Mr. Million?'

I told him about Mr. Million, and when I finished he said, 'It sounds as if you've got a ten nine unbound simulator here, which should be interesting. Only a few have ever been made.'

'A ten nine simulator?'

'A billion, ten to the ninth power. The human brain has several billion synapses, of course; but it's been found that you can simulate its action pretty well —'

It seemed to me that no time at all had passed since Nerissa had left, but she was back. She curtseyed to Dr. Marsch and said, 'Madame will see you.'

I blurted, 'Now?'

'Yes,' Nerissa said artlessly, 'Madame said right now.'

'I'll take him then. You mind the door.'

I escorted Dr. Marsch down the dark corridors, taking a long route to have more time, but he seemed to be arranging in his mind the questions he wished to ask my aunt as we walked past the spotted mirrors and warped little walnut tables, and he answered me in monosyllables when I tried to question him about Earth.

At my aunt's door I rapped for him. She opened it herself, the hem of her black skirt hanging emptily over the untrodden carpet, but I do not think he noticed that. He said, 'I'm really very sorry to bother you, Madame, and I only do so because your nephew thought you might be able to help me locate the author of Veil's Hypothesis.'

My aunt said, 'I am Dr. Veil, please come in,' and shut the door behind him.

*

I mentioned the incident to Phaedria the next time we met, but she was more interested in learning about my father's house. Phaedria was the girl who had sat near me while I watched David play squash. She had been introduced to me on my next visit to the park by no less than the monster herself, who had helped her to a seat beside me and, miracle of miracles, promptly retreated to a point which, though not out of sight, was at least out of earshot. Phaedria had thrust her broken ankle out before her, halfway across the gravelled path, and smiled a most charming smile. 'You don't object to my sitting here?' She had perfect teeth.

'I'm delighted.'

'You're surprised too. Your eyes get big when you're surprised, did you know that?'

'I am surprised. I've come here looking for you several times, but you haven't been here.'

'We've come looking for you, and you haven't been here either, but I suppose one can't really spend a great deal of time in a park.'

'I would have,' I said, 'if I'd known you were looking for me. I went here as much as I could anyway. I was afraid that she' – I jerked my head at the monster – 'wouldn't let you come back. How did you persuade her?'

'I didn't,' Phaedria said. 'Can't you guess? Don't you know anything?'

'I confessed that I did not. I felt stupid, and I was stupid, at least in the things I said, because so much of my mind was caught up not in formulating answers to her remarks but in committing to memory the lilt of her voice, the purple of her eyes, even the faint perfume of her skin and the soft, warm touch of her breath on my cool cheek.

'So you see,' Phaedria was saying, 'that's how it is with me. When Aunt Uranie – she's only a poor cousin of mother's really – got home and told him about you he found out who you are, and here I am.'

'Yes,' I said, and she laughed.

Phaedria was one of those girls raised between the hope of marriage and the thought of sale. Her father's affairs, as she herself said, were 'unsettled'. He speculated in ship cargoes, mostly from the south – drugs and slaves. He owed, most of the time, large sums which the lenders could not hope to collect unless they were willing to allow him more to recoup. He might die a pauper, but in the meanwhile he had raised his daughter with every detail of education and plastic surgery attended to. If, when she reached marriageable age, he could afford a good dowry, she would link him with some wealthy family. If he were pressed for money instead, a girl would bring fifty times the price of a common street child. Our family, of course, would be ideal for either purpose.

'Tell me about your house,' she said. 'Do you know what the kids call it? The Cave Canem, or sometimes just the Cave. The boys all think it's a big thing to have been there and they lie about it. Most of them haven't.'

But I wanted to talk about Dr. Marsch and the sciences of Earth, and I was nearly as anxious to find out about her own world, 'the kids' she mentioned so casually, her school and family, as she was to learn about us. Also, although I was willing to detail the services my father's girls rendered their benefactors, there were some things, such as my aunt's floating down the stairwell, that I was averse to discussing. But we bought egg rolls from the same old woman to eat in the chill sunlight, and exchanged confidences, and somehow parted not only lovers but friends, promising to meet again the next day.

At some time during the night, I believe at almost the same time that I returned – or to speak more accurately *was* returned since I could scarcely walk – to my bed after a session of hours with my father, the weather changed. The musked exhalation of late spring or early summer crept through the shutters, and the fire in our little grate seemed to extinguish itself for shame almost at once. My father's valet opened the window for me and there poured into the room that fragrance that tells of the melting of the last snows beneath the deepest and darkest evergreens on the north sides of mountains. I had arranged with Phaedria to meet at ten, and before going to my father's library I had posted a note, asking that I be awakened an hour earlier, on the escritoire beside my bed; and that night

I slept with the fragrance in my nostrils and the thought – half plan, half dream – that by some means Phaedria and I would elude her aunt entirely and find a deserted lawn where blue and yellow flowers dotted the short grass.

When I woke it was an hour past noon, and rain drove in sheets past the window. Mr. Million, who was reading a book on the far side of the room, told me that it had been raining like that since six, and for that reason he had not troubled to wake me. I had a splitting headache, as I often did after a long session with my father, and took one of the powders he had prescribed to relieve it. They were grey, and smelled of anise.

'You look unwell,' Mr. Million said.

'I was hoping to go to the park.'

'I know.' He rolled across the room towards me, and I recalled that Dr. Marsch had called him an 'unbound' simulator. For the first time since I had satisfied myself about them when I was quite small I bent over (at some cost to my head) and read the almost obliterated stampings on his main cabinet. There was only the name of a cybernetics company on Earth and, in French as I had always supposed, his name: M. Million – 'Monsieur' or 'Mister' Million. Then, as startling as a blow from behind to a man musing in a comfortable chair, I remembered that a dot was employed in some algebras for multiplication. He saw my change of expression at once. 'A thousand-million-word core capacity,' he said. 'An English billion or a French milliard, the M being the Roman numeral for one thousand, of course. I thought you understood that some time ago.'

'You are an unbound simulator. What is a bound simulator, and whom are you simulating – my father?'

'No.' The face in the screen, Mr. Million's face as I had always thought of it, shook its head. 'Call me, call the person simulated, at least, your great-grandfather. He – I – am dead. In order to achieve simulation it is necessary to examine the cells of the brain, layer by layer, with a beam of accelerated particles so that the neural patterns can be reproduced, we say "core imaged", in the computer. The process is fatal.'

I asked after a moment, 'And a bound simulator?'

'If the simulation is to have a body that looks human the mechanical body must be linked – "bound" – to a remote core, since the smallest billion-word core cannot be made even approximately as small as a human brain.' He paused again, and for an instant his face dissolved into a myriad sparkling dots, swirling like dust motes in a sunbeam. 'I am sorry. For once you wish to listen but I do not wish to lecture. I was told, a very long time ago, just before the operation, that my simulation – this – would be capable of emotion in certain circumstances. Until today I had always thought they lied.' I would have stopped him if I could, but he rolled out of the room before I could recover from my surprise.

For a long time, I suppose an hour or more, I sat listening to the drumming of the rain and thinking about Phaedria and about what Mr. Million had said, all of it confused with my father's questions of the night before, questions which had seemed to steal their answers from me so that I was empty, and dreams had come to flicker in the emptiness, dreams of fences and walls and the concealing ditches called ha-has, that contain a barrier you do not see until you are about to tumble on it. Once I had dreamed of standing in a paved court fenced with Corinthian pillars so close-set that I could not force my body between them, although in the dream I was only a child of three or four. After trying various places for a long time I had noticed that each column was carved with a word – the only one that I could remember was 'carapace' – and that the paving stones of the courtyard were mortuary tablets like those set into the floors in some of the old French churches, with my own name and a different date on each.

This dream pursued me even when I tried to think of Phaedria, and when a maid brought me hot water – for I now shaved twice a week – I found that I was already holding my razor in my hand, and had in fact cut myself with it so that the blood had streaked my nightclothes and run down on to the sheets.

The next time I saw Phaedria, which was four or five days afterwards, she was engrossed by a new project in which she enlisted both David and me. This was nothing less than a theatrical company, composed mostly of girls her own age, which was to present plays during the summer in a natural amphitheatre in the park. Since the company, as I have said, consisted principally of girls, male actors were at a premium, and David and I soon found ourselves deeply embroiled. The play had been written by a committee of the cast, and – inevitably – revolved about the loss of political power by the original French-speaking colonists. Phaedria, whose ankle would not be mended in time for our performance, would play the crippled daughter of the French governor, David her lover (a dashing captain of chasseurs), and I the governor himself – a part I accepted readily because it was a much better one than David's, and offered scope for a great deal of fatherly affection towards Phaedria.

The night of our performance, which was early in June, I recall vividly for two reasons. My aunt, whom I had not seen since she had closed the door behind Dr. Marsch, notified me at the last moment that she wished to attend and that I was to escort her. And we players had grown so afraid of having an empty house that I had asked my father if it would be possible for him to send some of his girls – who would thus lose only the earliest part of the evening, when there was seldom much business in any event. To my great surprise he consented (I suppose because he felt it would be good advertising), stipulating only that they should return at the end of the third act if he sent a messenger saying they were needed.

Because I would have to arrive at least an hour early to make up, it was no more than late afternoon when I called for my aunt. She showed me in herself, and immediately asked my help for her maid, who was trying to wrestle some heavy object from the upper shelf of a closet. It proved to be a folding wheelchair, and under my aunt's direction we set it up. When we had finished she said abruptly, 'Give me a hand in, you two,' and taking our arms lowered herself into the seat. Her black skirt, lying emptily against the leg boards of the chair like a collapsed tent, showed legs no thicker than my wrists; but also an odd thickening almost like a saddle, below her hips. Seeing me staring she snapped, 'Won't be needing that until I come back, I suppose. Lift me up a little. Stand in back and get me under the arms.'

I did so, and her maid reached unceremoniously under my aunt's skirt and drew out a little leather-padded device on which she had been resting. 'Shall we go?' my aunt sniffed. 'You'll be late.'

Our play went smoothly enough, with predictable cheers from members of the audience who were, or at least wished to be thought, descended from the original French. The audience, in fact, was better than we had dared hope, five hundred or so besides the inevitable sprinkling of pickpockets, police, and streetwalkers. The incident I most vividly recall came towards the latter half of the first act, when for ten minutes or so I sat with few lines at a desk listening to my fellow actors. Our stage faced west, and the setting sun had left the sky a welter of lurid colour: purple-reds striped gold and flame and black. Against this violent ground, which might have been the massed banners of hell, there began to appear, in ones and twos, like the elongate shadows of fantastic grenadiers crenellated and plumed, the heads, the slender necks, the narrow shoulders, of a platoon of my father's demimondaines; arriving late, they were taking the last seats at the upper rim of our theatre, encircling it like the soldiery of some ancient, bizarre government surrounding a treasonous mob.

They sat at last, my cue came, and I forgot them; and that is all I can now remember of our first performance, except that at one point some motion of mine suggested to the audience a mannerism of my father's and there was a shout of misplaced laughter – and that at the beginning of the second act Sainte Anne rose, with its sluggish rivers and great, grassy meadow-meres clearly visible, flooding the audience with green light; and at the close of the third I saw my father's crooked little valet bustling among the upper rows, and the girls, green-edged black shadows, filing out.

We produced three more plays that summer, all with some success, and David and Phaedria and I became an accepted partnership, with Phaedria dividing herself more or less equally between us – whether by her own inclination or her parents' orders I could never be quite sure. When her ankle knit she was a companion fit for David in athletics, a better player of the ball and racquet games than any of the other girls who came to the park; but she would as often drop everything and come to sit with me, where she sympathized with (though she did not actually share) my interest in botany and biology, and gossiped, and delighted in showing me off to her friends, since my reading had given me a sort of talent for puns and repartee.

It was Phaedria who suggested, when it became apparent that the ticket money from our first play would be insufficient for the costumes and scenery we coveted for our second, that at the close of future performances the cast circulate among the audience to take up a collection; and this, of course, in the press and bustle easily lent itself to the accomplishment of petty thefts for our cause. Most people, however, had too much sense to bring to our theatre, in the evening, in the gloomy park, more money than was required to buy tickets and perhaps an ice or a glass of wine during intermission; so no matter how dishonest we were the profit remained small, and we, and especially Phaedria and David, were soon talking of going forward to more dangerous and lucrative adventures.

At about this time, I suppose as a result of my father's continued and intensified probing of my subconscious, a violent and almost nightly examination whose purpose was still unclear to me and which, since I had been accustomed to it for so long, I scarcely questioned, I became more and more subject to frightening lapses of conscious control. I would, so David and Mr. Million told me, seem quite myself though perhaps rather more quiet than usual, answering questions intelligently if absently, and then, suddenly, come to myself, start, and stare at the familiar rooms, the familiar faces, among which I now found myself, perhaps after the mid-afternoon, without the slightest memory of having awakened, dressed, shaved, eaten, gone for a walk.

Although I loved Mr. Million as much as I had when I was a boy, I was never able, after that conversation in which I learned the meaning of the familiar lettering on his side, quite to re-establish the old relationship. I was always conscious, as I am conscious now, that the personality I loved had perished years before I was born; and that I addressed an imitation of it, fundamentally mathematical in nature, responding as that personality might to the stimuli of human speech and action. I could never determine whether Mr. Million is really aware in that sense which would give him the right to say, as he always has, 'I think' and 'I feel'. When I asked him about it he could only explain that he did not know the answer himself, that having no standard of comparison he could not be positive whether his own mental processes represented true consciousness or not; and I, of course, could not know whether this answer represented the deepest meditation of a soul somehow alive in the dancing abstractions of the simulation, or whether it was merely triggered, a phonographic response, by my question.

Our theatre, as I have said, continued through the summer and gave its last performance with the falling leaves drifting, like the obscure, perfumed old letters from some attic, upon our stage. When the curtain calls were over we who had written and acted the plays of our season were too disheartened to do more than remove our costumes and cosmetics, and drift, with the last of our departing audience, down the whippoorwill-haunted paths to the city streets and home. I was prepared, as I remember, to take up my duties at my father's door, but that night he had stationed his valet in the foyer to wait for me and I was ushered directly into the library, where he explained brusquely that he would have to devote the latter part of the evening to business and for that reason would speak to me (as he put it) early. He looked tired and ill, and it occurred to me, I think for the first time, that he would one day die – and that I would, on that day, become at once both rich and free.

What I said under the drugs that evening I do not of course recall, but I remember as vividly as if I had only this morning awakened from it the dream that followed. I was on a ship, a white ship like one of those the oxen pull, so slowly the sharp prows make no wake at all, through the green water of the canal beside the park. I was the only crewman, and indeed the only living man aboard. At the stern, grasping the huge wheel in such a flaccid way that it seemed to support and guide and steady him rather than he it, stood the corpse of a tall, thin man whose face, when the rolling of his head presented it to me, was the face that floated in Mr. Million's screen. This face, as I have said, was very like my father's, but I knew the dead man at the wheel was not he.

I was aboard the ship a long time. We seemed to be running free, with the wind a few points to port and strong. When I went aloft at night, masts and spars and rigging quivered and sang in the wind, and sail upon sail towered above me, and sail upon white sail spread below me, and more masts clothed in sails stood before me and behind me. When I worked on deck by day, spray wet my shirt and left tear-shaped spots on the planks which dried quickly in the bright sunlight.

I cannot remember ever having really been on such a ship, but perhaps, as a very small child, I was; for the sounds of it, the creaking of the masts in their sockets, the whistling of the wind in the thousand ropes, the crashing of the waves against the wooden hull, were all as distinct, and as real, as much *themselves*, as the sounds of laughter and breaking glass overhead had been when, as a child, I had tried to sleep; or the bugles from the citadel which sometimes, then, woke me in the morning.

I was about some work, I do not know just what, aboard this ship. I carried buckets of water with which I dashed clotted blood from the decks, and I pulled at ropes which seemed attached to nothing – or rather, firmly tied to immovable objects still higher in the rigging. I watched the surface of the sea from bow and rail, from the mastheads, and from atop a large cabin amidships, but when a star-crosser, its entry shields blinding bright with heat, plunged hissing into the sea far off I reported it to no one.

And all this time the dead man at the wheel was talking to me. His head hung limply, as though his neck were broken, and the jerkings of the wheel he held, as big waves struck the rudder, sent it from one shoulder to the other, or back to stare at the sky, or down. But he continued to speak, and the few words I caught suggested that he was lecturing upon an ethical theory whose postulates seemed doubtful even to him. I felt a dread of hearing this talk and tried to keep myself as much as possible towards the bow, but the wind at times carried the words to me with great clarity, and whenever I looked up from my work I found myself much nearer the stern, sometimes in fact almost touching the dead steersman, than I had supposed.

After I had been on this ship a long while, so that I was very tired and very lonely, one of the doors of the cabin opened and my aunt came out, floating quite upright about two feet above the tilted deck. Her skirt did not hang vertically as I had always seen it, but whipped in the wind like a streamer so that she seemed on the point of blowing away. For some reason I said, 'Don't get close to that man at the wheel, Aunt. He might hurt you.'

She answered, as naturally as if we had met in the corridor outside my bedroom, 'Nonsense. He's far past doing anyone any good, Number Five, or any harm either. It's my brother we have to worry about.'

'Where is he?'

'Down there.' She pointed at the deck as if to indicate that he was in the hold. 'He's trying to find out why the ship doesn't move.'

I ran to the side and looked over, and what I saw was not water but the night sky. Stars – innumerable stars – were spread at an infinite distance below me, and as I looked at them I realized that the ship, as my aunt had said, did not make headway or even roll, but remained heeled over, motionless. I looked back at her and she told me, 'It doesn't move because he has fastened it in place until he finds out why it doesn't move,' and at this point I found myself sliding down a rope into what I supposed was the hold of the ship. It smelled of animals. I had awakened, though at first I did not know it.

My feet touched the floor, and I saw that David and Phaedria were beside me. We were in a huge, loftlike room, and as I looked at Phaedria, who was very pretty but tense and biting her lips, a cock crowed.

David said, 'Where do you think the money is?' He was carrying a tool kit.

And Phaedria, who I suppose had expected him to say something else, or in answer to her own thoughts, said, 'We'll have lots of time; Marydol is watching.' Marydol was one of the girls who appeared in our plays.

'If she doesn't run away. Where do you think the money is?'

'Not up here. Downstairs behind the office.' She had been crouching, but she rose now and began to creep forward. She was all in black, from her ballet slippers to a black ribbon binding her black hair, with her white face and arms in striking contrast, and her carmine lips an error, a bit of colour left by mistake. David and I followed her.

Crates were scattered, widely separated, on the floor; and as we passed them I saw that they held poultry, a single bird in each. It was not until we were nearly to the hatch in the floor at the opposite corner of the room that I realized that these birds were gamecocks. Then a shaft of sun from one of the skylights struck a crate and the cock rose and stretched himself, showing fierce red eyes and plumage as gaudy as a macaw's. 'Come on,' Phaedria said, 'the dogs are next,' and we followed her down the ladder. Pandemonium broke out on the floor below.

The dogs were chained in stalls, with dividers too high for them to see the dogs on either side, and wide aisles between the rows of stalls. They were all fighting dogs, but of every size from ten-pound terriers to mastiffs larger than small horses, brutes with heads as misshapen as the growths that appear on old trees and jaws that could sever both a man's legs at a bite. The din of the barking was incredible, a solid substance that shook us as we descended the ladder, and at the bottom I took Phaedria's arm and tried to indicate by signs that we should leave at once. She shook her head and then, when I was unable to understand what she said, wrote on a dusty wall with her moistened forefinger, 'They do this all the time – a noise in the street – anything.'

Access to the floor below was by stairs, reached through a heavy but unbolted door which I think had been installed largely to exclude the din. I felt better when we had closed it behind us even though the noise was still very loud. I had fully come to myself by this time, and I should have explained to David and Phaedria that I did not know where I was or what we were doing there, but shame held me back. And in any event I could guess easily enough what our purpose was. We had often talked – talk I had considered at the time to be more than half empty boasting – about a single robbery that would free us from the necessity of further petty crime.

Where we were I discovered later when we left; and how we had come to be there I pieced together from casual conversations. The building had been originally designed as a warehouse, and stood on the Rue des Egouts close to the bay. Its owner supplied those enthusiasts who staged combats of all kinds for sport, and was credited with maintaining the largest assemblage of these creatures in the Department. Phaedria's father, who for a fee would assume a part of any shipping risk, had taken her with him when he called on this man, who had just disposed of a quantity of merchandise; and, since the place was known not to open its doors until after the last Angelus, we had come the next day a little after the second and entered through one of the skylights.

I find it difficult to describe what we saw when we descended from the floor of the dogs to the next, which was the second floor of the building. I had seen fighting slaves many times before when Mr. Million, David and I had traversed the slave market to reach the library; but never more than one or two together, heavily manacled. Here they lay, sat, and lounged everywhere, and for a moment I wondered why they did not tear one another to pieces, and the three of us as well. Then I saw that each was held by a short chain stapled to the floor, and it was not difficult to tell, from the scraped and splintered circles in the boards, just how far the slave in the centre could reach. Such furniture as they had, straw pallets and a few chairs and benches, was either too light to do harm if thrown or very stoutly made and spiked down. I had expected them to shout and threaten us as I had heard they threatened each other in the pits before closing, but they seemed to understand that as long as they were chained they could do nothing. Every head turned towards us as we came down the steps, but we had no food for them, and after that first examination they were far less interested in us than the dogs had been.

'They aren't people, are they?' Phaedria said. She was walking erectly as a soldier on parade now, and looking at the slaves with interest; studying her, it occurred to me that she was taller and less plump than the Phaedria I pictured to myself when I thought of her. She was not just a pretty but a beautiful girl. 'They're a kind of animal, really,' she said.

From my studies I was better informed, and I told her that they had been human as infants – in some cases even as children or older – and that they differed from normal people only as a result of surgery (some of it on their brains) and chemically induced alterations in their endocrine systems. And of course in appearance, because of their scars.

'Your father does that sort of thing to little girls, doesn't he? For your house?'

David said, 'Only once in a while. It takes a lot of time, and most people prefer normals, even when they prefer pretty odd normals.'

'I'd like to see some of them. I mean the ones he's worked on.'

I was still thinking of the fighting slaves around us, and said, 'Don't you know about these things? I thought you'd been here before. You knew about the dogs.'

'Oh, I've seen them before, and the man told me about them. I suppose I was just thinking out loud. It would be awful if they were still people.'

Their eyes followed us, and I wondered if they could understand her.

The ground floor was very different from the ones above. The walls were panelled, there were framed pictures of dogs and cocks, and of the slaves, and curious animals. The windows, opening towards Egouts Street and the bay, were high and narrow and admitted only slender beams of the bright sunlight to pick out of the gloom the arm alone of a rich, red leather chair, a square of maroon carpet no bigger than a book, a half-full decanter. I took three steps into this room and knew that we had been discovered. Striding towards us was a tall, high-shouldered young man – who halted, with a startled look, just when I did. He was my own reflection in a gilt-framed pier glass, and I felt the momentary dislocation that comes when a stranger, an unrecognized shape, turns or moves his head and is some familiar friend glimpsed, perhaps for the first time, from outside. The sharp-chinned, grim-looking boy I had seen when I did not know him to be myself had been myself as Phaedria and David, Mr. Million and my aunt, saw me.

'This is where he talks to customers,' Phaedria said. 'If he's trying to sell something he has his people bring them down one at a time so you don't see the others, but you can hear the dogs bark even from way down here, and he took Papa and I upstairs and showed us everything.'

David asked, 'Did he show you where he keeps the money?'

'In back. See that tapestry? It's really a curtain, because while Papa was talking to him a man came that owed him for something and paid, and he went through there with it.'

The door behind the tapestry opened on a small office, with still another door in the wall opposite. There was no sign of a safe or strongbox. David broke the lock on the desk with a pry bar from his tool kit, but there was only the usual clutter of papers, and I was about to open the second door when I heard a sound, a scraping or shuffling, from the room beyond.

For a minute or more none of us moved. I stood with my hand on the latch. Phaedria, behind me and to my left, had been looking under the carpet for a cache in the floor – she remained crouched, her skirt a black pool. From somewhere near the broken desk I could hear David's breathing. The shuffling came again, and a board creaked. David said very softly, 'It's an animal.'

I drew my fingers away from the latch and looked at him. He was still gripping the pry bar and his face was pale, but he smiled, 'An animal tethered in there, shifting its feet. That's all.'

I said, 'How do you know?'

'Anybody in there would have heard us, especially when I cracked the desk. If it were a person he would have come out, or if he were afraid he'd hide and be quiet.'

Phaedria said, 'I think he's right. Open the door.'

'Before I do, if it isn't an animal?'

David said, 'It is.'

'But if it isn't?'

I saw the answer on their faces; David gripped his pry bar, and I opened the door.

The room beyond was larger than I had expected, but bare and dirty. The only light came from a single window high in the far wall. In the middle of the floor stood a big chest, of dark wood bound with iron, and before it lay what appeared to be a bundle of rags. As I stepped from the carpeted office the rags moved and a face, a face triangular as a mantis', turned towards me. Its chin was hardly more than an inch from the floor, but under deep brows the eyes were tiny scarlet fires.

'That must be it,' Phaedria said. She was looking not at the face but at the iron-banded chest. 'David, can you break into that?'

'I think so,' David said, but like me, he was watching the ragged thing's eyes. 'What about that?' he said after a moment, and gestured towards it. Before Phaedria or I could answer, its mouth opened showing long, narrow teeth, grey-yellow. 'Sick,' it said.

None of us, I think, had thought it could speak. It was as though a mummy had spoken. Outside a carriage went past, its iron wheels rattling on the cobbles.

'Let's go,' David said. 'Let's get out.'

Phaedria said, 'It's sick. Don't you see, the owner's brought it down here where he can look in on it and take care of it. It's sick.'

'And he chained his sick slave to the cash box?' David cocked an eyebrow at her.

'Don't you see? It's the only heavy thing in the room. All you have to do is go over there and knock the poor creature on the head. If you're afraid, give me the bar and I'll do it myself.'

'I'll do it.'

I followed him to within a few feet of the chest. He gestured at the slave imperiously with the steel pry bar. 'You! Move away from there.'

The slave made a gurgling sound and crawled to one side, dragging his chain. He was wrapped in a filthy, tattered blanket and seemed hardly larger than a child, though I noticed that his hands were immense.

I turned and took a step toward Phaedria, intending to urge that we leave if David were unable to open the chest in a few minutes. I remember that before I heard or felt anything I saw her eyes open wide, and I was still wondering why, when David's kit of tools clattered on the floor and David himself fell with a thud and a little gasp. Phaedria screamed, and all the dogs on the third floor began to bark.

All this, of course, took less than a second. I turned to look almost as David fell. The slave had darted out an arm and caught my brother by the ankle, and then in an instant had thrown off his blanket and bounded on top of him.

I caught him by the neck and jerked him backward, thinking that he would cling to David and that it would be necessary to tear him away, but the instant he felt my hands he flung David aside and writhed like a spider in my grip. *He had four arms.*

I saw them flailing as he tried to reach me, and I let go of him and jerked back as if a rat had been thrust at my face. That instinctive repulsion saved me; he drove his feet backwards in a kick, which, if I had still been holding him tightly enough to give him a fulcrum, would have surely ruptured my liver or spleen and killed me.

Instead it shot him forward and me back, gasping for breath. I fell and rolled, and was outside the circle permitted him by his chain; David had already scrambled away, and Phaedria was well out of his reach.

For a moment, while I shuddered and tried to sit up, the three of us simply stared at him. Then David quoted wryly:

'Arms and the man I sing, who forc'd by fate,
  And haughty Juno's unrelenting hate,
  Expell'd and exil'd, left the Trojan shore.'

Neither Phaedria nor I laughed, but Phaedria let out her breath in a long sigh and asked me, 'How did they do that? Get him like that?'

I told her I supposed they had transplanted the extra pair after suppressing his body's natural resistance to the implanted foreign tissue, and that the operation had probably replaced some of his ribs with the donor's shoulder structure. 'I've been teaching myself to do the same sort of thing with mice – on a much less ambitious scale, of course – and the striking thing to me is that he seems to have full use of the grafted pair. Unless you've got identical twins to work with, the nerve endings almost never join properly, and whoever did this probably had a hundred failures before he got what he wanted. That slave must be worth a fortune.'

David said, 'I thought you threw your mice out. Aren't you working with monkeys now?'

I wasn't, although I hoped to; but whether I was or not, it seemed clear that talking about it wasn't going to accomplish anything. I told David that.

'I thought you were hot to leave.'

I had been, but now I wanted something else much more. I wanted to perform an exploratory operation on that creature much more than David or Phaedria had ever wanted money. David liked to think that he was bolder than I, and I knew when I said, 'You may want to get away, but don't use me as an excuse, brother,' that that would settle it.

'All right, how are we going to kill him?' He gave me an angry look.

Phaedria said, 'It can't reach us. We could throw things at it.'

'And he could throw the ones that missed back.'

While we talked, the thing, the four-armed slave, was grinning at us. I was fairly sure it could understand at least a part of what we were saying, and I motioned to David and Phaedria to indicate that we should go back into the room where the desk was. When we were there I closed the door. 'I didn't want him to hear us. If we had weapons on poles, spears of some kind, we might be able to kill him without getting close. What could we use for the sticks? Any ideas?'

David shook his head, but Phaedria said, 'Wait a minute, I remember something.' We both looked at her and she knitted her brows, pretending to search her memory and enjoying the attention.

'Well?' David asked.

She snapped her fingers. 'Window rods. You know, long things with a little hook on the end. Remember the windows out there where he talks to customers? They're high up in the wall, and while he and Papa were talking one of the men who works for him brought one and opened a window. They ought to be around somewhere.'

We found two after a five-minute search. They looked satisfactory: about six feet long and an inch and a quarter in diameter, of hardwood. David flourished his and pretended to thrust at Phaedria, then asked me, 'Now what do we use for points?'

The scalpel I always carried was in its case in my breast pocket, and I fastened it to the rod with electrical tape, but we could find nothing to make a second spearhead for David until he himself suggested broken glass.

'You can't break a window,' Phaedria said, 'they'd hear you outside. Besides, won't it just snap off when you try to get him with it?'

'Not if it's thick glass. Look here, you two.'

I did, and saw – again – my own face. He was pointing towards the large mirror that had surprised me when I came down the steps. While I looked, his shoe struck it and it shattered with a crash that set the dogs barking again. He selected a long, almost straight, triangular piece and held it up to the light, where it flashed like a gem. 'That's about as good as they used to make them from agate and jasper on Sainte Anne, isn't it?'

*

By prior agreement we approached from opposite sides. The slave leaped to the top of the chest, and from there watched us quite calmly, his deepset eyes turning from David to me until at last when we were both quite close David rushed him.

He spun around as the glass point grazed his ribs, and caught David's spear by the shaft and jerked him forward. I thrust at him but missed, and before I could recover he had dived from the chest and was grappling with David on the far side. I bent over it and jabbed down at him, and it was not until David screamed that I realized I had driven my scalpel into his thigh. I saw the blood, bright arterial blood, spurt up and drench the shaft, and let it go and threw myself over the chest on top of them.

He was ready for me, on his back and grinning, with his legs and all four arms raised like a dead spider's. I am certain he would have strangled me in the next few seconds if it had not been that David, how consciously I do not know, threw one arm across the creature's eyes so that he missed his grip and I fell between those outstretched arms.

There is not a great deal more to tell. He jerked free of David and, pulling me to him, tried to bite my throat; but I hooked a thumb in one of his eye sockets and held him off. Phaedria, with more courage than I would have credited her with, put David's glass-tipped spear into my free hand and I stabbed him in the neck – I believe I severed both jugulars and the trachea before he died. We put a tourniquet on David's leg and left without either the money or the knowledge of technique I had hoped to get from the body of the slave. Marydol helped us get David home, and we told Mr. Million he had fallen while we were exploring an empty building – though I doubt that he believed us.

There is one other thing to tell about that incident – I mean the killing of the slave – although I am tempted to go on and describe instead a discovery I made immediately afterwards that had, at the time, a much greater influence on me. It is only an impression, and one that I have, I am sure, distorted and magnified in recollection. While I was stabbing the slave, my face was very near his and I saw (I suppose because of the light from the high windows behind us) my own face reflected and doubled in the corneas of his eyes, and it seemed to me that it was a face very like his. I have been unable to forget, since then, what Dr. Marsch told me about the production of any number of identical individuals by cloning, and that my father had, when I was younger, a reputation as a child broker. I have tried since my release to find some trace of my mother, the woman in the photograph shown me by my aunt; but that picture was surely taken long before I was born – perhaps even on Earth.

The discovery I spoke of I made almost as soon as we left the building where I killed the slave, and it was simply this: that it was no longer autumn, but high summer. Because all four of us – Marydol had joined us by that time – were so concerned about David, and busy concocting a story to explain his injury, the shock was somewhat blunted, but there could be no doubt about it. The weather was warm with that torpid damp heat peculiar to summer. The trees I remembered nearly bare were in full leaf and filled with orioles. The fountain in our garden no longer played, as it always did after the danger of frost and burst pipes had come, with warmed water: I dabbed my hand in the basin as we helped David up the path, and it was as cool as dew.

My periods of unconscious action then, my sleepwalking, had increased to devour an entire winter and the spring, and I felt that I had lost myself.

When we entered the house, an ape which I thought at first was my father's sprang to my shoulder. Later Mr. Million told me that it was my own, one of my laboratory animals I had made a pet. I did not know the little beast, but scars under his fur, and the twist of his limbs, showed he knew me.

(I have kept Popo ever since, and Mr. Million took care of him for me while I was imprisoned. He climbs still, in fine weather, on the grey and crumbling walls of this house; and as he runs along the parapets and I see his hunched form against the sky I think, for a moment, that my father is still alive, and that I may be summoned again for the long hours in his library – but I forgive my pet that.)

My father did not call a physician for David, but treated him himself; and if he was curious about the manner in which he had received his injury he did not show it. My own guess – for whatever it may be worth, this late – is that he believed I had stabbed him in some quarrel. I say this because he seemed, after this, apprehensive whenever I was alone with him. He was not a fearful man, and he had been accustomed for years to deal occasionally with the worst sort of criminals; but he was no longer at ease with me – he guarded himself. It may have been, of course, merely the result of something I had said or done during the forgotten winter.

Both Marydol and Phaedria, as well as my aunt and Mr. Million, came frequently to visit David, so that his sickroom became a sort of meeting place for us all, only disturbed by my father's occasional visits. Marydol was a slight, fair-haired, kind-hearted girl, and I became very fond of her. Often when she was ready to go home I escorted her, and on the way back stopped at the slave market, as Mr. Million and David and I had done so often, to buy fried bread and the sweet black coffee and to watch the bidding. The faces of slaves are the dullest in the world; but I would find myself staring into them, and it was a long time, a month at least, before I understood why I did. A young male, a sweeper, was brought to the block. His face as well as his back had been scarred by the whip, and his teeth were broken; but recognized him: the scarred face was my own or my father's. I spoke to him and would have bought and freed him, but he answered me in the servile way of slaves and I turned away in disgust and went home.

That night when my father had me brought to the library, for the first time in several nights, I watched our reflections in the mirror that concealed the entrance to his laboratories. He looked younger than he was; I older. We might almost have been the same man, and when he faced me and I, staring over his shoulder, saw no image of my own body, but only his arms and mine, we might have been the fighting slave.

I cannot say who first suggested that we kill him. I only remember that one evening, as I prepared for bed after taking Marydol and Phaedria to their homes, I realized that earlier when the three of us, with Mr. Million and my aunt, had sat around David's bed, we had been talking of that.

Not openly, of course. Perhaps we had not admitted even to ourselves what it was we were thinking. My aunt had mentioned the money he was supposed to have hidden; and Phaedria, then, a yacht luxurious as a palace; David talked about hunting in the grand style, and the political power money could buy.

And I, saying nothing, had thought of the hours and weeks, and the months he had taken from me; of the destruction of my *self*, which he had gnawed at night after night. I thought of how I might enter the library that night and find myself when next I woke an old man and perhaps a beggar.

Then I knew that I must kill him, since if I told him those thoughts while I lay drugged on the peeling leather of the old table he would kill *me* without a qualm.

While I waited for his valet to come I made my plan. There would be no investigation, no death certificate for my father. I would replace him. To our patrons it would appear that nothing had changed. Phaedria's friends would be told that I had quarrelled with him and left home. I would allow no one to see me for a time, and then, in makeup, in a dim room, speak occasionally to some favoured caller. It was an impossible plan, but at the time I believed it possible and even easy. My scalpel was ready. The body could be destroyed in his own laboratory.

He read it in my face. He spoke to me as he always had, but I think he knew. There were flowers in the room, something that had never been before, and I wondered if he had not known even earlier and had them brought in, as for a special event. Instead of telling me to lie on the leather-covered table he gestured towards a chair and seated himself at his writing desk. 'We will have company today,' he said.

I looked at him.

'You're angry with me. I've seen it growing in you. Don't you know who —'

He was about to say something further when there was a tap at the door, and when he called, 'Come in!' it was opened by Nerissa, who ushered in a demimondaine and Dr. Marsch. I was surprised to see him; still more surprised to see one of the girls in my father's library. She seated herself beside Marsch in a way that showed he was her benefactor for the night.

'Good evening, Doctor,' my father said. 'Have you been enjoying yourself?'

Marsch smiled, showing large, square teeth. He wore clothing of the most fashionable cut now, but the contrast between his beard and the colourless skin of his cheeks was as remarkable as ever. 'Both sensually and intellectually,' he said. 'I've seen a naked girl, a giantess twice the height of a man, walk through a wall.'

I said, 'That's done with holographs.'

He smiled again. 'I know. And I have seen a great many other things as well. I was going to recite them all, but perhaps I would only bore my audience; I will content myself with saying that you have a remarkable establishment – but you know that.'

My father said, 'It is always flattering to hear it again.'

'And now are we going to have the discussion we spoke of earlier?'

My father looked at the demimondaine; she rose, kissed Dr. Marsch, and left the room. The heavy library door swung shut behind her with a soft click.

Like the sound of a switch, or old glass breaking.

I have thought since, many times, of that girl as I saw her leaving: the high-heeled platform shoes and grotesquely long legs, the backless dress dipping an inch below the coccyx. The bare nape of her neck; her hair piled and teased and threaded with ribbons and tiny lights. As she closed the door she was ending, though she could not have known it, the world she and I had known.

'She'll be waiting when you come out,' my father said to Marsch.

'And if she's not, I'm sure you can supply others.' The anthropologist's green eyes seemed to glow in the lamp light. 'But now, how can I help you?'

'You study race. Could you call a group of similar men thinking similar thoughts a race?'

'And women,' Marsch said smiling.

'And here,' my father continued, 'here on Sainte Croix, you are gathering material to take back with you to Earth?'

'I am gathering material, certainly. Whether or not I shall return to the mother planet is problematical.'

I must have looked at him sharply; he turned his smile towards me, and it became, if possible, even more patronizing than before. 'You're surprised?'

'I've always considered Earth the centre of scientific thought,' I said. 'I can easily imagine a scientist leaving it to do field work, but —'

'But it is inconceivable that one might want to stay in the field? Consider my position. You are not alone – happily for me – in respecting the mother world's grey hairs and wisdom. As an Earth-trained man I've been offered a department in your university at almost any salary I care to name, with a sabbatical every second year. And the trip from here to Earth requires twenty years of Newtonian time; only six months subjectively for me, of course, but when I return, if I do, my education will be forty years out of date. No, I'm afraid your planet may have acquired an intellectual luminary.'

My father said, 'We're straying from the subject, I think.'

Marsch nodded. 'But I was about to say that an anthropologist is peculiarly equipped to make himself at home in any culture – even in so strange a one as this family has constructed about itself. I think I may call it a family, since there are two members resident besides yourself. You don't object to my addressing the pair of you in the singular?'

He looked to me as if expecting a protest, then when I said nothing: 'I mean your son David – that, and not brother is his real relationship to your continuing personality – and the woman you call your aunt. She is in reality daughter to an earlier – shall we say version? – of yourself.'

'You're both trying to tell me I'm a cloned duplicate of my father, and I see both of you expect me to be shocked. I'm not. I've suspected it for some time.'

My father said, 'I'm glad to hear that. Frankly, when I was your age the discovery disturbed me a great deal; I came into my father's library – this room – to confront him, and I intended to kill him.'

Dr. Marsch asked, 'And did you?'

'I don't think that matters – the point is that it was my intention. I hope that having you here will make things easier for Number Five.'

'Is that what you call him?'

'It's more convenient since his name is the same as my own.'

'He is your fifth clone-produced child?'

'My fifth experiment? No.' My father's hunched, high shoulders, wrapped in the dingy scarlet of his old dressing gown, made him look like some savage bird, and I remembered having read, in a book of natural history, of one called the red-shouldered hawk. His pet monkey, grizzled now with age, had climbed on to the desk. 'No, more like my fiftieth, if you must know. I used to do them for drill. You people who have never tried it think the technique is simple because you've heard it can be done, but you don't know how difficult it is to prevent spontaneous differences. Every gene dominant in myself had to remain dominant, and people are not garden peas – few things are governed by simple Mendelian pairs.'

Marsch asked, 'You destroyed your failures?'

I said, 'He sold them. When I was a child I used to wonder why Mr. Million stopped to look at the slaves in the market. Since then I've found out.' My scalpel was still in its case in my pocket; I could feel it.

'Mr. Million,' my father said, 'is perhaps a bit more sentimental than I – besides, I don't like to go out. You see, Doctor, your supposition that we are all truly the same individual will have to be modified. We have our little variations.'

Dr. Marsch was about to reply, but I interrupted him.

'Why?' I said. 'Why David and me? Why Aunt Jeannine a long time ago? Why go on with it?'

'Yes,' my father said, 'why? We ask the question to ask the question.'

'I don't understand you.'

'I seek self-knowledge. If you want to put it this way, *we* seek self-knowledge. You are here because I did and do, and I am here because the individual behind me did – who was himself originated by the one whose mind is simulated in Mr. Million. And one of the questions whose answers we seek is why we seek. But there is more than that.' He leaned forward, and the little ape lifted its white muzzle and bright, bewildered eyes to stare into his face. 'We wish to discover why we fail, why others rise and change and we remain here.'

I thought of the yacht I had talked about with Phaedria and said, 'I won't stay here.' Dr. Marsch smiled.

My father said, 'I don't think you understand me. I don't necessarily mean here physically, but *here*, socially and intellectually. I have travelled, and you may, but —'

'But you end here,' Dr. Marsch said.

'We end at this level!' It was the only time, I think, that I ever saw my father excited. He was almost speechless as he waved at the notebooks and tapes that thronged the walls. 'After how many generations? We do not achieve fame or the rule of even this miserable little colony planet. Something must be changed, but what?' He glared at Dr. Marsch.

'You are not unique,' Dr. Marsch said, then smiled. 'That sounds like a truism, doesn't it? But I wasn't referring to your duplicating yourself. I meant that since it became possible, back on Earth during the last quarter of the twentieth century, it has been done in such chains a number of times. We have borrowed a term from engineering to describe it, and call it the process of relaxation – a bad nomenclature, but the best we have. Do you know what relaxation in the engineering sense is?'

'No.'

'There are problems which are not directly soluble, but which can be solved by a succession of approximations. In heat transfer, for example, it may not be possible to calculate initially the temperature at every point on the surface of an unusually shaped body. But the engineer, or his computer, can assume reasonable temperatures, see how nearly stable the assumed values would be, then make new assumptions based on the result. As the levels of approximation progress, the successive sets become more and more similar until there is essentially no change. That is why I said the two of you are essentially one individual.'

'What I want you to do,' my father said impatiently, 'is to make Number Five understand that the experiments I have performed on him, particularly the narcotherapeutic examinations he resents so much, are necessary. That if we are to become more than we have been we must find out —' He had been almost shouting, and he stopped abruptly to bring his voice under control. 'That is the reason he was produced, the reason for David too – I hoped to learn something from an outcrossing.'

'Which was the rationale, no doubt,' Dr. Marsch said, 'for the existence of Dr. Veil as well, in an earlier generation. But as far as your examinations of your younger self are concerned, it would be just as useful for him to examine you.'

'Wait a moment,' I said. 'You keep saying that he and I are identical. That's incorrect. I can see that we're similar in some respects, but I'm not really like my father.'

'There are no differences that cannot be accounted for by age. You are what? Eighteen? And you' – he looked towards my father – 'I should say are nearly fifty. There are only two forces, you see, which act to differentiate between human beings: they are heredity and environment, nature and nurture. And since the personality is largely formed during the first three years of life it is the environment provided by the home which is decisive. Now every person is born into *some* home environment, though it may be such a harsh one that he dies of it; and no person, except in this situation we call anthropological relaxation, provides that environment himself – it is furnished for him by the preceding generation.'

'Just because both of us grew up in this house —'

'Which you built and furnished and filled with the people you chose. But wait a moment. Let's talk about a man neither of you has ever seen, a man born in a place provided by parents quite different from himself: I mean the first of you. . . .'

I was no longer listening. I had come to kill my father, and it was necessary that Dr. Marsch leave. I watched him as he leaned forward in his chair, his long white hands making incisive little gestures, his cruel lips moving in a frame of black hair: I watched him and I heard nothing. It was as though I had gone deaf, or as if he could communicate only by his thoughts, and I, knowing the thoughts were silly lies, had shut them out. I said, 'You are from Sainte Anne.'

He looked at me in surprise, halting in the midst of a sound-less sentence. 'I have been there, yes. I spent a year on Sainte Anne before coming here.'

'You were born there. You studied your anthropology there from books written on Earth a hundred years ago. You are an abo, or at least half abo; but we are men.'

Marsch glanced at my father, then said, 'The abos are gone. They've been extinct for almost a century.'

'You didn't believe that when you came to see my aunt.'

'I've never accepted Veil's Hypothesis. I called on every-one here who had published anything in my field. Really, I don't have time to listen to this.'

'You are an abo and not from Earth.'

And in a short time my father and I were alone.

Most of my sentence I served in a labour camp in the Tat-tered Mountains. It was a small camp, housing usually only a hundred and fifty prisoners – sometimes less than eighty when the winter deaths had been bad. We cut wood and burned char-coal, and made skis when we found good birch. Above the timberline we gathered a saline moss supposed to be medicinal and knotted long plants for rock slides that would crush the stalking machines that were our guards – though somehow the moment never came, the stones never slid. The work was hard, and these guards administered exactly the mixture of severity and fairness some prison board had decided upon when they

were programmed and the problem of brutality and favourit-
ism by hirelings was settled for ever, so that only well-dressed
men at meetings could be cruel or kind.

Or so they thought. I sometimes talked to my guards for
hours about Mr. Million, and once I found a piece of meat, and
once a cake of hard sugar, brown and gritty as sand, hidden in
the corner where I slept.

A criminal may not profit by his crime, but the court – so
I was told much later – could find no proof that David was
indeed my father's son, and made my aunt his heir.

She died and a letter from an attorney informed me that by
her favour I had inherited 'a large house in the city of Port-
Mimizon, together with the furniture and chattels apper-
taining thereto'. And that this house 'located at 666 Saltimbanque, is presently under the care of a robot servitor'. Since
the robot servitors under whose direction I found myself did
not allow me writing materials, I could not reply.

Time passed on the wings of birds. I found dead larks at
the feet of north-facing cliffs in autumn, at the feet of south-
facing cliffs in spring.

I received a letter from Mr. Million. Most of my father's
girls had left during the investigation of his death; the re-
mainder he had been obliged to send away when my aunt died,
finding that as a machine he could not enforce the necessary
obedience. David had gone to the capital. Phaedria had married well. Marydol had been sold by her parents. The date on
his letter was three years later than the date of my trial, but
how long the letter had been in reaching me I could not tell.
The envelope had been opened and resealed many times and
was soiled and torn.

A seabird, I believe a gannet, came fluttering down into our
camp after a storm, too exhausted to fly. We killed and ate it.

One of our guards went berserk, burned fifteen prisoners
to death and fought the other guards all night with swords of
white and blue fire. He was not replaced.

I was transferred with some others to a camp farther north
where I looked down chasms of red stone so deep that if I
kicked a pebble in I could hear the rattle of its descent grow

to a roar of slipping rock – and hear that, in half a minute, fade with distance, yet never strike the bottom lost somewhere in darkness.

I pretended the people I had known were with me. When I sat shielding my basin of soup from the wind, Phaedria sat upon a bench nearby and smiled and talked about her friends. David played squash for hours on the dusty ground of our compound, slept against the wall near my own corner. Marydol put her hand in mine while I carried my saw into the mountains.

In time they all grew dim, but even in the last year I never slept without telling myself, just before sleep, that Mr. Million would take us to the city library in the morning; never woke without fearing that my father's valet had come for me.

Then I was told that I was to go, with three others, to another camp. We carried our food, and nearly died of hunger and exposure on the way. From there we were marched to a third camp where we were questioned by men who were not prisoners like ourselves but free men in uniforms who made notes of our answers and at last ordered that we bathe, and burned our old clothing, and gave us a thick stew of meat and barley.

I remember very well that it was then I allowed myself to realize, at last, what these things meant. I dipped my bread into my bowl and pulled it out soaked with the fragrant stock, with bits of meat and grains of barley clinging to it; and I thought then of the fried bread and coffee at the slave market not as something of the past but as something in the future, and my hands shook until I could no longer hold my bowl, and I wanted to rush shouting at the fences.

In two more days we, six of us now, were put into a mule cart that drove on winding roads always downhill until the winter that had been dying behind us was gone, and the birches and firs were gone, and the tall chestnuts and oaks beside the road had spring flowers under their branches.

The streets of Port-Mimizon swarmed with people. I would have been lost in a moment if Mr. Million had not hired a chair for me, but I made the bearers stop, and bought (with money he gave me) a newspaper from a vendor so that I could know the date with certainty at last.

My sentence had been the usual one of two to fifty years, and though I had known the month and year of the beginning of my imprisonment, it had been impossible to know, in the camps, the number of the current year, which everyone counted, and no one knew. A man took fever, and in ten days, when he was well enough again to work, said that two years had passed or had never been. Then you yourself took fever. I do not recall any headline, any article from the paper I bought I read only the date at the top, all the way home.

It had been nine years.

I had been eighteen when I had killed my father. I was now twenty-seven. I had thought I might be forty.

The flaking grey walls of our house were the same. The iron dog with his three wolf-heads still stood in the front garden, but the fountain was silent and the beds of fern and moss were full of weeds. Mr. Million paid my chairmen and unlocked with a key the door that was always guard-chained but unbolted in my father's day – but as he did so an immensely tall and lanky woman who had been hawking pralines in the street came running towards us. It was Nerissa, and I now had a servant and might have had a bedfellow if I wished, though I could pay her nothing.

And now I must, I suppose, explain why I have been writing this account, which has already been the labour of days; and I must even explain why I explain. Very well then. I have written to disclose myself to myself, and I am writing now because I will, I know, sometime read what I am now writing and wonder.

Perhaps by the time I do, I will have solved the mystery of myself; or perhaps I will no longer care.

It has been three years since my release. This house, when Nerissa and I re-entered it, was in a very confused state, my aunt having spent her last days, so Mr. Million told me, in a search for my father's supposed hoard. She did not find it, and

I do not think it is to be found; knowing his character better than she, I believe he spent most of what his girls brought him on his experiments and apparatus. I needed money badly myself at first, but the reputation of the house brought people. Seeking buyers or seeking to buy. It is hardly necessary, as I told myself when we began, to do more than introduce them, and I have a good staff now. Phaedria lives with us and works too; the brilliant marriage was a failure after all. Last night while I was working in my surgery I heard her at the library door. I opened it and she had the child with her. Some day they'll want us.

WHEN WE WENT TO SEE THE END OF THE WORLD

Satire has its own spectrum, too. It can be as sunny and gentle as that of Robert Benchley or Jack Benny, which takes one's self as chief target, or of Charles Schulz, which makes you feel affection for the objects satirized. Or it can be as intensely bitter as that of Ambrose Bierce or Jonathan Swift, and makes you feel ashamed of and disgusted by the whole human race.

And, of course, all gradations in between.

It is to be expected that satire in science fiction would have a similar spectrum and we can see that right in this volume.

Silverberg's story here is as intensely satirical as the story by Pohl which you will find earlier in the volume. It is as light-hearted in some ways and it is nowhere as immediately tragic as is the end of Pohl's story.

And yet while Pohl's story I recall with a smile, Silverberg's I think of with a shudder. 'When We Went to See the End of the World' is a bitter story written in anger, and it is a measure of its effectiveness that when you are done you share the anger.

Nor must it be forgotten that this story is a satire of science fiction itself. Read it and see.

WHEN WE WENT TO SEE THE END OF THE WORLD

Robert Silverberg

Nick and Jane were glad that they had gone to see the end of the world, because it gave them something special to talk about at Mike and Ruby's party. One always likes to come to a party armed with a little conversation. Mike and Ruby give marvellous parties. Their home is superb, one of the finest in the neighbourhood. It is truly a home for all seasons, all moods. Their very special corner-of-the-world. With more space indoors and out . . . more wide-open freedom. The living room with its exposed ceiling beams is a natural focal point for entertaining. Custom-finished, with a conversation pit and fireplace. There's also a family room with beamed ceiling and wood panelling . . . plus a study. And a magnificent master suite with 12-foot dressing room and private bath. Solidly impressive exterior design. Sheltered courtyard. Beautifully wooded $\frac{1}{3}$-acre grounds. Their parties are highlights of any month. Nick and Jane waited until they thought enough people had arrived. Then Jane nudged Nick and Nick said gaily, 'You know what we did last week? Hey, we went to see the end of the world!'

'The end of the world?' Henry asked.

'You went to see it?' said Henry's wife Cynthia.

'How did you manage that?' Paula wanted to know.

'It's been available since March,' Stan told her. 'I think a division of American Express runs it.'

Nick was put out to discover that Stan already knew. Quickly, before Stan could say anything more, Nick said, 'Yes, it's just started. Our travel agent found out for us. What they do is they put you in this machine, it looks like a tiny teeny submarine, you know, with dials and levers up front behind a plastic wall to keep you from touching anything, and they send you into the future. You can charge it with any of the regular credit cards.'

'It must be very expensive,' Marcia said.

'They're bringing the costs down rapidly,' Jane said. 'Last year only millionaires could afford it. Really, haven't you heard about it before?'

'What did you see?' Henry asked.

'For a while, just greyness outside the porthole,' said Nick. 'And a kind of flickering effect.' Everybody was looking at him. He enjoyed the attention. Jane wore a rapt, loving expression. 'Then the haze cleared and a voice said over a loudspeaker that we had now reached the very end of time, when life had become impossible on Earth. Of course we were sealed into the submarine thing. Only looking out. On this beach, this empty beach. The water a funny grey colour with a pink sheen. And then the sun came up. It was red like it sometimes is at sunrise, only it stayed red as it got to the middle of the sky, and it looked lumpy and sagging at the edges. Like a few of us, hah hah. Lumpy and sagging at the edges. A cold wind blowing across the beach.'

'If you were sealed in the submarine, how did you know there was a cold wind?' Cynthia asked.

Jane glared at her. Nick said, 'We could see the sand blowing around. And it *looked* cold. The grey ocean. Like in winter.'

'Tell them about the crab,' said Jane.

'Yes, and the crab. The last life-form on Earth. It wasn't really a crab, of course, it was something about two feet wide and a foot high, with thick shiny green armour and maybe a dozen legs and some curving horns coming up, and it moved slowly from right to left in front of us. It took all day to cross the beach. And towards nightfall it died. Its horns went limp and it stopped moving. The tide came in and carried it away The sun went down. There wasn't any moon. The stars didn't seem to be in the right places. The loudspeaker told us we had just seen the death of Earth's last living thing.'

'How *eerie*!' cried Paula.

'Were you gone very long?' Ruby asked.

'Three hours,' Jane said. 'You can spend weeks or days at the end of the world, if you want to pay extra, but they always bring you back to a point three hours after you went. To hold down the baby-sitter expenses.'

Mike offered Nick some pot. 'That's really something,' he said. 'To have gone to the end of the world. Hey, Ruby, maybe we'll talk to the travel agent about it.'

Nick took a deep drag and passed the joint to Jane. He felt pleased with himself about the way he had told the story. They had all been very impressed. That swollen red sun, that scuttling crab. The trip had cost more than a month in Japan, but it had been a good investment. He and Jane were the first in the neighbourhood who had gone. That was important. Paula was staring at him in awe. Nick knew that she regarded him in a completely different light now. Possibly she would meet him at a motel on Tuesday at lunchtime. Last month she had turned him down but now he had an extra attractiveness for her. Nick winked at her. Cynthia was holding hands with Stan. Henry and Mike both were crouched at Jane's feet. Mike and Ruby's twelve-year-old son came into the room and stood at the edge of the conversation pit. He said, 'There just was a bulletin on the news. Mutated amoebas escaped from a government research station and got into Lake Michigan. They're carrying a tissue-dissolving virus and everybody in seven states is supposed to boil his water until further notice.' Mike scowled at the boy and said, 'It's after your bedtime, Timmy.' The boy went out. The doorbell rang. Ruby answered it and returned with Eddie and Fran.

Paula said, 'Nick and Jane went to see the end of the world. They've just been telling us all about it.'

'Gee,' said Eddie, 'we did that too, on Wednesday night.'

Nick was crestfallen. Jane bit her lip and asked Cynthia quietly why Fran always wore such flashy dresses. Ruby said, 'You saw the whole works, eh? The crab and everything?'

'The crab?' Eddie said. 'What crab? We didn't see the crab.'

'It must have died the time before,' Paula said. 'When Nick and Jane were there.'

Mike said, 'A fresh shipment of Cuernavaca Lightning is in. Here, have a toke.'

'How long ago did you do it?' Eddie said to Nick.

'Sunday afternoon. I guess we were about the first.'

'Great trip, isn't it?' Eddie said. 'A little sombre, though. When the last hill crumbles into the sea.'

'That's not what we saw,' said Jane. 'And you didn't see the crab? Maybe we were on different trips.'

Mike said, 'What was it like for you, Eddie?'

Eddie put his arms around Cynthia from behind. He said, 'They put us into this little capsule, with a porthole, you know, and a lot of instruments and —'

'We heard that part,' said Paula. 'What did you *see*?'

'The end of the world,' Eddie said. 'When water covers everything. The sun and the moon were in the sky at the same time —'

'We didn't see the moon at all,' Jane remarked. 'It just wasn't there.'

'It was on one side and the sun was on the other,' Eddie went on. 'The moon was closer than it should have been. And a funny colour, almost like bronze. And the ocean creeping up. We went halfway around the world and all we saw was ocean. Except in one place, there was this chunk of land sticking up, this hill, and the guide told us it was the top of Mount Everest.' He waved to Fran. 'That was groovy, huh, floating in our tin boat next to the top of Mount Everest. Maybe ten feet of it sticking up. And the water rising all the time. Up, up, up. Up and over the top. Glub. No land left. I have to admit it was a little disappointing, except of course the *idea* of the thing. That human ingenuity can design a machine that can send people billions of years forward in time and bring them back, wow! But there was just this ocean.'

'How strange,' said Jane. 'We saw an ocean too, but there was a beach, a kind of nasty beach, and the crab-thing walking along it, and the sun – it was all red, was the sun red when you saw it?'

'A kind of pale green,' Fran said.

'Are you people talking about the end of the world?' Tom asked. He and Harriet were standing by the door taking off their coats. Mike's son must have let them in. Tom gave his coat to Ruby and said, 'Man, what a spectacle!'

'So you did it too?' Jane asked, a little hollowly.

'Two weeks ago,' said Tom. 'The travel agent called and said, Guess what we're offering now, the end of the goddamned world! With all the extras it didn't really cost so much. So we went right down there to the office, Saturday, I think – was it a Friday? – the day of the big riot, anyway, when they burned St. Louis —'

'That was a Saturday,' Cynthia said. 'I remember I was coming back from the shopping centre when the radio said they were using nuclears —'

'Saturday, yes,' Tom said. 'And we told them we were ready to go, and off they sent us.'

'Did you see a beach with crabs,' Stan demanded, 'or was it a world full of water?'

'Neither one. It was a big ice age. Glaciers covered everything. No oceans showing, no mountains. We flew clear around the world and it was all a huge snowball. They had floodlights on the vehicles because the sun had gone out.'

'I was sure I could see the sun still hanging up there,' Harriet put in. 'Like a ball of cinders in the sky. But the guide said no, nobody could see it.'

'How come everybody gets to visit a different kind of the end of the world?' Henry asked. 'You'd think there'd be only one kind of end of the world. I mean, it ends, and this is how it ends, and there can't be more than one way.'

'Could it be a fake?' Stan asked. Everybody turned around and looked at him. Nick's face got very red. Fran looked so mean that Eddie let go of Cynthia and started to rub Fran's shoulders. Stan shrugged. 'I'm not suggesting it is,' he said defensively. 'I was just wondering.'

'Seemed pretty real to me,' said Tom. 'The sun burned out. A big ball of ice. The atmosphere, you know, frozen. The end of the goddamned world.'

The telephone rang. Ruby went to answer it. Nick asked Paula about lunch on Tuesday. She said yes. 'Let's meet at the motel,' he said, and she grinned. Eddie was making out with Cynthia again. Henry looked very stoned and was having trouble staying awake. Phil and Isabel arrived. They heard

Tom and Fran talking about their trips to the end of the world and Isabel said she and Phil had gone only the day before yesterday. 'Goddamn,' Tom said, 'everybody's doing it! What was your trip like?'

Ruby came back into the room. 'That was my sister calling from Fresno to say she's safe. Fresno wasn't hit by the earthquake at all.'

'Earthquake?' Paula said.

'In California,' Mike told her. 'This afternoon. You didn't know? Wiped out most of Los Angeles and ran right up the coast practically to Monterey. They think it was on account of the underground bomb test in the Mohave Desert.'

'California's always having such awful disasters,' Marcia said.

'Good thing those amoebas got loose back east,' said Nick.

'Imagine how complicated it would be if they had them in L.A. now too.'

'They will,' Tom said. 'Two to one they reproduce by airborne spores.'

'Like the typhoid germs last November,' Jane said.

'That was typhus,' Nick corrected.

'Anyway,' Phil said, 'I was telling Tom and Fran about what we saw at the end of the world. It was the sun going nova. They showed it very cleverly, too. I mean, you can't actually sit around and *experience* it, on account of the heat and the hard radiation and all. But they give it to you in a peripheral way, very elegant in the McLuhanesque sense of the word. First they take you to a point about two hours before the blowup, right? It's I don't know how many jillion years from now, but a long way, anyhow, because the trees are all different, they've got blue scales and ropy branches, and the animals are like things with one leg that jump on pogo sticks —'

'Oh, I don't *believe* that,' Cynthia drawled.

Phil ignored her gracefully. 'And we didn't see any sign of human beings, not a house, not a telephone pole, nothing, so I suppose we must have been extinct a long time before. Anyway, they let us look at that for a while. Not getting out of our time machine, naturally, because they said the atmosphere was wrong. Gradually the sun started to puff up. We were nervous – weren't we, Iz? – I mean, suppose they miscalculated things? This whole trip is a very new concept and things might go wrong. The sun was getting bigger and bigger, and then this thing like an arm seemed to pop out of its left side, a big fiery arm reaching out across space, getting closer and closer. We saw it through smoked glass, like you do an eclipse. They gave us about two minutes of the explosion, and we could feel it getting hot already. Then we jumped a couple of years forward in time. The sun was back to its regular shape, only it was smaller, sort of like a little white sun instead of a big yellow one. And on Earth everything was ashes.'

'Ashes,' Isabel said, with emphasis.

'It looked like Detroit after the union nuked Ford,' Phil said. 'Only much, much worse. Whole mountains were melted. The oceans were dried up. Everything was ashes.' He shuddered and took a joint from Mike. 'Isabel was crying.'

'The things with one leg,' Isabel said. 'I mean, they must have all been wiped *out*.' She began to sob. Stan comforted her. 'I wonder why it's a different way for everyone who goes,' he said. 'Freezing. Or the oceans. Or the sun blowing up. Or the thing Nick and Jane saw.'

'I'm convinced that each of us had a genuine experience in the far future,' said Nick. He felt he had to regain control of the group somehow. It had been so good when he was telling his story, before those others had come. 'That is to say, the world suffers a variety of natural calamities, it doesn't just have *one* end of the world, and they keep mixing things up and sending people to different catastrophes. But never for a moment did I doubt that I was seeing an authentic event.'

'We have to do it,' Ruby said to Mike. 'It's only three hours. What about calling them first thing Monday and making an appointment for Thursday night?'

'Monday's the President's funeral,' Tom pointed out. 'The travel agency will be closed.'

'Have they caught the assassin yet?' Fran asked.

'They didn't mention it on the four o'clock news,' said Stan. 'I guess he'll get away like the last one.'

'Beats me why anybody wants to be President,' Phil said.

Mike put on some music. Nick danced with Paula. Eddie danced with Cynthia. Henry was asleep. Dave, Paula's husband, was on crutches because of his mugging and he asked Isabel to sit and talk with him. Tom danced with Harriet even though he was married to her. She hadn't been out of the hospital more than a few months after the transplant and he treated her extremely tenderly. Mike danced with Fran. Phil danced with Jane. Stan danced with Marcia. Ruby cut in on Eddie and Cynthia. Afterwards Tom danced with Jane and Phil danced with Paula. Mike and Ruby's little girl woke up and came out to say hello. Mike sent her back to bed. Far away there was the sound of an explosion. Nick danced with Paula again, but he didn't want her to get bored with him before Tuesday, so he excused himself and went to talk with Dave. Dave handled most of Nick's investments. Ruby said to Mike, 'The day after the funeral, will you call the travel agent?' Mike said he would, but Tom said somebody would probably shoot the new President too and there'd be another funeral. These funerals were demolishing the gross national product, Stan observed, on account of how everything had to close all the time. Nick saw Cynthia wake Henry up and ask him sharply if he would take her on the end-of-the-world trip. Henry looked embarrassed. His factory had been blown up at Christmas in a peace demonstration and everybody knew he was in bad shape financially. 'You can *charge* it,' Cynthia said, her fierce voice carrying above the chitchat. 'And it's so *beautiful,* Henry. The ice. Or the sun exploding. I want to go.'

'Lou and Janet were going to be here tonight too,' Ruby said to Paula. 'But their younger boy came back from Texas with that new kind of cholera and they had to cancel.'

Phil said, 'I understand that one couple saw the moon come apart. It got too close to the Earth and split into chunks and the chunks fell like meteors. Smashing everything up, you know. One big piece nearly hit their time machine.'

'I wouldn't have liked that at all,' Marcia said.

'Our trip was very lovely,' said Jane. 'No violent things at all. Just the big red sun and the tide and that crab creeping along the beach. We were both deeply moved.'

'It's amazing what science can accomplish nowadays,' Fran said.

Mike and Ruby agreed they would try to arrange a trip to the end of the world as soon as the funeral was over. Cynthia drank too much and got sick. Phil, Tom, and Dave discussed the stock market. Harriet told Nick about her operation. Isabel flirted with Mike, tugging her neckline lower. At midnight someone turned on the news. They had some shots of the earthquake and a warning about boiling your water if you lived in the affected states. The President's widow was shown visiting the last President's widow to get some pointers for the funeral. Then there was an interview with an executive of the time-trip company. 'Business is phenomenal,' he said. 'Time-tripping will be the nation's number one growth industry next year.' The reporter asked him if his company would soon be offering something besides the end-of-the-world trip. 'Later on, we hope to,' the executive said. 'We plan to apply for Congressional approval soon. But meanwhile the demand for our present offering is running very high. You can't imagine. Of course, you have to expect apocalyptic stuff to attain immense popularity in times like these.' The reporter said, 'What do you mean, times like these?' but as the time-trip man started to reply, he was interrupted by the commercial. Mike shut off the set. Nick discovered that he was extremely depressed. He decided that it was because so many of his friends had made the journey, and he had thought he and Jane were the only ones who had. He found himself standing next to Marcia and tried to describe the way the crab had moved, but Marcia only shrugged. No one was talking about time-trips now. The party had moved beyond that point. Nick and Jane left quite early and went right to sleep, without making love. The next morning the Sunday paper wasn't delivered because of the Bridge Authority strike, and the radio said that the mutant amoebas were proving harder to eradicate than originally anticipated. They were spreading into Lake Superior and everyone in the region would have to boil all drinking water. Nick and Jane discussed where they would go for their next vacation. 'What about going to see the end of the world all over again?' Jane suggested, and Nick laughed quite a good deal.

GOAT SONG

Anderson, somehow, breaks the rules I set up so easily. I said that science-fiction writers rarely write good fantasies, particularly if they are writers of hard science fiction; and that fantasy writers rarely write good science fiction. Yet here comes Poul Anderson, who does both with equal skill. He can write a science-fiction story of the hardest variety as well as anyone, and he can write a fantasy of the most soaring type as well as anyone.

And do I say, as I do in the introduction, that the essential fact of the present is change and that science fiction is the literature of change and that any form of literature that does not take change into account is irrelevant?

Well, all that is so, but Anderson can take up the thesis that some things don't change and that when we have covered ourselves with all the glitter of a mechanized future, we can still probe deeply and come up with the human condition once again as it always was.

Anyway, come and listen once again to the old Greek tale of the master-musician and his lost love, and remember that 'Goat Song' in Greek is 'tragoidia', which we pronounce 'tragedy'.

GOAT SONG

Poul Anderson

Three women: one is dead; one is alive; One is both and neither, and will never live and never die, being immortal in SUM.

On a hill above that valley through which runs the high-road, I await Her passage. Frost came early this year, and the grasses have paled. Otherwise the slope is begrown with blackberry bushes that have been harvested by men and birds, leaving only briars, and with certain apple trees. They are very old, those trees, survivors of an orchard raised by generations which none but SUM now remembers (I can see a few fragments of wall thrusting above the brambles) – scattered crazily over the hill-side and as crazily gnarled. A little fruit remains on them. Chill across my skin, a gust shakes loose an apple. I hear it knock on the earth, another stroke of some eternal clock. The shrubs whisper to the wind.

Elsewhere the ridges around me are wooded, afire with scarlets and brasses and bronzes. The sky is huge, the westering sun wan-bright. The valley is filling with a deeper blue, a haze whose slight smokiness touches my nostrils. This is Indian summer, the funeral pyre of the year.

There have been other seasons. There have been other life-times, before mine and hers; and in those days they had words to sing with. We still allow ourselves music, though, and I have spent much time planting melodies around my rediscovered words. '*In the greenest growth of the Maytime* —' I unsling the harp on my back, and tune it afresh, and sing to her, straight into autumn and the waning day.

 Nebula Award, Best Novelette 1972

'– *You came, and the sun came after,*
    And the green grew golden above;
  And the flag-flowers lightened with laughter,
    And the meadowsweet shook with love.'

A footfall stirs the grasses, quite gently, and the woman says, trying to chuckle, 'Why, thank you.'

Once, so soon after my one's death that I was still dazed by it, I stood in the home that had been ours. This was on the hundred-and-first floor of a most desirable building. After dark the city flamed for us, blinked, glittered, flung immense sheets of radiance forth like banners. Nothing but SUM could have controlled the firefly dance of a million aircars among the towers: or, for that matter, have maintained the entire city, from nuclear powerplants through automated factories, physical and economic distribution networks, sanitation, repair, services, education, culture, order, everything as one immune immortal organism. We had gloried in belonging to this as well as to each other.

But that night I told the kitchen to throw the dinner it had made for me down the waste chute, and ground under my heel the chemical consolations which the medicine cabinet extended to me, and kicked the cleaner as it picked up the mess, and ordered the lights not to go on, anywhere in our suite. I stood by the vieWall, looking out across megalopolis, and it was tawdry. In my hands I had a little clay figure she had fashioned herself. I turned it over and over and over.

But I had forgotten to forbid the door to admit visitors. It recognized this woman and opened for her. She had come with the kindly intention of teasing me out of a mood that seemed to her unnatural. I heard her enter, and looked around through the gloom. She had almost the same height as my girl did, and her hair chanced to be bound in a way that my girl often favoured, and the figurine dropped from my grasp and shattered, because for an instant I thought she was my girl. Since then I have been hard put not to hate Thrakia.

This evening, even without so much sundown light, I would not make that mistake. Nothing but the silvery bracelet about her left wrist bespeaks the past we share. She is in wildcountry garb: boots, kilt of true fur and belt of true leather, knife at hip and rifle slung on shoulder. Her locks are matted and snarled, her skin brown from weeks of weather; scratches and smudges show beneath the fantastic zigzags she has painted in many colours on herself. She wears a necklace of bird skulls.

How that one who is dead was, in her own way, more a child of trees and horizons than Thrakia's followers. She was so much at home in the open that she had no need to put off clothes or cleanliness, reason or gentleness, when we sickened of the cities and went forth beyond them. From this trait I got many of the names I bestowed on her, such as Wood's Colt or Fallow Hind or, from my prowlings among ancient books, Dryad and Elven. (She liked me to choose her names, and this pleasure had no end, because she was inexhaustible.)

I let my harpstring ring into silence. Turning about, I say to Thrakia, 'I wasn't singing for you. Not for anyone. Leave me alone.'

She draws a breath. The wind ruffles her hair and brings me an odour of her: not female sweetness, but fear. She clenches her fists and says, 'You're crazy.'

'Wherever did you find a meaningful word like that?' I gibe; for my own pain and – to be truthful – my own fear must strike out at something, and here she stands. 'Aren't you content any longer with "untranquil" or "disequilibrated"?'

'I got it from you,' she says defiantly, 'you and your damned archaic songs. There's another word, "damned". And how it suits you! When are you going to stop this morbidity?'

'And commit myself to a clinic and have my brain laundered nice and sanitary? Not soon, darling.' I use *that* last word aforethought, but she cannot know what scorn and sadness are in it for me, who know that once it could also have been a name for my girl. The official grammar and pronunciation of language is as frozen as every other aspect of our civilization, thanks to electronic recording and neuronic teaching; but meanings shift and glide about like subtle serpents. (O adder that stung my Foalfoot!)

I shrug and say in my driest, most city-technological voice,

'Actually, I'm the practical, non-morbid one. Instead of running away from my emotions – via drugs, or neuroadjustment, or playing at savagery like you, for that matter – I'm about to implement a concrete plan for getting back to the person who made me happy.'

'By disturbing Her on Her way home?'

'Anyone has the right to petition the Dark Queen while She's abroad on earth.'

'But this is past the proper time —'

'No law's involved, just custom. People are afraid to meet Her outside a crowd, a town, bright flat lights. They won't admit it, but they are. So I came here precisely not to be part of a queue. I don't want to speak into a recorder for subsequent computer analysis of my words. How could I be sure She was listening? I want to meet Her as myself, a unique being, and look in Her eyes while I make my prayer.'

Thrakia chokes a little. 'She'll be angry.'

'Is She able to be angry, any more?'

'I . . . I don't know. What you mean to ask for is so impossible, though. So absurd. That SUM should give you back your girl. You know It never makes exceptions.'

'Isn't She Herself an exception?'

'That's different. You're being silly. SUM has to have a, well, a direct human liaison. Emotional and cultural feedback, as well as statistics. How else can It govern rationally? And She must have been chosen out of the whole world. Your girl, what was she? Nobody!'

'To me, she was everybody.'

'You —' Thrakia catches her lip in her teeth. One hand reaches out and closes on my bare forearm, a hard hot touch, the grimy fingernails biting. When I make no response, she lets go and stares at the ground. A V of outbound geese passes overhead. Their cries come shrill through the wind, which is loudening in the forest.

'Well,' she says, 'you are special. You always were. You went to space and came back, with the Great Captain. You're maybe the only man alive who understands about the ancients. And your singing, yes, you don't really entertain, your songs trouble people and can't be forgotten. So maybe She will listen to you. But SUM won't. It can't give special resurrections. Once that was done, a single time, wouldn't it have to be done for everybody? The dead would overrun the living.'

'Not necessarily,' I say. 'In any event, I mean to try.'

'Why can't you wait for the promised time? Surely, then, SUM will re-create you two in the same generation.'

'I'd have to live out this life, at least, without her,' I say, looking away also, down to the highroad which shines through shadow like death's snake, the length of the valley. 'Besides, how do you know there ever will be any resurrections? We have only a promise. No, less than that. An announced policy.'

She gasps, steps back, raises her hands as if to fend me off. Her soul bracelet casts light into my eyes. I recognize an embryo exorcism. She lacks ritual; every 'superstition' was patiently scrubbed out of our metal-and-energy world, long ago. But if she has no word for it, no concept, nevertheless she recoils from blasphemy.

So I say, wearily, not wanting an argument, wanting only to wait here alone: 'Never mind. There could be some natural catastrophe, like a giant asteroid striking, that wiped out the system before conditions had become right for resurrections to commence.'

'That's impossible,' she says, almost frantic. 'The homeostats, the repair functions —'

'All right, call it a vanishingly unlikely theoretical contingency. Let's declare that I'm so selfish I want Swallow Wing back now, in this life of mine, and don't give a curse whether that'll be fair to the rest of you.'

You won't care either, anyway, I think. None of you. You don't grieve. It is your own precious private consciousnesses that you wish to preserve; no one else is close enough to you to matter very much. Would you believe me if I told you I am quite prepared to offer SUM my own death in exchange for It releasing Blossom-in-the-Sun?

I don't speak that thought, which would be cruel, nor repeat what is crueller: my fear that SUM lies, that the dead never will be disgorged. For (I am not the All-Controller, I think not with vacuum and negative energy levels but with ordinary earth-begotten molecules; yet I can reason somewhat dispassionately, being disillusioned) consider —

The object of the game is to maintain a society stable, just, and sane. This requires satisfaction not only of somatic, but of symbolic and instinctual needs. Thus children must be allowed to come into being. The minimum number per generation is equal to the maximum: that number which will maintain a constant population.

It is also desirable to remove the fear of death from men. Hence the promise: At such time as it is socially feasible, SUM will begin to refashion us, with our complete memories but in the pride of our youth. This can be done over and over, life after life across the millennia. So death is, indeed, a sleep.

– in that sleep of death, what dreams may come — No. I myself dare not dwell on this. I ask merely, privately: Just when and how does SUM expect conditions (in a stabilized society, mind you) to have become so different from today's that the reborn can, in their millions, safely be welcomed back?

I see no reason why SUM should not lie to us. We, too, are objects in the world that It manipulates.

'We've quarrelled about this before, Thrakia,' I sigh. 'Often. Why do you bother?'

'I wish I knew,' she answers low. Half to herself, she goes on: 'Of course I want to copulate with you. You must be good, the way that girl used to follow you about with her eyes, and smile when she touched your hand, and – But you can't be better than everyone else. That's unreasonable. There are only so many possible ways. So why do I care if you wrap yourself up in silence and go off alone? Is it that that makes you a challenge?'

'You think too much,' I say. 'Even here. You're a pretend primitive. You visit wildcountry to "slake inborn atavastic impulses" . . . but you can't dismantle that computer inside yourself and simply feel, simply be.'

She bristles. I touched a nerve there. Looking past her, along the ridge of fiery maple and sumac, brassy elm and great dun oak, I see others emerge from beneath the trees. Women exclusively, her followers, as unkempt as she; one has a brace of ducks lashed to her waist, and their blood has trickled down her thigh and dried black. For this movement, this unadmitted mystique has become Thrakia's by now: that not only men should forsake the easy routine and the easy pleasure of the cities, and become again, for a few weeks each year, the carnivores who begot our species; women too should seek out starkness, the better to appreciate civilization when they return.

I feel a moment's unease. We are in no park, with laid-out trails and campground services. We are in wildcountry. Not many men come here, ever, and still fewer women; for the region is, literally, beyond the law. No deed done here is punishable. We are told that this helps consolidate society, as the most violent among us may thus vent their passions. But I have spent much time in wildcountry since my Morning Star went out – myself in quest of nothing but solitude – and I have watched what happens through eyes that have also read anthropology and history. Institutions are developing; ceremonies, tribalisms, acts of blood and cruelty and acts elsewhere called unnatural are becoming more elaborate and more expected every year. Then the practitioners go home to their cities and honestly believe they have been enjoying fresh air, exercise, and good tension-releasing fun.

Let her get angry enough and Thrakia can call knives to her aid.

Wherefore I make myself lay both hands on her shoulders, and meet the tormented gaze, and say most gently, 'I'm sorry. I know you mean well. You're afraid She will be annoyed and bring misfortune on your people.'

Thrakia gulps. 'No,' she whispers. 'That wouldn't be logical. But I'm afraid of what might happen to you. And then —' Suddenly she throws herself against me. I feel arms, breasts, belly press through my tunic, and smell meadows in her hair and musk in her mouth. 'You'd be gone!' she wails. 'Then who'd sing to us?'

'Why, the planet's crawling with entertainers,' I stammer.

'You're more than that,' she says. 'So much more. I don't

like what you sing, not really – and what you've sung since that stupid girl died, oh, meaningless, horrible! – but, I don't know why, I *want* you to trouble me.'

Awkward, I pat her back. The sun now stands very little above the treetops. Its rays slant interminably through the booming, frosting air. I shiver in my tunic and buskins and wonder what to do.

A sound rescues me. It comes from one end of the valley below us, where further view is blocked off by two cliffs; it thunders deep in our ears and rolls through the earth into our bones. We have heard that sound in the cities, and been glad to have walls and lights and multitudes around us. Now we are alone with it, the noise of Her chariot.

The women shriek, I hear them faintly across wind and rumble and my own pulse, and they vanish into the woods. They will seek their camp, dress warmly, build enormous fires; presently they will eat their ecstatics, and rumours are uneasy about what they do after that.

Thrakia seizes my left wrist, above the soul bracelet, and hauls. 'Harper, come with me!' she pleads. I break loose from her and stride down the hill towards the road. A scream follows me for a moment.

Light still dwells in the sky and on the ridges, but as I descend into that narrow valley I enter dusk, and it thickens. Indistinct bramblebushes whicker where I brush them, and claw back at me. I feel the occasional scratch on my legs, the tug as my garment is snagged, the chill that I breathe, but dimly. My perceived-outer-reality is overpowered by the rushing of Her chariot and my blood. My inner-universe is fear, yes, but exaltation too, a drunkenness which sharpens instead of dulling the senses, a psychedelia which opens the reasoning mind as well as the emotions; I have gone beyond myself, I am embodied purpose. Not out of need for comfort, but to voice what Is, I return to words whose speaker rests centuries dust, and lend them my own music. I sing:

> '– *Gold is my heart, and the world's golden,*
> *And one peak tipped with light;*

> *And the air lies still about the hill*
>   *With the first fear of night;*
>
> *Till mystery down the soundless valley*
>   *Thunders, and dark is here;*
> *And the wind blows, and the light goes,*
>   *And the night is full of fear.*
>
> *And I know one night, on some far height,*
>   *In the tongue I never knew,*
> *I yet shall hear the tidings clear*
>   *From them that were friends of you.*
>
> *They'll call the news from hill to hill,*
>   *Dark and uncomforted,*
> *Earth and sky and the winds; and I*
>   *Shall know that you are dead —.'*

But I have reached the valley floor, and She has come in sight.

Her chariot is unlit, for radar eyes and inertial guides need no lamps, nor sun nor stars. Wheelless, the steel tear rides on its own roar and thrust of air. The pace is not great, far less than any of our mortals' vehicles are wont to take. Men say the Dark Queen rides thus slowly in order that She may perceive with Her own senses and so be the better prepared to counsel SUM. But now Her annual round is finished; She is homeward bound; until spring She will dwell with It Which is our lord. Why does She not hasten tonight?

Because Death has never a need of haste? I wonder. And as I step into the middle of the road, certain lines from the yet more ancient past rise tremendous within me, and I strike my harp and chant them louder than the approaching car:

> '*I that in heill was and gladness*
>   *Am trublit now with great sickness*
>   *And feblit with infirmitie: —*
>   Timor mortis conturbat me.'

The car detects me and howls a warning. I hold my ground.
The car could swing around, the road is wide and in any event
a smooth surface is not absolutely necessary. But I hope, I
believe that She will be aware of an obstacle in Her path, and
tune in Her various amplifiers, and find me abnormal enough
to stop for. Who, in SUM's world – who, even among the
explorers that It has sent beyond in Its unappeasable hunger
for data – would stand in a cold wild-country dusk and shout
while his harp snarls

> *'Our plesance here is all vain glory,*
> *This fals world is but transitory,*
> *The flesh is bruckle, the Feynd is slee:–*
> Timor mortis conturbat me.
>
> *The state of man does change and vary,*
> *Now sound, now sick, now blyth, now sary,*
> *Now dansand mirry, now like to die:–*
> Timor mortis conturbat me.
>
> *No state in Erd here standis sicker;*
> *As with the wynd wavis the wicker*
> *So wannis this world's vanite:–*
> Timor mortis conturbat me — ?'

The car draws alongside and sinks to the ground. I let my
strings die away into the wind. The sky overhead and in the
west is grey-purple; eastward it is quite dark and a few early
stars peer forth. Here, down in the valley, shadows are heavy
and I cannot see very well.

The canopy slides back. She stands erect in the chariot, thus
looming over me. Her robe and cloak are black, fluttering like
restless wings; beneath the cowl Her face is a white blur. I
have seen it before, under full light, and in how many thousands
of pictures; but at this hour I cannot call it back to my mind,
not entirely. I list sharp-sculptured profile and pale lips, sable
hair and long green eyes, but these are nothing more than
words.

'What are you doing?' She has a lovely low voice; but is it, as oh, how rarely since SUM took Her to Itself, is it the least shaken? 'What is that you were singing?'

My answer comes so strong that my skull resonates; for I am borne higher and higher on my tide. 'Lady of Ours, I have a petition.'

'Why did you not bring it before Me when I walked among men? Tonight I am homebound. You must wait till I ride forth with the new year.'

'Lady of Ours, neither You nor I would wish living ears to hear what I have to say.'

She regards me for a long while. Do I indeed sense fear also in Her? (Surely not of me. Her chariot is armed and armoured, and would react with machine speed to protect Her should I offer violence. And should I somehow, incredibly, kill Her, or wound Her beyond chemosurgical repair, She of all beings has no need to doubt death. The ordinary bracelet cries with quite sufficient radio loudness to be heard by more than one thanatic station, when we die; and in that shielding the soul can scarcely be damaged before the Winged Heels arrive to bear it off to SUM. Surely the Dark Queen's circlet can call still further, and is still better insulated, than any mortal's. And She will most absolutely be re-created. She has been, again and again; death and rebirth every seven years keep Her eternally young in the service of SUM. I have never been able to find out when She was first born.)

Fear, perhaps, of what I have sung and what I might speak?

At last She says — I can scarcely hear through the gusts and creakings in the trees — 'Give me the Ring, then.'

The dwarf robot which stands by Her throne when She sits among men appears beside Her and extends the massive dull-silver circle to me. I place my left arm within, so that my soul is enclosed. The tablet on the upper surface of the Ring, which looks so much like a jewel, slants away from me; I cannot read what flashes on to the bezel. But the faint glow picks Her features out of murk as She bends to look.

Of course, I tell myself, the actual soul is not scanned. That would take too long. Probably the bracelet which contains the soul has an identification code built in. The Ring sends this to an appropriate part of SUM, Which instantly sends back what is recorded under that code. I hope there is nothing more to it. SUM has not seen fit to tell us.

'What do you call yourself at the moment?' She asks.

A current of bitterness crosses my tide. 'Lady of Ours, why should You care? Is not my real name the number I got when I was allowed to be born?'

Calm descends once more upon Her. 'If I am to evaluate properly what you say, I must know more about you than these few official data. Name indicates mood.'

I too feel unshaken again, my tide running so strong and smooth that I might not know I was moving did I not see time recede behind me. 'Lady of Ours, I cannot give You a fair answer. In this past year I have not troubled with names, or with much of anything else. But some people who knew me from earlier days call me Harper.'

'What do you do besides make that sinister music?'

'These days, nothing, Lady of Ours. I've money to live out my life, if I eat sparingly and keep no home. Often I am fed and housed for the sake of my songs.'

'What you sang is unlike anything I have heard since —' Anew, briefly, that robot serenity is shaken. 'Since before the world was stabilized. You should not wake dead symbols, Harper. They walk through men's dreams.'

'Is that bad?'

'Yes. The dreams become nightmares. Remember: mankind, every man who ever lived, was insane before SUM brought order, reason, and peace.'

'Well, then,' I say, 'I will cease and desist if I may have my own dead wakened for me.'

She stiffens. The tablet goes out. I withdraw my arm and the Ring is stored away by Her servant. So again She is faceless, beneath flickering stars, here at the bottom of this shadowed valley. Her voice falls cold as the air: 'No one can be brought back to life before Resurrection Time is ripe.'

I do not say, 'What about You?' for that would be vicious. What did She think, how did She weep, when SUM chose Her of all the young on earth? What does She endure in Her centuries? I dare not imagine.

Instead, I smite my harp and sing, quietly this time:

> '*Strew on her roses, roses,*
>   *And never a spray of yew.*
> *In quiet she reposes:*
>   *Ah! would that I did too.*'

The Dark Queen cries, 'What are you doing? Are you really insane?' I go straight to the last stanza.

> '*Her cabin'd, ample Spirit*
>   *It flutter'd and fail'd for breath.*
> *Tonight it doth inherit*
>   *The vasty hall of Death.*'

I know why my songs strike so hard: because they bear dreads and passions that no one is used to – that most of us hardly know could exist – in SUM's ordered universe. But I had not the courage to hope She would be as torn by them as I see. Has She not lived with more darkness and terror than the ancients themselves could conceive? She calls, 'Who has died?'

'She has many names, Lady of Ours,' I say. 'None was beautiful enough. I can tell You her number, though.'

'Your daughter? . . . sometimes I am asked if a dead child cannot be brought back. Not often, any more, when they go so soon to the crèche. But sometimes. I tell the mother she may have a new one; but if ever We started re-creating dead infants, at what age level could We stop?'

'No, this was my woman.'

'Impossible!' Her tone seeks to be not unkindly but is, instead, well-nigh frantic. 'You will have no trouble finding others. You are handsome, and your psyche is, is, is extraordinary. It burns like Lucifer.'

'Do You remember the name Lucifer, Lady of Ours?' I pounce. 'Then You are old indeed. So old that You must also remember how a man might desire only one woman, but her above the whole world and heaven.'

She tries to defend Herself with a jeer: 'Was that mutual, Harper? I know more of mankind than you do, and surely I am the last chaste woman in existence.'

'Now that she is gone, Lady, yes, perhaps You are. But we – Do You know how she died? We had gone to a wild-country area. A man saw her, alone, while I was off hunting gem rocks to make her a necklace. He approached her. She refused him. He threatened force. She fled. This was desert land, viper land, and she was barefoot. One of them bit her. I did not find her till hours later. By then the poison and the unshaded sun – She died quite soon after she told me what had happened and that she loved me. I could not get her body to chemosurgery in time for normal revival procedures. I had to let them cremate her and take her soul away to SUM.'

'What right have you to demand her back, when no one else can be given their own?'

'The right that I love her, and she loves me. We are more necessary to each other than sun or moon. I do not think You could find another two people of whom this is so, Lady. And is not everyone entitled to claim what is necessary to his life? How else can society be kept whole?'

'You are being fantastic,' She says thinly. 'Let me go.'

No, Lady, I am speaking sober truth. But poor plain words won't serve me. I sing to You because then maybe You will understand.' And I strike my harp anew; but it is more to her than Her that I sing.

'If I had thought thou couldst have died,
    I might not weep for thee;
But I forgot, when by thy side,
    That thou couldst mortal be:
It never through my mind had past
    The time would e'er be o'er,
And I on thee should look my last,
    And thou shouldst smile no more!'

'I cannot —' She falters. 'I did not know – any such feelings – so strong – existed any longer.'

'Now You do, Lady of Ours. And is that not an important datum for SUM?'

'Yes. If true.' Abruptly She leans towards me. I see Her shudder in the murk, under the flapping cloak, and hear Her jaws clatter with cold. 'I cannot linger here. But ride with Me. Sing to Me. I think I can bear it.'

So much have I scarcely expected. But my destiny is upon me. I mount into the chariot. The canopy slides shut and we proceed.

The main cabin encloses us. Behind its rear door must be facilities for her living on earth; this is a big vehicle. But here is little except curved panels. They are true wood of different comely grains: so She also needs periodic escape from our machine existence, does She? Furnishing is scant and austere. The only sound is our passage, muffled to a murmur for us; and, because their photomultipliers are not activated, the scanners show nothing outside but night. We huddle close to a glower, hands extended towards its fieriness. Our shoulders brush, our bare arms, Her skin is soft and Her hair falls loose over the thrown-back cowl, smelling of the summer which is dead. What, is She still human?

After a timeless time, She says, not yet looking at me: 'The thing you sang, there on the highroad as I came near – I do not remember it. Not even from the years before I became what I am.'

'It is older than SUM,' I answer, 'and its truth will outlive It.'

'Truth?' I see Her tense Herself. 'Sing Me the rest.'

My fingers are no longer too numb to call forth chords.

> '– *Unto the Death gois all Estatis,*
> *Princis, Prelattis, and Potestatis,*
> *Baeith rich and poor of all degree:–*
>   Timor mortis conturbat me.
>
> *He takis the knichtis in to the field*
> *Enarmit under helm and scheild;*
> *Victor he is at all mellie:–*
>   Timor mortis conturbat me.

That strong unmerciful tyrand
Takis, on the motheris breast sowkand,
The babe full of benignitie:–
    Timor mortis conturbat me.

He takis the campion in the stour,
The captain closit in the tour,
The ladie in bour full of bewtie:–'

(There I must stop a moment.)

'Timor mortis conturbat me.

He sparis no lord for his piscence.
Na clerk for his intelligence;
His awful straik may no man flee:–
    Timor mortis conturbat me.'

She breaks me off, clapping hands to ears and half shrieking, 'No!'

I, grown unmerciful, pursue Her: 'You understand now, do You not? You are not eternal either. SUM isn't. Not Earth, not sun, not stars. We hid from the truth. Every one of us. I too, until I lost the one thing which made everything make sense. Then I had nothing left to lose, and could look with clear eyes. And what I saw was Death.'

'Get out! Let Me alone!'

'I will not let the whole world alone, Queen, until I get her back. Give me her again, and I'll believe in SUM again. I'll praise It till men dance for joy to hear Its name.'

She challenges me with wildcat eyes. 'Do you think such matters to It?'

'Well,' I shrug, 'songs could be useful. They could help achieve the great objective sooner. Whatever that is. "Optimization of total human activity" – wasn't that the programme? I don't know if it still is. SUM has been adding to Itself so long. I doubt if You Yourself understand Its purposes, Lady of Ours.'

'Don't speak as if It were alive,' She says harshly. 'It is a computer-effector complex. Nothing more.'

'Are You certain?'

'I – Yes. It thinks, more widely and deeply than any human ever did or could; but It is not alive, not aware, It has no consciousness. That is one reason why It decided It needed Me.'

'Be that as it may, Lady,' I tell Her, 'the ultimate result, whatever It finally does with us, lies far in the future. At present I care about that; I worry; I resent our loss of self-determination. But that's because only such abstractions are left to me. Give me back my Lightfoot, and she, not the distant future, will be my concern. I'll be grateful, honestly grateful, and You Two will know it from the songs I then choose to sing. Which, as I said, might be helpful to It.'

'You are unbelievably insolent,' She says without force.

'No, Lady, just desperate,' I say.

The ghost of a smile touches Her lips. She leans back, eyes hooded, and murmurs, 'Well, I'll take you there. What happens then, you realize, lies outside My power. My observations, My recommendations, are nothing but a few items to take into account, among billions. However . . . we have a long way to travel this night. Give me what data you think will help you, Harper.'

I do not finish the Lament. Nor do I dwell in any other fashion on grief. Instead, as the hours pass, I call upon those who dealt with the joy (not the fun, not the short delirium, but the joy) that man and woman might once have of each other.

Knowing where we are bound, I too need such comfort.

And the night deepens, and the leagues fall behind us, and finally we are beyond habitation, beyond wildcountry, in the land where life never comes. By crooked moon and waning starlight I see the plain of concrete and iron, the missiles and energy projectors crouched like beasts, the robot aircraft wheeling aloft: and the lines, the relay towers, the scuttling beetle-shaped carriers, that whole transcendent nerve-blood-sinew by which SUM knows and orders the world. For all the flitting about, for all the forces which seethe, here is altogether

still. The wind itself seems to have frozen to death. Hoarfrost
is grey on the steel shapes. Ahead of us, tiered and mountainous,
begins to appear the castle of SUM.

She Who rides with me does not give sign of noticing that
my songs have died in my throat. What humanness She showed
is departing; Her face is cold and shut, Her voice bears a ring
of metal. She looks straight ahead. But She does speak to me
for a little while yet:

'Do you understand what is going to happen? For the next
half year I will be linked with SUM, integral, another compo-
nent of It. I suppose you will see Me, but that will merely be
My flesh. What speaks to you will be SUM.'

'I know.' The words must be forced forth. My coming this
far is more triumph than any man in creation before me has
won; and I am here to do battle for my Dancer-on-Moonglades;
but none the less my heart shakes me, and is loud in my skull,
and my sweat stinks.

I manage, though, to add: 'You *will* be a part of It, Lady of
Ours. That gives me hope.'

For an instant She turns to me, and lays Her hand across
mine, and something makes Her again so young and untaken
that I almost forget the girl who died; and she whispers, 'If
you knew how I hope!'

The instant is gone, and I am alone among machines.

We must stop before the castle gate. The wall looms sheer
above, so high and high that it seems to be toppling upon me
against the westward march of the stars, so black and black
that it does not only drink down every light, it radiates blind-
ness. Challenge and response quiver on electronic bands I
cannot sense. The outer-guardian parts of It have perceived
a mortal aboard this craft. A missile launcher swings about to
aim its three serpents at me. But the Dark Queen answers –
She does not trouble to be peremptory – and the castle opens
its jaws for us.

We descend. Once, I think, we cross a river. I hear a rushing
and hollow echoing and see droplets glitter where they are cast
on to the viewports and outlined against dark. They vanish at
once: liquid hydrogen, perhaps, to keep certain parts near

absolute zero?

Much later we stop and the canopy slides back. I rise with Her. We are in a room, or cavern, of which I can see nothing, for there is no light except a dull bluish phosphorescence which streams from every solid object, also from Her flesh and mine. But I judge the chamber is enormous, for a sound of great machines at work comes very remotely, as if heard through dream, while our own voices are swallowed up by distance. Air is pumped through, neither warm nor cold, totally without odour, a dead wind.

We descend to the floor. She stands before me, hands crossed on breast, eyes half shut beneath the cowl and not looking at me nor away from me. 'Do what you are told, Harper,' She says in a voice that has never an overtone, 'precisely as you are told.' She turns and departs at an even pace. I watch Her go until I can no longer tell Her luminosity from the formless swirlings within my own eyeballs.

A claw plucks my tunic. I look down and am surprised to see that the dwarf robot has been waiting for me this whole time. How long a time that was, I cannot tell.

Its squat form leads me in another direction. Weariness crawls upward through me, my feet stumble, my lips tingle, lids are weighted and muscles have each their separate aches. Now and then I feel a jag of fear, but dully. When the robot indicates *Lie down here*, I am grateful.

The box fits me well. I let various wires be attached to me, various needles be injected which lead into tubes. I pay little attention to the machines which cluster and murmur around me. The robot goes away. I sink into blessed darkness.

I wake renewed in body. A kind of shell seems to have grown between my forebrain and the old animal parts. Far away I can feel the horror and hear the screaming and thrashing of my instincts; but awareness is chill, calm, logical. I have also a feeling that I slept for weeks, months, while leaves blew loose and snow fell on the upper world. But this may be wrong, and in no case does it matter. I am about to be judged by SUM.

The little faceless robot leads me off, through murmurous black corridors where the dead wind blows. I unsling my harp and clutch it to me, my sole friend and weapon. So the tranquillity of the reasoning mind which has been decreed for me cannot be absolute. I decide that It simply does not want to be bothered by anguish. (No; wrong; nothing so human-like; It has no desires; beneath that power to reason is nullity.)

At length a wall opens for us and we enter a room where She sits enthroned. The self-radiation of metal and flesh is not apparent here, for light is provided, a featureless white radiance with no apparent source. White, too, is the muted sound of the machines which encompass Her throne. White are Her robe and face. I look away from the multitudinous unwinking scanner eyes, into Hers, but She does not appear to recognize me. Does She even see me? SUM has reached out with invisible fingers of electromagnetic induction and taken Her back into Itself. I do not tremble or sweat – I cannot – but I square my shoulders, strike one plangent chord, and wait for It to speak.

It does, from some invisible place. I recognize the voice It has chosen to use: my own. The overtones, the inflections are true, normal, what I myself would use in talking as one reasonable man to another. Why not? In computing what to do about me, and in programming Itself accordingly, SUM must have used so many billion bits of information that adequate accent is a negligible sub-problem.

No . . . there I am mistaken again . . . SUM does not do things on the basis that I might as well do them as not. This talk with myself is intended to have some effect on me. I do not know what.

'Well,' It says pleasantly, 'you made quite a journey, didn't you? I'm glad. Welcome.'

My instincts bare teeth to hear those words of humanity used by the unfeeling unalive. My logical mind considers replying with an ironic 'Thank you', decides against it, and holds me silent.

'You see,' SUM continues after a moment that whirrs, 'you are unique. Pardon Me if I speak a little bluntly. Your sexual monomania is just one aspect of a generally atavistic, superstition-oriented personality. And yet, unlike the ordinary misfit, you're both strong and realistic enough to cope with the world. This chance to meet you, to analyse you while you rested, has opened new insights for Me on human psycho-physiology. Which may lead to improved techniques for governing it and its evolution.'

'That being so,' I reply, 'give me my reward.'

'Now look here,' SUM says in a mild tone, 'you if anyone should know I'm not omnipotent. I was built originally to help govern a civilization grown too complex. Gradually, as My programme of self-expansion progressed, I took over more and more decision-making functions. They were *given* to Me. People were happy to be relieved of responsibility, and they could see for themselves how much better I was running things than any mortal could. But to this day, My authority depends on a substantial consensus. If I started playing favourites, as by re-creating your girl, well, I'd have troubles.'

'The consensus depends more on awe than on reason,' I say. 'You haven't abolished the gods, You've simply absorbed them into Yourself. If You choose to pass a miracle for me, your prophet singer – and I will be Your prophet if You do this – why, that strengthens the faith of the rest.'

'So you think. But your opinions aren't based on any exact data. The historical and anthropological records from the past before Me are unquantitative. I've already phased them out of the curriculum. Eventually, when the culture's ready for such a move, I'll order them destroyed. They're too misleading. Look what they've done to you.'

I grin into the scanner eyes. 'Instead,' I say, 'people will be encouraged to think that before the world was, was SUM. All right. I don't care, as long as I get my girl back. Pass me a miracle, SUM, and I'll guarantee You a good payment.'

'But I have no miracles. Not in your sense. You know how the soul works. The metal bracelet encloses a pseudovirus, a set of giant protein molecules with taps directly to the blood-stream and nervous system. They record the chromosome pattern, the synapse flash, the permanent changes, everything. At the owner's death, the bracelet is dissected out. The Winged Heels bring it here, and the information contained is trans-

ferred to one of My memory banks. I can use such a record to
guide the growing of a new body in the vats: a young body, on
which the former habits and recollections are imprinted. But
you don't understand the complexity of the process, Harper.
It takes Me weeks, every seven years, and every available biochemical facility, to re-create My human liaison. And the
process isn't perfect, either. The pattern is affected by storage.
You might say that this body and brain you see before you
remembers each death. And those are short deaths. A longer
one – man, use your sense. Imagine.'

I can; and the shield between reason and feeling begins to
crack. I had sung, of my darling dead,

> *'No motion has she now, no force;*
> *She neither hears nor sees;*
> *Roll'd round in earth's diurnal course,*
> *With rocks, and stones, and trees.'*

Peace, at least. But if the memory-storage is not permanent
but circulating; if, within those gloomy caverns of tubes and
wire and outer-space cold, some remnant of her psyche must
flit and flicker, alone, unremembering, aware of nothing but
having lost life – No!

I smite the harp and shout so the room rings: 'Give her back!
Or I'll kill you!'

SUM finds it expedient to chuckle; and, horribly, the smile
is reflected for a moment on the Dark Queen's lips, though
otherwise She never stirs. 'And how do you propose to do
that?' It asks me.

It knows, I know, what I have in mind, so I counter: 'How
do You propose to stop me?'

'No need. You'll be considered a nuisance. Finally someone
will decide you ought to have psychiatric treatment. They'll
query My diagnostic outlet. I'll recommend certain excisions.'

'On the other hand, since You've sifted my mind by now,
and since You know how I've affected people with my songs
– even the Lady yonder, even Her – wouldn't you rather have
me working for You? With words like, "*O taste, and see, how*

gracious the Lord is; blessed is the man that trusteth in Him. O fear the Lord, ye that are his saints: for they that fear Him lack nothing." I can make You into God.'

'In a sense, I already am God.'

'And in another sense not. Not yet.' I can endure no more. 'Why are we arguing? You made Your decision before I woke. Tell me and let me go!'

With an odd carefulness, SUM responds: 'I'm still studying you. No harm in admitting to you, My knowledge of the human psyche is as yet imperfect. Certain areas won't yield to computation. I don't know precisely what you'd do, Harper. If to that uncertainty I added a potentially dangerous precedent —'

'Kill me, then.' Let my ghost wander forever with hers, down in Your cryogenic dreams.

'No, that's also inexpedient. You've made yourself too conspicuous and controversial. Too many people know by now that you went off with the Lady.' Is it possible that, behind steel and energy, a non-existent hand brushes across a shadow face in puzzlement? My heartbeat is thick in the silence.

Suddenly It shakes me with decision: 'The calculated probabilities do favour your keeping your promises and making yourself useful. Therefore I shall grant your request. However —'

I am on my knees. My forehead knocks on the floor until blood runs into my eyes. I hear through stormwinds:

'– testing must continue. Your faith in Me is not absolute; in fact, you're very sceptical of what you call My goodness. Without additional proof of your willingness to trust Me, I can't let you have the kind of importance which your getting your dead back from Me would give you. Do you understand?'

The question does not sound rhetorical. 'Yes,' I sob.

'Well, then,' says my civilized, almost amiable voice, 'I computed that you'd react much as you have done, and prepared for the likelihood. Your woman's body was recreated while you lay under study. The data which make personality are now being fed back into her neurones. She'll be ready to leave this place by the time you do.

'I repeat, though, there has to be a testing. The procedure is also necessary for its effect on you. If you're to be My prophet, you'll have to work pretty closely with Me; you'll have to undergo a great deal of reconditioning; this night we begin the process. Are you willing?'

'Yes, yes, yes, what must I do?'

'Only this: follow the robot out. At some point, she, your woman, will join you. She'll be conditioned to walk so quietly you can't hear her. Don't look back. Not once, until you're in the upper world. A single glance behind you will be an act of rebellion against Me, and a datum indicating you can't really be trusted . . . and that ends everything. Do you understand?'

'Is that all?' I cry. 'Nothing more?'

'It will prove more difficult than you think,' SUM tells me. My voice fades, as if into illimitable distances: 'Farewell, worshipper.'

The robot raises me to my feet. I stretch out my arms to the Dark Queen. Half blinded with tears, I none the less see that She does not see me. 'Goodbye,' I mumble, and let the robot lead me away.

Our walking is long through those mirk miles. At first I am in too much of a turmoil, and later too stunned, to know where or how we are bound. But later still, slowly, I become aware of my flesh and clothes and the robot's alloy, glimmering blue in blackness. Sounds and smells are muffled; rarely does another machine pass by, unheeding of us. (What work does SUM have for them?) I am so careful not to look behind me that my neck grows stiff.

Though it is not prohibited, is it, to lift my harp past my shoulder, in the course of strumming a few melodies to keep up my courage, and see if perchance a following illumination is reflected in this polished wood?

Nothing. Well, her second birth must take time – O SUM, be careful of her! – and then she must be led through many tunnels, no doubt, before she makes rendezvous with my back. Be patient, Harper.

Sing. Welcome her home. No, these hollow spaces swallow all music; and she is as yet in that trance of death from which only the sun and my kiss can wake her; if, indeed, she has joined me yet. I listen for other footfalls than my own.

Surely we haven't much further to go. I ask the robot, but of course I get no reply. Make an estimate. I know about how fast the chariot travelled coming down . . . The trouble is, time does not exist here. I have no day, no stars, no clock but my heartbeat and I have lost the count of that. Nevertheless, we must come to the end soon. What purpose would be served by walking me through this labyrinth till I die?

Well, if I am totally exhausted at the outer gate, I won't make undue trouble when I find no Rose-in-Hand behind me.

No, now that's ridiculous. If SUM didn't want to heed my plea, It need merely say so. I have no power to inflict physical damage on Its parts.

Of course, It might have plans for me. It did speak of reconditioning. A series of shocks, culminating in that last one, could make me ready for whatever kind of gelding It intends to do.

Or It might have changed Its mind. Why not? It was quite frank about an uncertainty factor in the human psyche. It may have re-evaluated the probabilities and decided: better not to serve my desire.

Or It may have tried and failed. It admitted the recording process is imperfect. I must not expect quite the Gladness I knew; she will always be a little haunted. At best. But suppose the tank spawned a body with no awareness behind the eyes? Or a monster? Suppose, at this instant, I am being followed by a half rotten corpse?

No! Stop that! SUM would know, and take corrective measures.

Would It? *Can It?*

I comprehend how this passage through night, where I never look to see what follows me, how this is an act of sub-mission and confession. I am saying, with my whole existent being, that SUM is all-powerful, all-wise, all-good. To SUM I offer the love I came to win back. Oh, It looked more deeply into me than ever I did myself.

But I shall not fail.

Will SUM, though? If there has indeed been some grisly error . . . let me not find it out under the sky. Let her, my only, not. For what then shall we do? Could I lead her here again, knock on the iron gate, and cry, 'Master, You have given me a thing unfit to exist. Destroy it and start over? —' For what might the wrongness be? Something so subtle, so pervasive, that it does not show in any way save my slow, resisted discovery that I embrace a zombie? Doesn't it make better sense to look – make certain while she is yet drowsy with death – use the whole power of SUM to correct what may be awry?

No, SUM wants me to believe that It makes no mistakes. I agreed to that price. And to much else . . . I don't know how much else, I am daunted to imagine, but that word 'recondition' is ugly. . . . Does not my woman have some rights in the matter too? Shall we not at least ask her if she wants to be the wife of a prophet; shall we not, hand in hand, ask SUM what the price of her life is to her?

Was that a footfall? Almost, I whirl about. I check myself and stand shaking; names of hers break from my lips. The robot urges me on.

Imagination. It wasn't her step. I am alone. I will always be alone.

The halls wind upwards. Or as I think; I have grown too weary for much kinesthetic sense. We cross the sounding river and I am bitten to the bone by the cold which blows upward around the bridge, and I may not turn about to offer the naked newborn woman my garment. I lurch through endless chambers where machines do meaningless things. She hasn't seen them before. Into what nightmare has she risen; and why don't I, who wept into her dying senses that I loved her, why don't I look at her, why don't I speak?

Well, I could talk to her. I could assure the puzzled mute dead that I have come to lead her back into sunlight. Could I not? I ask the robot. It does not reply. I cannot remember if I may speak to her. If indeed I was ever told. I stumble forward.

I crash into a wall and fall bruised. The robot's claw closes on my shoulder. Another arm gestures. I see a passageway, very long and narrow, through the stone. I will have to crawl through. At the end, at the end, the door is swinging wide. The dear real dusk of Earth pours through into this darkness. I am blinded and deafened.

Do I hear her cry out? Was that the final testing; or was my own sick, shaken mind betraying me; or is there a destiny which, like SUM with us, makes tools of suns and SUM? I don't know. I know only that I turned, and there she stood. Her hair flowed long, loose, past the remembered face from which the trance was just departing, on which the knowing and the love of me had just awakened – flowed down over the body that reached forth arms, that took one step to meet me and was halted.

The great grim robot at her own back takes her to it. I think it sends lightning through her brain. She falls. It bears her away.

My guide ignores my screaming. Irresistible, it thrusts me out through the tunnel. The door clangs in my face. I stand before the wall which is like a mountain. Dry snow hisses across concrete. The sky is bloody with dawn; stars still gleam in the west, and arc lights are scattered over the twilit plain of the machines.

Presently I go dumb. I become almost calm. What is there left to have feelings about? The door is iron, the wall is stone fused into one basaltic mass. I walk some distance off into the wind, turn around, lower my head and charge. Let my brains be smeared across Its gate; the pattern will be my hieroglyphic for hatred.

I am seized from behind. The force that stops me must needs be bruisingly great. Released, I crumple to the ground before a machine with talons and wings. My voice from it says, 'Not here. I'll carry you to a safe place.'

'What more can You do to me?' I croak.

'Release you. You won't be restrained or molested on any orders of Mine.'

'Why not?'

'Obviously you're going to appoint yourself My enemy forever. This is an unprecedented situation, a valuable chance to collect data.'

'You tell me this, You warn me, deliberately?'

'Of course. My computation is that these words will have the effect of provoking your utmost effort.'

'You won't give her again? You don't want my love?'

'Not under the circumstances. Too uncontrollable. But your hatred should, as I say, be a useful experimental tool.'

'I'll destroy You,' I say.

It does not deign to speak further. Its machine picks me up and flies off with me. I am left on the fringes of a small town further south. Then I go insane.

I do not much know what happens during that winter, nor care. The blizzards are too loud in my head. I walk the ways of Earth, among lordly towers, under neatly groomed trees, into careful gardens, over bland, bland campuses. I am unwashed, uncombed, unbarbered; my tatters flap about me and my bones are near thrusting through the skin; folk do not like to meet these eyes sunken so far into this skull, and perhaps for that reason they give me to eat. I sing to them.

> *'From the hag and hungry goblin*
> *That into rags would rend ye*
> *And the spirit that stan' by the naked man*
> *In the Book of Moons defend ye!*
> *That of your five sound senses*
> *You never be forsaken*
> *Nor travel from yourselves with Tom*
> *Abroad to beg your bacon.'*

Such things perturb them, do not belong in their chrome-edged universe. So I am often driven away with curses, and sometimes I must flee those who would arrest me and scrub my brain smooth. An alley is a good hiding place, if I can find one in the oldest part of a city; I crouch there and yowl with the cats. A forest is also good. My pursuers dislike to enter any place where any wildness lingers.

But some feel otherwise. They have visited parklands, preserves, actual wildcountry. Their purpose was over-conscious – measured, planned savagery, and a clock to tell them when they must go home – but at least they are not afraid of silences and unlighted nights. As spring returns, certain among them begin to follow me. They are merely curious, at first. But slowly, month by month, especially among the young ones, my madness begins to call to something in them.

> *'With an host of furious fancies*
> *Whereof I am commander*
> *With a burning spear, and a horse of air,*
> *To the wilderness I wander.*
> *By a knight of ghosts and shadows*
> *I summoned am to tourney*
> *Ten leagues beyond the wide world's edge.*
> *Methinks it is no journey.'*

They sit at my feet and listen to me sing. They dance, crazily, to my harp. The girls bend close, tell me how I fascinate them, invite me to copulate. This I refuse, and when I tell them why they are puzzled, a little frightened maybe, but often they strive to understand.

For my rationality is renewed with the hawthorn blossoms. I bathe, have my hair and beard shorn, find clean raiment and take care to eat what my body needs. Less and less do I rave before anyone who will listen; more and more do I seek solitude, quietness, under the vast wheel of the stars, and think.

What is man? Why is man? We have buried such questions; we have sworn they are dead – that they never really existed, being devoid of empirical meaning – and we have dreaded that they might raise the stones we heaped on them, rise and walk the world again of nights. Alone, I summon them to me. They cannot hurt their fellow dead, among whom I now number myself.

I sing to her who is gone. The young people hear and wonder. Sometimes they weep.

> *'Fear no more the heat o' the sun,*
> *Nor the furious winter's rages;*
> *Thou thy worldly task hast done,*

> *Home art gone, and ta'en thy wages:*
> *Golden lads and girls all must,*
> *As chimney-sweepers, come to dust.'*

'But this is not so!' they protest. 'We will die and sleep a while, and then we will live forever in SUM.'

I answer as gently as may be: 'No. Remember I went there. So I know you are wrong. And even if you were right, it would not be right that you should be right.'

'What?'

'Don't you see, it is not right that a thing should be the lord of man. It is not right that we should huddle through our whole lives in fear of finally losing them. You are not parts in a machine, and you have better ends than helping the machine run smoothly.'

I dismiss them and stride off, solitary again, into a canyon where a river clangs, or on to some gaunt mountain peak. No revelation is given me. I climb and creep towards the truth.

Which is that SUM must be destroyed, not in revenge, not in hate, not in fear, simply because the human spirit cannot exist in the same reality as It.

But what, then, is our proper reality? And how shall we attain to it?

I return with my songs to the lowlands. Word about me has gone widely. They are a large crowd who follow me down the highroad until it has changed into a street.

'The Dark Queen will soon come to these parts,' they tell me. 'Abide till She does. Let Her answer those questions you put to us, which make us sleep so badly.'

'Let me retire to prepare myself,' I say. I go up a long flight of steps. The people watch from below, dumb with awe, till I vanish. Such few as were in the building depart. I walk down vaulted halls, through hushed high-ceilinged rooms full of tables, among shelves made massive by books. Sunlight slants dusty through the windows.

The half memory has plagued me of late: once before, I know not when, this year of mine also took place. Perhaps in this library I can find the tale that – casually, I suppose, in my abnormal childhood – I read. For man is older than SUM: wiser, I swear; his myths hold more truth than Its mathematics. I spend three days and most of three nights in my search. There is scant sound but the rustling of leaves between my hands. Folk place offerings of food and drink at the door. They tell themselves they do so out of pity, or curiosity, or to avoid the nuisance of having me die in an unconventional fashion. But I know better.

At the end of the three days I am little further along. I have too much material; I keep going off on sidetracks of beauty and fascination. (Which SUM means to eliminate.) My education was like everyone else's, science, rationality, good sane adjustment. (SUM writes our curricula, and the teaching machines have direct connections to It.) Well, I can make some of my lopsided training work for me. My reading has given me sufficient clues to prepare a search program. I sit down before an information retrieval console and run my fingers across its keys. They make a clattery music.

Electron beams are swift hounds. Within seconds the screen lights up with words, and I read who I am.

It is fortunate that I am a fast reader. Before I can press the Clear button, the unreeling words are wiped out. For an instant the screen quivers with formlessness, then appears.

I HAD NOT CORRELATED THESE DATA WITH THE FACTS CONCERNING YOU. THIS INTRODUCES A NEW AND INDETERMINATE QUANTITY INTO THE COMPUTATIONS.

The nirvana which has come upon me (yes, I found that word among the old books, and how portentous it is) is not passiveness, it is a tide more full and strong than that which bore me down to the Dark Queen those ages apast in wildcountry, I say, as coolly as may be, 'An interesting coincidence. If it is a coincidence.' Surely sonic receptors are emplaced hereabouts.

EITHER THAT, OR A CERTAIN NECESSARY CONSEQUENCE OF THE LOGIC OF EVENTS.

The vision dawning within me is so blinding bright that I cannot refrain from answering, 'Or a destiny, SUM?'

MEANINGLESS. MEANINGLESS. MEANINGLESS.

'Now why did You repeat Yourself in that way? Once would have sufficed. Thrice, though, makes an incantation. Are You by any chance hoping Your words will make me stop existing?'

I DO NOT HOPE. YOU ARE AN EXPERIMENT. IF I COMPUTE A SIGNIFICANT PROBABILITY OF YOUR CAUSING SERIOUS DISTURBANCE, I WILL HAVE YOU TERMINATED.

I smile. 'SUM,' I say, 'I am going to terminate You.' I lean over and switch off the screen. I walk out into the evening.

Not everything is clear to me yet, that I must say and do. But enough is that I can start preaching at once to those who have been waiting for me. As I talk, others come down the street, and hear, and stay to listen. Soon they number in the hundreds.

I have no immense new truth to offer them: nothing that I have not said before, although piecemeal and unsystematically; nothing they have not felt themselves, in the innermost darknesses of their beings. Today, however, knowing who I am and therefore why I am, I can put these things in words. Speaking quietly, now and then drawing on some forgotten song to show my meaning, I tell them how sick and starved their lives are; how they have made themselves slaves; how the enslavement is not even to a conscious mind, but to an insensate inanimate thing which their own ancestors began; how that thing is not the centrum of existence, but a few scraps of metal and bleats of energy, a few sad stupid patterns, adrift in unbounded space-time. Put not your faith in SUM, I tell them. SUM is doomed, even as you and I. Seek out mystery; what else is the whole cosmos but mystery? Live bravely, die and be done, and you will be more than any machine. You may perhaps be God.

They grow tumultuous. They shout replies, some of which are animal howls. A few are for me, most are opposed. That doesn't matter. I have reached into them, my music is being played on their nervestrings, and this is my entire purpose.

The sun goes down behind the buildings. Dusk gathers. The city remains unilluminated. I soon realize why. She is coming, the Dark Queen Whom they wanted me to debate with. From afar we hear Her chariot thunder. Folk wail in terror. They are not wont to do that either. They used to disguise their feelings from Her and themselves by receiving Her with grave sparse ceremony. Now they would flee if they dared. I have lifted the masks.

The chariot halts in the street. She dismounts, tall and shadowy cowled. The people make way before Her like water before a shark. She climbs the stairs to face me. I see for the least instant that Her lips are not quite firm and Her eyes abrim with tears. She whispers, too low for anyone else to hear, 'Oh, Harper, I'm sorry.'

'Come join me,' I invite. 'Help me set the world free.'

'No. I cannot. I have been too long with It.' She straightens. Imperium descends upon Her. Her voice rises for everyone to hear. The little television robots flit close, bat shapes in the twilight, that the whole planet may witness my defeat. 'What is this freedom you rant about?' She demands.

'To feel,' I say. 'To venture. To wonder. To become men again.'

'To become beasts, you mean. Would you demolish the machines that keep us alive?'

'Yes. We must. Once they were good and useful, but we let them grow upon us like a cancer, and now nothing but destruction and a new beginning can save us.'

'Have you considered the chaos?'

'Yes. It too is necessary. We will not be men without the freedom to know suffering. In it is also enlightenment. Through it we travel beyond ourselves, beyond earth and stars, space and time, to Mystery.'

'So you maintain that there is some undefined ultimate vagueness behind the measurable universe?' She smiles into the bat eyes. We have each been taught, as children, to laugh on hearing sarcasms of this kind. 'Please offer me a little proof.'

'No,' I say. 'Prove to me instead, beyond any doubt, that there is *not* something we cannot understand with words and equations. Prove to me likewise that I have no right to seek for it.

'The burden of proof is on You Two, so often have You lied

to us. In the name of rationality, You resurrected myth. The better to control us! In the name of liberation, You chained our inner lives and castrated our souls. In the name of service, You bound and blinkered us. In the name of achievement, You held us to a narrower round than any swine in its pen. In the name of beneficence, You created pain, and horror, and darkness beyond darkness.' I turn to the people. 'I went there. I descended into the cellars. I know!'

'He found that SUM would not pander to his special wishes, at the expense of everyone else,' cries the Dark Queen. Do I hear shrillness in Her voice? 'Therefore he claims SUM is cruel.'

'I saw my dead,' I tell them. 'She will not rise again. Nor yours, nor you. Not ever. SUM will not, cannot raise us. In Its house is death indeed. We must seek life and rebirth elsewhere, among the mysteries.'

She laughs aloud and points to my soul bracelet, glimmering faintly in the grey-blue thickening twilight. Need She say anything?

'Will someone give me a knife and an axe?' I ask.

The crowd stirs and mumbles. I smell their fear. Street lamps go on, as if they could scatter more than this corner of the night which is rolling upon us. I fold my arms and wait. The Dark Queen says something to me. I ignore Her.

The tools pass from hand to hand. He who brings them up the stairs comes like a flame. He kneels at my feet and lifts what I have desired. The tools are good ones, a broad-bladed hunting knife and a long double-bitted axe.

Before the world, I take the knife in my right hand and slash beneath the bracelet on my left wrist. The connections to my inner body are cut. Blood flows, impossibly brilliant under the lamps. It does not hurt; I am too exalted.

The Dark Queen shrieks. 'You meant it! Harper, Harper!'

'There is no life in SUM,' I say. I pull my hand through the circle and cast the bracelet down so it rings.

A voice of brass: '*Arrest that maniac for correction. He is deadly dangerous.*'

The monitors who have stood on the fringes of the crowd

try to push through. They are resisted. Those who seek to help them encounter fists and fingernails.

I take the axe and smash downward. The bracelet crumples. The organic material within, starved of my secretions, exposed to the night air, withers.

I raise the tools, axe in right hand, knife in bleeding left. 'I seek eternity where it is to be found,' I call. 'Who goes with me?'

A score or better break loose from the riot, which is already calling forth weapons and claiming lives. They surround me with their bodies. Their eyes are the eyes of prophets. We make haste to seek a hiding place, for one military robot has appeared and others will not be long in coming. The tall engine strides to stand guard over Our Lady, and this is my last glimpse of Her.

My followers do not reproach me for having cost them all they were. They are mine. In me is the godhead which can do no wrong.

And the war is open, between me and SUM. My friends are few, my enemies many and mighty. I go about the world as a fugitive. But always I sing. And always I find someone who will listen, will join us, embracing pain and death like a lover.

With the Knife and the Axe I take their souls. Afterwards we hold for them the ritual of rebirth. Some go thence to become outlaw missionaries; most put on facsimile bracelets and return home, to whisper my word. It makes little difference to me. I have no haste, who own eternity.

For my word is of what lies beyond time. My enemies say I call forth ancient bestialities and lunacies; that I would bring civilization down in ruin; that it matters not a madman's giggle to me whether war, famine, and pestilence will again scour the earth. With these accusations I am satisfied. The language of them shows me that here, too, I have reawakened anger. And that emotion belongs to us as much as any other. More than the others, maybe, in this autumn of mankind. We need a gale, to strike down SUM and everything It stands for. Afterwards will come the winter of barbarism.

And after that the springtime of a new and (perhaps) more

human civilization. My friends seem to believe this will come in their very lifetimes: peace, brotherhood, enlightenment, sanctity. I know otherwise. I have been in the depths. The wholeness of mankind, which I am bringing back, has its horrors.

When one day
    the Eater of the Gods returns
    the Wolf breaks his chain
    the Horsemen ride forth
    the Age ends
    the Beast is reborn
then SUM will be destroyed; and you, strong and fair, may go back to earth and rain.

I shall await you.

My aloneness is nearly ended, Daybright. Just one task remains. The god must die, that his followers may believe he is raised from the dead and lives forever. Then they will go on to conquer the world.

There are those who say I have spurned and offended them. They too, borne on the tide which I raised, have torn out their machine souls and seek in music and ecstasy to find a meaning for existence. But their creed is a savage one, which has taken them into wildcountry, where they ambush the monitors sent against them and practise cruel rites. They believe that the final reality is female. Nevertheless, messengers of theirs have approached me with the suggestion of a mystic marriage. This I refused; my wedding was long ago, and will be celebrated again when this cycle of the world has closed.

Therefore they hate me. But I have said I will come and talk to them.

I leave the road at the bottom of the valley and walk singing up the hill. Those few I let come this far with me have been told to abide my return. They shiver in the sunset; the vernal equinox is three days away. I feel no cold myself. I stride exultant among briars and twisted ancient apple trees. If my bare feet leave a little blood in the snow, that is good. The ridges around are dark with forest, which waits like the skeleton dead for leaves to be breathed across it again. The eastern sky is purple, where stands the evening star. Overhead, against blue, cruises an early flight of homebound geese. Their calls drift faintly down to me. Westward, above me and before me, smoulders redness. Etched black against it are the women.

THE NEBULA AWARDS

Winners of the Nebula Award are chosen by the members of Science Fiction Writers of America. Throughout the year SFWA members nominate the best science-fiction stories and novels as they are published. At the end of the year there is a final nominating ballot and then an awards ballot to determine the winners. Nebula Trophies are presented at the annual Nebula Awards Banquets, held simultaneously each spring in New York City, New Orleans, and on the West Coast.

Science Fiction Writers of America was organized in 1965, and the first Nebula Awards were made in the spring of 1966 for 1965 publications. The Nebula Trophy was designed by Judith Ann Lawrence (Mrs. James Blish) from a sketch by Kate Wilhelm (Mrs. Damon Knight). Each trophy is an individual creation, consisting of a block of lucite four inches square by nine inches high, into which a spiral nebula made of metallic glitter and a specimen of rock crystal are embedded.

The categories in which the awards are made have remained unchanged from the beginning. In the following list, the year given is the year of publication for the winning entries.

1965

Best Novel: *Dune* by Frank Herbert.

Best Novella: (tie) 'The Saliva Tree' by Brian W. Aldiss; 'He Who Shapes' by Roger Zelazny.

Best Novelette: 'The Doors of His Face, the Lamps of His Mouth' by Roger Zelazny.

Best Short Story: ' "Repent, Harlequin!" Said the Ticktockman' by Harlan Ellison.

1966

Best Novel: (tie) *Flowers for Algernon* by Daniel Keyes; *Babel-17* by Samuel R. Delany.
Best Novella: 'The Last Castle' by Jack Vance.
Best Novelette: 'Call Him Lord' by Gordon R. Dickson.
Best Short Story: 'The Secret Place' by Richard McKenna.

1967

Best Novel: *The Einstein Intersection* by Samuel R. Delany.
Best Novella: 'Behold the Man' by Michael Moorcock.
Best Novelette: 'Gonna Roll the Bones' by Fritz Leiber.
Best Short Story: 'Aye, and Gomorrah' by Samuel R. Delany.

1968

Best Novel: *Rite of Passage* by Alexei Panshin.
Best Novella: 'Dragonrider' by Anne McCaffrey.
Best Novelette: 'Mother to the World' by Richard Wilson.
Best Short Story: 'The Planners' by Kate Wilhelm.

1969

Best Novel: *The Left Hand of Darkness* by Ursula K. Le Guin.
Best Novella: 'A Boy and His Dog' by Harlan Ellison.
Best Novelette: 'Time Considered as a Helix of Semi-Precious Stones' by Samuel R. Delany.
Best Short Story: 'Passengers' by Robert Silverberg.

1970

Best Novel: *Ringworld* by Larry Niven.
Best Novella: 'I'll Met in Lankhmar' by Fritz Leiber.
Best Novelette: 'Slow Sculpture' by Theodore Sturgeon.
Best Short Story: No award.

1971

Best Novel: *A Time of Changes* by Robert Silverberg.
Best Novella: 'The Missing Man' by Katherine MacLean.
Best Novelette: 'The Queen of Air and Darkness' by Poul Anderson.
Best Short Story: 'Good News from the Vatican' by Robert Silverberg.

1972

Best Novel: *The Gods Themselves* by Isaac Asimov.
Best Novella: 'A Meeting with Medusa' by Arthur C. Clarke.
Best Novelette: 'Goat Song' by Poul Anderson.
Best Short Story: 'When it Changed' by Joanna Russ.

THE HUGO AWARDS

The Science Fiction Achievement Awards, a title rarely used, became known as 'Hugo' Awards shortly after the first such awards were presented, in 1953. The 'Hugo' is after Hugo Gernsback, author, editor, and publisher and one of the 'fathers' of modern science fiction. The Hugo Awards have been made annually since 1955, and their winners are determined by popular vote. Because each year's awards have been under the administration of a different group, the committee in charge of the year's World Science Fiction Convention, rules and categories have fluctuated from year to year, sometimes drastically.

From their inception, the Hugo Awards have been made for amateur as well as for professional achievement. Thus there are usually awards for Best Fanzine (the initiate's term for amateur magazine), Best Fan Writer, and Best Fan Artist as well as the awards for professional writing, for Best Professional Magazine, and for Best Professional Artist. Only the more standardized awards for professional writing are listed here.* In recent years voting on both the nominating and final ballot has been limited to those who have purchased memberships in the World Science Fiction Convention. The Hugo Trophy is a miniature rocket ship poised for take-off, though details of design and materials have varied from year to year. In the following list, the year given is the year of publication for the winning entries.

* The reader is referred to *A History of the Hugo, Nebula and International Fantasy Awards*, published by Howard DeVore, 4705 Weddel St., Dearborn, Mich., for the history of the awards and a detailed listing of Hugo winners and nominees in all categories. The book also contains a complete listing of Nebula Award nominees.

1965

Best Novel: (tie) . . . *And Call Me Conrad* by Roger Zelazny; *Dune* by Frank Herbert.

Best Short Fiction: ' "Repent, Harlequin!" Said the Ticktockman' by Harlan Ellison.

1966

Best Novel: *The Moon is a Harsh Mistress* by Robert A. Heinlein.

Best Novelette: 'The Last Castle' by Jack Vance.

Best Short Story: 'Neutron Star' by Larry Niven.

1967

Best Novel: *Lord of Light* by Roger Zelazny.

Best Novella: (tie) 'Riders of the Purple Wage' by Philip José Farmer; 'Weyr Search' by Anne McCaffrey.

Best Novelette: 'Gonna Roll the Bones' by Fritz Leiber.

Best Short Story: 'I Have No Mouth and I Must Scream' by Harlan Ellison.

1968

Best Novel: *Stand on Zanzibar* by John Brunner.

Best Novella: 'Nightwings' by Robert Silverberg.

Best Novelette: 'The Sharing of Flesh' by Poul Anderson.

Best Short Story: 'The Beast That Shouted Love at the Heart of the World' by Harlan Ellison.

1969

Best Novel: *The Left Hand of Darkness* by Ursula K. Le Guin.

Best Novella: 'Ship of Shadows' by Robert Silverberg.

Best Short Story: 'Time Considered as a Helix of Semi-Precious Stones' by Samuel R. Delany.

1970

Best Novel: *Ringworld* by Larry Niven.
Best Novella: 'Ill Met in Lankhmar' by Fritz Leiber.
Best Short Story: 'Slow Sculpture' by Theodore Sturgeon.

1971

Best Novel: *To Your Scattered Bodies Go* by Philip José Farmer.
Best Novella: 'The Queen of Air and Darkness' by Poul Anderson.
Best Short Story: 'Inconstant Moon' by Larry Niven.

1972

Best Novel: *The Gods Themselves* by Isaac Asimov.
Best Novella: 'The Word for World is Forest' by Ursula K. Le Guin.
Best Novelette: 'Goat Song' by Poul Anderson.
Best Short Story: (tie) 'Eurema's Dam' by R. A. Lafferty; 'The Meeting' by Frederik Pohl and C. M. Kornbluth.